BECK

BAR
28

Book Four

JJ HARPER

Cover design by Jay Aheer at Simply Defined Art

Edited by Tanja Ongkiehong

Formatted by Brenda Wright at Formatting Done Wright

BECK

Six months ago

In the years I'd worked at BAR 28, I'd found my family. The guys had become my brothers. The fact that we were all gay made it even better. It wasn't a gay bar, not by any standards, but it was a welcome and safe place for everyone, however they classified themselves, if they did at all.

It was a busy Saturday night, and thankfully, Leo, Sawyer, and Gus were on shift too. The room was packed to the rafters. Two large groups took up a corner each. Both were celebrating a birthday, and looking at the number of cocktails we were making, I might have to order a cab or two at the end of the night. Once the club downstairs opened, it would ease up in here. No doubt, the partyers would take their celebrations there.

I was right about one of the groups, but the other seemed content to stay put here. A few I recognised as regulars, but a couple of faces I didn't know. I caught the eye of one man. One gorgeous and sexy man. His dark hair was messily styled, or he'd run his hands through it too much. He was watching me, so I smiled and winked. He blushed and turned away. Okay, not gay, then.

But I caught him looking time and time again. I was used to people staring at me. The ton of ink covering me garnered a lot of attention. Some of it was good, and the negative opinions didn't bother me. It was my body to decorate as I wished.

When I glanced over at the corner table, the gorgeous man was staring at me again. So me being me, I grinned at him. His lips lifted in a hesitant smile, but one of his mates nudged him, and he quickly looked away. As much as I thought he was probably straight, he was totally my type.

"He likes you," Leo whispered as he passed behind me.

"I think he's straight," I muttered back.

Just then, a leggy blonde woman wrapped her arms around him and sat on his lap. Yep, straight as a die.

"Whatever he is, he's curious. Could be bi or pan."

Before I could answer, one of my regular hookups walked up to me. He had a wicked look in his eyes, and the cocky grin gave every intention he had away. "Hi, Beck, baby. What are you doing later?"

I laughed at his blatant invitation. "Hmm, I think I could do you."

"Excellent answer." He leant over the bar top and planted a big, fat kiss on my mouth. "I'll see you later, then." He sauntered back to the door, giving his tight ass an extra sway. The fucker knew it was his best asset.

Once he was gone, I looked back at the gorgeous man. The blonde now sat on the chair next to him, with a sulky look on her face. Sexy straight or perhaps bi-curious was frowning. I was the one to drop my gaze first.

Leo frowned at me. "What?" I asked, but I already knew his answer.

"Are you back with Barney again?"

"No, and I've never been with him. We just had a fun time together. No strings, nothing complicated, just damn good sex." I grinned and waggled my eyebrows. "Can you remember that far back? Or has your loved-up brain forgotten what no-strings sex feels like?"

"Oh, I remember, but it has nothing on what I've got now." He laughed and gave me a nudge. Leo had found love with a freaking supermodel. Bruno Alderton was hot TV property but totally in love with my friend.

"Maybe that's because you've got every gay man's wet dream for a boyfriend," Gus said.

Max scowled at Gus. "I thought *I* was your wet dream."

Gus rolled his eyes. "You keep thinking that, baby." But he smiled and kissed him. Yep, two more of my friends who were ridiculously in love.

When it was closing time, Sawyer's man, Devon, had turned up too. This place was like a dating site. Only I've never found my perfect match.

The last of the patrons to leave were the corner party. They all seemed to be drunk as skunks but happy and laughing still. It was good to know they'd had a great night. The guy who had been staring at me nearly all night walked toward the bar. He didn't come to me but spoke to Leo. They chatted while his card was debited. After accepting back his card, he gave me a sideways glance, then left.

Leo sidled up to me. "He was completely sober. Hadn't had any alcohol all night, but he just settled a six-hundred-quid bill."

"I'm sure they'll all chip in."

"Nope, he said it was his present to his friend."

"What was the name on the card?" Why did I even ask? If he'd wanted to speak to me, he could've approached me.

"I didn't look, sorry."

I shrugged. "It's okay. I was curious, that's all."

"He did say he thought this was a great bar. So he'll probably be here again," Leo said.

"Still, he screamed straight to me."

BECK

Now

"Beck, wait up!" The voice from the office stopped me in my tracks in the corridor. I closed my eyes and calmed myself, then turned back and stepped inside. Jonas, my boss—and my ex-lover—looked me over and frowned. "Are you okay? You've seemed distracted lately." Damn him for knowing me so well.

"Yeah, I'm good. I've had a lot on my mind lately, but it's all sorted now." *Please don't ask. Please don't ask.*

"Anything I can help with?" He was such a genuine guy, a great man. If only it could've worked out for us. He was a protector, a carer, and I didn't need one of those. I wanted an equal.

"No, like I said, it's all sorted. I'm good. I promise." I plastered my brightest smile on my face and turned away, conscious of his eyes still on me.

"You know where I am if you need anything, Beck." The kindness in his voice made my heart hurt, and I had to blink hard a couple of times to fight back the sting of tears.

"I know. Thank you, Jonas." I walked to the breakroom, which was empty. I was always early, a habit I'd had my whole life, thanks to my parents. They'd always prided themselves on the fact that they were never late. It was a shame they didn't pride themselves on loving their son.

It was going to be a busy night, which was exactly what I needed. A night to take my mind off the total fuck-up my life was right now. Not my love life. I hadn't got that. No, it was my sex life that was fucked up. I must have a sign on my forehead that said 'SUCKER' flashing in pink neon lights. I was a sucker for a sad smile and a sob story, which was why I ended up alone after my so-called date decided to call his ex and, with a gabbled apology, rushed off back to him. I'd spent all damn night trying to cheer him up so that I could get him back to my place, not for him to friend-zone me before he left.

The others were arriving as well. Max had Gus tucked under his arm, and Sawyer sported a hickey or two, courtesy of Devon. Leo was already working and would be leaving after his shift ended to go home to Bruno. Happy couples everywhere.

Fuck. My. Life.

"Hi, Beck," Gus said cheerfully as he extricated himself from Max. "How was your night off? Did you meet up with that cute guy?"

"Jack? Yeah, it was okay. Not going to see him again, though." I shrugged. They were used to me turning men down after one time together. Jonas was the last real relationship I'd had, and it had ended a long while ago. It hadn't even been public knowledge. Max had known but never had an opinion that I was aware of. If Max had known, then Gus would have too, but he could keep quiet about information that wasn't his to share.

"What was wrong with this one?" Sawyer shook his head. "He seemed keen."

"On the rebound, but still totally hung up on his ex." That was as much as they were getting from me. "I'm not even looking anymore. I can't be arsed with all the drama. I'll stick to Grindr or my right hand."

"Eww, nasty man!" Gus fake gagged.

"Which one are you more offended by, babe? The app or the palm?" Max asked as he nuzzled Gus's neck.

Sawyer poked Max. "Leave him alone. Christ, this is work, not your bedroom."

"Anyway"—I stowed my bag into my locker—"like I said, I'm not looking for anyone, not if it means I end up as sappy as you all are. It's sickening." I nudged Sawyer, letting him know I was only teasing, then walked out of the breakroom and towards the bar.

The thing was, I meant it this time.

"That totally hot guy is here again, watching every move you make," Sawyer whispered to me. I grunted in reply. I knew exactly who he was talking about. For the last six months, I'd seen the guy in just about every pub or bar I'd been in. He had never spoken to me, even though he looked my way constantly. Besides, he always had his girlfriend with him. Tonight was no different. He was sitting with a mixed group of people. He was still hot as fuck and was staring at me every now and then. The same girl was hanging onto his every word and touched him at every opportunity.

"Not interested. He's with that girl."

"Not really. She just wants him to be," Sawyer said with a grin. "He's not interested in her."

I shook my head. "Are you sure? I've seen her with him a ton of times."

I wasn't going to be some guy's experiment, which was how it felt after all this time. The last hour of the night, I studiously ignored the table Hot Guy was sitting at. Sawyer seemed to get the hint and took over serving that group.

Finally, time was called, and they all settled their tabs and left. I let out a long breath and relaxed. Sheesh, had I really been that wound up by him? Hot Guy was the last one out the door, but not without one more long drink-me-in gaze. I stared back, unable to look away however much I wanted to.

We cashed up quickly. Sawyer wanted to get home to Devon, and Max and Gus had their own agenda to fill. I had no one. I was okay with that. Or so I told myself.

When we were back in the breakroom, Sawyer handed me a piece of paper. "You can chuck it away if you want."

I took it but didn't open it, and stupidly I didn't throw it away either. Sawyer gave me a wink as he pulled his coat on. That smug fucker.

As I walked home, the slip of paper seemed to be burning a hole in my back pocket.

I closed my door behind me and took in a deep breath, glad that my shift was over. I knew the guys wanted me to be as happy as they were, but I couldn't imagine my prince charming would walk into the bar. They just got lucky. And everyone knew I wasn't lucky. I was the guy who always got picked last, the one who got refused entrance when all my mates had already gone inside. The sight of my tattoos had little old ladies clutching their handbags tight, even when I gave them my seat on the bus. So the chance of finding my man was pretty slim. I'd wished it was Jonas, and he might even have wished the same. Our relationship had been good, really good, right up until it wasn't. Neither of us had wanted to make a commitment, and after we realised that, there didn't seem much point in carrying on. But we remained friends, and that worked well for us.

I pulled the piece of paper out of my pocket. He hadn't written his name, just his number. I hesitated. Why should I keep it? I scrunched it into a ball and tossed it into the bin. If he couldn't make the effort to walk up to me in the bar or tell me his name, then he wasn't worth my time. I stripped out of my clothes, dropped them in the laundry basket, and went for a shower.

I was feeling proud of myself for making the sensible decision. Why then was his face still bothering me when I got into bed? Why did it feel like I shouldn't have thrown his number away?

But hell, I doubted he would disappear just because I didn't call him. With that settled, I closed my eyes and fell asleep, his shy smile from all those months ago the last thing I saw.

Chapter 3

Munro

My phone rang. I looked at the screen. Bollocks. It was Lucie. She wasn't going to take no for an answer. Last night, she'd been all over me, and as much as I'd shifted away from her, she'd still managed to stay glued to my side. Her obsession with me was getting out of hand.

"Hi, Lu," I answered, trying to sound interested, even though I rolled my eyes.

"How can you sound so jolly? My head is killing me." Why had she called me if she felt like shit?

"I'm not feeling bad because I didn't down porn-star martinis like they were water." Martinis she didn't pay for, not even one.

"God, you're so grumpy. But please, I'm going to need a big greasy fry-up to cure this one. Let's meet at Joe's café."

"Sorry, no can do. I'm at work. I've got too much to do." This, at least, was true, and I didn't have to lie to get out of seeing her. I was a dreadful liar; my face would go red before I'd even spoken. All my friends knew this.

"You're the boss, Munro. You don't need to be there on a Sunday at the arse crack of dawn," she grumbled. Her sulky voice really grated on me today. "Please, please, pretty please with knobs on, meet me. I wanted to ask you something. I couldn't last night because we were with the others."

I could guess what it was, and that only sharpened my resolve to stay away from her. "Another time, Lucie." I almost said,

"I promise," but I managed to swallow the words down. She would pester me until I gave in. "I've got to go. Catch up soon, okay?"

"Whatever, you big meanie." Before I could end the call, she spoke again. "Who were you watching all night? You hardly spoke at all."

Fuck. It was bad enough that Ed had caught me checking out the sexy barman. Now Lucie had noticed as well. "I wasn't looking at anyone, Lucie."

"Whatever." She hung up without saying goodbye.

My office window looked down over the main part of the gymnasium, over the running machines and weights section. The place was already filling up. Eight o'clock wasn't the arse crack Lucie claimed it to be. It was no surprise she had a hangover after all the strong cocktails she'd drunk all night.

The barman's face popped into my mind again. Damn, he was beautiful. I hadn't been able to keep my eyes off him, but I needed to be careful. Will had noticed, as had Ed. Even though they were my friends, they didn't know I was gay. I'd kept my sexuality a secret my whole life. It wasn't something I'd planned to do. When I went to uni, I'd thought I'd be free to explore, but there had never seemed to be a right time. My dream to open a gym became a reality, and thanks to Instagram, it quickly turned into the place to be. One gym became two, then three and on and on it went. The fitness companies started contacting me as they wanted to sponsor me to promote their products, and my followers grew. Suddenly announcing I was gay hadn't seemed like a good idea. I'd spent ten years of my life building this business. I couldn't watch it all fall apart when my followers, sponsors, and gym members rejected me. How could they trust me? All my life, I'd told people the most important thing in life was to be true to yourself. They'd see me as a fake—a fraud.

So now I was twenty-eight, had made a brilliant business, and was more than financially stable, but the worst of it was I'd locked myself so deep in the closet I should be having tea and crumpets with Mr Tumnus. And I hated it. I wanted to feel a man's body on mine, to trail my lips over an unmapped body, and to sense being filled. I didn't think I'd be able to hold back much longer. The idea of popping my gay cherry with a Grindr hookup wasn't the way I wanted to go, so I'd been pushing it further and further from my mind.

I was coping with it until I saw the bartender at BAR 28, and then I seemed to see him everywhere. Every pub or bar I visited, he seemed to show up. He intrigued me, excited me. He made me think of all the fantasies I'd ever had. I wanted to do them with him. I didn't know what drew me to him first. Was it the sexy, floppy hair, the gorgeous smile with perfectly straight white teeth, or the myriad of colourful tattoos covering his arms, his neck, even the back of one of his hands? They were a contrast to the beautiful face that appeared calm, pensive when he wasn't laughing. He had an innocent look, then. But his laugh was raw and deep, intoxicating. So like Lucie just had called me out on, I was left staring at the gorgeous man and not doing anything about it. Until it got to closing time, and I couldn't stop myself from writing my number on the back of the bar bill and thrusting it into the hands of the tall, blond, and Viking godlike barman. Thankfully, he'd taken it without joking about it but with the promise to give it to his colleague. If I'd gone up to the object of my desires, I would have made a total fool of myself.

Now I had to wait and wonder if he would call.

He didn't on Sunday. Monday, Tuesday, and Wednesday passed without a call. Now it was Friday, and I found a seat in the corner of BAR 28—by myself—and watched him again. When my friends told me where they were going, I'd cried off and come here alone. He hadn't seen me, which was fine with me. I got to see him laughing and joking with his co-workers and the patrons. He flirted with both the men and the women. Was he bi? Would I care if he was? No, I wouldn't. I just wanted him to flirt with me, to be with me. I stared at his lips. Were they as soft as they looked? What would they taste like? Christ, I was screwed.

I had finished my first drink and went to the bar for a refill rather than wait for a server. It was crazy busy now, and I could be in for a long wait, but if he served me, it would be worth it.

He hadn't noticed me until he looked up to take my order. His sage-green eyes widened, and he swallowed hard, his Adam's apple bobbing in his throat, the tattoo rippling with the motion.

"Hi," he croaked, then cleared his throat as a delicious blush spread over his cheeks. "Hi, I'm Beck. What can I get for you?"

Oh, he wasn't totally unaffected by me, so why hadn't he called me? "Just a beer, please."

"We've got Peroni, Staropramen, San Miguel, or Beck's."

I smiled. Hopefully, he'd give me one of his smiles he'd shared with the other patrons in return. "Beck's, please."

"Sure." He turned to one of the under-counter fridges behind him and took out a bottle of Beck's, then collected a glass. When he placed them on the bar, he did smile, but it wasn't the bright, cheeky, eye-sparkling smile I wanted.

I handed him a ten-pound note. "You didn't call."

"No." He rang up my drink, then came back with my change. "Why not?"

His eyes slid away from mine and settled on one of the other bartenders, then back to me. "I didn't think it was a good idea." He moved away to serve another customer, not giving me the time to answer.

A bar stool became available, so like the persistent fool I was, I took it and stayed watching Beck. He captivated me the way no one ever had. The tattoos on his arms seemed to come to life as he flexed and stretched. Whoever his artist was, he was a genius.

Beck chatted and laughed with the other patrons, but his shoulders were tense, and his jaw ticked as he approached me again. "Another one?" he pointed to my empty bottle.

"No, I'm good." I slid off the stool and handed him my number again. "Try to call me this time. I don't think you'll regret it." I gave him a smile, then strolled out of the bar, knowing his eyes were boring into my back.

I knew that if he called, I'd have to come out, and god, that scared the crap out of me. But I didn't think I'd have to worry about that. He didn't look like he had any intention of using my number. More was the pity. On the other hand, my life would change dramatically if he did want to go on a date with me. I fell asleep, relief warring with disappointment

When I woke up, my thoughts immediately went back to Beck. I knew I'd piqued his interest, but was it enough to make him call me? I'd never been so captivated by a man before. What would I have to do to get to spend time with him?

Stop hiding in the closet.

The cold truth in those snarky words brought me up short. What the hell was I thinking? I couldn't be seen with him, and he sure as hell wasn't one to hide.

Please don't let him call.

BECK

Turning up without your girlfriend doesn't take away from the fact that you have one, arsehole. I didn't even bother pocketing the card and tossed it straight into the bin.

"Was that your admirer?" Sawyer asked.

"Yep. And I'm still not interested." I was pleased with my self-control because he screamed everything I loved in a man. Tall, rugged, muscled, and just enough stubble to leave burn marks in places I'd feel for days. His gorgeous eyes were the colour of dark chocolate but had flashed with sparkles of gold when he spoke to me.

"Liar." He grinned. "That man has everything you go for, and you know it."

"Yeah, and he was with a girl last week. I'm not going to be part of that. I deserve more."

He stared at me for a moment, then nodded. "Yeah, you do." He patted my shoulder and got back to work.

I worked in the nightclub downstairs tonight, and the place was heaving. The new university year had started, and kids were everywhere. They were fun to watch as they flirted and tried to one-up each other with dumb drinking games. The supposed girlfriend of my admirer was here as well, but she was with another man, or rather all over him, virtually climbing him like a tree. Was she here alone? I looked around the room, searching all the tables for Hot Guy. Why I did it, I had no clue. Then I found him. He had a weird expression on his face as he stared at the girl, not anger, more like...relief. What was that all about?

His eyes met mine, flashing briefly, but he glanced away just as quickly. Damn. Not that I had any right to be disappointed. I'd not called him, and now he'd got the message. Shrugging it off, I got back to work, but damn he was good-looking. Maybe, only maybe, if he spoke to me tonight, I would see if he wanted to wait for my shift to end. One night couldn't hurt me, right?

But he didn't. He didn't come up to the bar once. And like an idiot, I was disappointed.

At the end of the night, I walked out, messing around with Leo and Gus and their boyfriends, and stopped dead in my tracks. Hot Guy was leaning against the wall.

"You go ahead," I said to the guys, then ambled over to him. "Hey, you okay? Waiting for someone?"

He looked nervously at my friends, but they said goodnight and walked on. "Um, yeah. You, actually. Although I don't know why. You made it clear you don't want anything to do with me. But you're kind of stuck in my head."

I smiled just a little. I liked that idea. "So you decided to wait?"

He scrubbed the back of his head and nodded. "Yeah, I decided to wait. This isn't something I usually do, so I'm a bit out of my depth."

"Are you talking about being with a guy or waiting for one?" This wasn't the way I'd thought the conversation would go. I was expecting "your place or mine?". He hesitated. Oh shit, he's not done this before. "Look, I'm flattered that you like me, but I'm not into playing games. Maybe you should work out what you want or who you are before you do this. If you're still interested, then come back and see me." I turned on my heel.

"No, wait." He grabbed my wrist, not firmly, but the shock of his touch raced up my arm and through my body. His eyes widened. He must've felt it too, and he let go as if he'd burnt his fingers. "Please don't go. I haven't ever waited for someone. I haven't felt like this before."

"What do you want? I mean, it's gone three in the morning, and I've just worked for eight hours. If you want a coffee, then now isn't the time."

Then his mouth was on mine. Like with his fingers around my wrist, it wasn't aggressive, but fuck, it was powerful. His tongue swept over my lips, and instinctively I opened for him, and I got my first taste—rich with the faint taste of the beer he'd drunk. It was heat and passion, mixed with heady desire. As he deepened the kiss, I grasped his hips and pulled him against me. His hard-on pressed heavily to mine, and he groaned. I broke off the kiss. His lips were slick with spit, swollen from the intensity, and his eyes burnt with lust.

"Your place or mine?" I growled, not caring what was happening around us.

"Yours." His voice was as husky as mine.

I looked around for a cab, but at this time, the pickings were slim. "I have my car," he said and took my hand.

Was I really going to do this again? Christ, I didn't even know his name. This was so wrong, but damn, that kiss had been the best I'd ever had. "How much have you had to drink?" I wasn't getting into a car with anyone who'd been drinking.

"One beer at about ten o'clock, water since then." He didn't smell of alcohol, and I believed him.

"What's your name?" I asked as he led me around the corner to a black BMW. A really bloody expensive, sporty BMW. Who was this guy?

He chuckled. "I can't believe I haven't told you. It's Munro." He tensed slightly. Why? Should the name mean anything?

"Good to meet you, Munro. Shall we go?" I climbed into the passenger seat and told him my address. "Do you know where that is?"

"Yeah, I do." He leant over the centre console and placed a chaste kiss on my mouth, setting my insides alight again.

The drive was quiet and mercifully short. Music was playing softly. I couldn't work out who it was, but it was comfortable. When he pulled up outside my flat, he stayed silent, his eyes facing forward, his hands on the steering wheel. "We don't have to do this, Munro. In fact, please don't come in if you're having any second thoughts."

He closed his eyes for a moment, then seemed to come back to the present and smiled. "I've never wanted anything more than I want this. To be with you."

"Then let's go." I opened my door and stepped out of possibly the most expensive car I'd ever been in. He followed me into the building and towards my door.

"Do you live alone?" His mouth was so close to my ear his breath warmed my skin. The key was already in the lock, and yet I could only nod. "That's good to know."

"Are you a screamer?" I chuckled, then shivered as he pressed his lips to my neck.

"I don't think so," he said as I opened the door. Strange answer, but I let it go.

I led him straight to my bedroom, where I turned on the lamp, then opened the drawer and took out a bottle of lube and a condom. I held up the foil packet. "How many of these are we going to need?" I grinned.

For a second, he looked as if I'd asked a trick question. "As many as you can handle." He ran his hand through his hair. The action made his shirt lift, and I got a glimpse of a tanned, well-defined six-pack. I held back an appreciative moan, now eager to see the rest of him.

I threw the supplies onto the bed, then slipped my hands up under his shirt, revelling in the delicious tight skin. I pressed my mouth to his stomach, licked lazily over the perfect squares of muscle, and dipped into his belly button. Munro took over removing his T-shirt and dropped it on the floor. I was still enjoying the smooth skin that tasted like honey and warm sunlight. He tangled his hands in my hair as I moved up to his nipples. I licked the left one while tugging on its twin. He groaned and gripped my head tightly, holding me against his chest.

When I bit down, he groaned again, thrusting his hips forward. My hands shook as I unzipped his jeans, his cock now hidden only behind a pair of briefs. I palmed his thick length through the fabric and stroked my thumb over the crown. A damp patch appeared as precum leaked from the tip. I stood upright and captured his mouth, delving my tongue between his lips, licking over every surface as I stroked his shaft.

"God, I'm going to come before you get inside me." Munro broke away from me.

"Then get naked." I stripped off my clothes, and in record time, I was naked and lying on my bed. I grabbed the lube and fisted my length.

He pulled the last of his clothes off, then stood hesitantly by the bed, his eyes glued on my hand and its slow movement up and down my cock.

"Are you going to join me, or do you want to watch me get myself off? I can suck you off after if you don't want to get fucked." He was so transfixed with my actions I wasn't even sure he'd heard me. He was acting like he'd never seen another man jack off, or was it the row of piercings running up the underside of my cock? His dick was definitely into it if the amount of precum dripping down his length was anything to go by.

"Munro," I said. His eyes snapped back to my face. "Are you joining me?"

Chapter 5

Munro

Shit. I'd been staring like a fucking fool. I had to get back in the game. But those piercings, I'd never seen anything like them. How much must that have hurt? He'd said he was going to fuck me, and god, yes, please. My arsehole clenched at the thought, eager for the stretch and burn of a real cock. How would those metal balls feel? Definitely different from the dildos and vibrators I'd been using for too fucking long.

"Y...yes, god yes. But what about those? I've never seen that before." I put one knee on the bed, then the other and crawled up to him. I wanted, *needed,* him to take control, to show me what he wanted to do to me. I didn't think there was a single thing I'd say no to.

Beck shifted onto his knees and pushed me down to lie on my back. "It's a Jacob's ladder, and it's going to make you scream." He grabbed the lube and squirted some onto his hand. "God, you've got a great dick. Maybe after I've fucked you, I'll let you fuck me." He wrapped his lube-slicked hand around my dick and pumped up and down a couple of times. His grip was hard, firm, assured, and so fucking hot I bucked up as more precum burst from my slit. He flicked his tongue out and lapped at the shimmering liquid. I groaned as more broke free. He slid his mouth over the head and swirled his tongue around and around. I needed him to stop, or it was game over.

"Beck, stop. I don't want to come yet."

He grinned, and with a final flick over my slit, he moved back. "Then we'd better get to it."

He leant over me and kissed me. I moaned when I tasted the precum on his tongue and deepened the kiss. Beck stroked down my cock and over my balls, which drew up under his touch. He didn't linger there. Oh god, he was going to touch my hole.

The moment his slick fingertip nudged me, I knew I had to relax. Not that I hadn't had anything up my arse before, but this was different. Another man was touching me. I sighed as he circled my entrance. It was so fucking good.

"Let me in, Munro," he whispered against my lips. He circled again and again. With only the slightest pressure, he slipped inside me. "You're so tight. God, I can't wait for you to grip my cock as hard as this." He pushed some more, then pumped in and out a few times until a second finger joined the fun.

I couldn't take my eyes off his face as he looked down between our bodies. He was equally as entranced as he slid two fingers in and out. What would he say if I told him he was the first man to do this to me? Would he have turned me down at the bar, or would he be more careful now? He didn't need to be. This was perfect.

"That's enough, Beck. I'm ready." He stroked over my prostate, sending fireworks through my body. "Christ, yeah."

Then he withdrew his fingers, leaving me empty. A foil wrapper tore, and my heart beat sped up. This was it. Finally, I would get my cherry popped. I'd been waiting so long for this. If Beck had turned me down again, I might have hired an escort. This was way better. And we might do this again after tonight. I spread my legs wide, bent my knees, and brought them up to my chest. I expected to be embarrassed to be so open and exposed, but it felt right, that it was worth waiting this long for it to be with Beck.

When Beck moved and took his dick in his hand, I reached up, needing his kiss. And as he parted his lips for me, I opened up for him. Shit, he was big. I panted, squeezing my eyes shut. Beck paused but kept kissing me until the burn eased. When I relaxed, he pushed farther, every tiny bead scraping against my walls. He went slowly, allowing me to adjust to the fullness, until his nuts hit my arse. I opened my eyes, wanting to see his face.

Beck pulled back, his eyes shut tight, his jaw slack. "Hey, are you okay?" I asked as I stroked his cheek and down his neck.

"Yeah, I've got the same problem as you. If I move, I'll come. You have the tightest arse ever, and damn, it feels good."

I chuckled, and he cursed, shaking his head. "Not fucking helping." He opened his eyes and winked.

Then he moved, and however hard I thought I'd fucked my dildo, it was nothing to having Beck withdraw, then plunge back in. He leant over me, pushing my legs back and my arse higher in the air. Thank fuck I was supple, or I'd be snapped in half, but god, if he didn't fill me even more this way.

I grabbed my dick as he pegged my prostate with every punch of his hips. Pants, curses, and the squelch of my lubed arse filled the room, and it sounded better than any porn I'd ever watched. He knelt up, lifting my legs from over my head to up his chest. It wasn't quite as deep this way, but still every inch of him hit me as he slid in and out. With his next stroke over my prostate, my back stiffened, and the tingle of my imminent orgasm rippled through me.

"I'm getting close, Beck," I said. "Very fucking close."

"Stroke yourself. I want to see you come." He let my legs drop and leant over me again. "You look so fucking hot. Cover those sexy abs with your spunk." He kissed me hard, a bruising kiss that sent sparks all the way to my toes. He sped up, and my whole body lit up as my balls drew up into my body and detonated, releasing a lifetime of pent-up sexual frustration and deprivation. I'd been so fucking stupid; I should have done this years ago.

"Fuck, yes!" Beck cried out. He pulled out and ripped off the condom. His climax hit him, and he shuddered and covered my abs and chest with his jizz. I'd seen some cumshots before, but they were nothing like the copious amount he sprayed over me.

Beck must have thought the same thing because he let out a dry chuckle. He swiped his fingers through the mess. I grabbed his wrist and brought his fingers up to my mouth. I wanted to taste us both, wanted to know his flavour. After I licked his fingers clean, he did it again, painting my lips, then me sucking them clean. It was so hot my dick gave a twitch of approval.

The kisses became sloppy as we fed each other the cooling cum. With a laugh, he broke away.

"We need a shower," he said and swung his legs off the bed.

I wasn't going to turn that down. A shared shower was something I'd always wanted to do. It was such an intimate act, which sounded ridiculous after what we'd just done, but it was true. I got off the bed too and followed him to the room next door.

"It'll be a bit of a squeeze." He laughed as he opened the shower door.

The bathroom was small indeed. It didn't have a bath, just a shower cubicle, a loo, and a sink. Shelves under the mirror held his toothbrush, some soap, and a razor. The rest of his toiletries must be in the cabinet over the toilet.

"I don't mind having to be close to you." Now, wasn't that the understatement of the year?

We washed each other, and my dick twitched the whole way through, stiffening and lengthening again. As much as I would've liked to fuck in here, there wasn't enough space. We finished rinsing the soap off our bodies, and Beck turned off the water.

As we dried off, he bit his lip, a nervous gesture I hadn't expected from him. "Are you going to leave?"

"Do you want me to?" I really didn't want to go. I wanted to lie with him wrapped around me and sleep.

"No, I'd like you to stay."

"Good, because I don't want to leave you. I'm not ready for this to be over," I told him honestly.

He led me back to the bedroom and his bed. My nerves started up again. What if I snored or drooled, or god, the worst, farted? *No, calm down, Munro.* It was almost daylight, and he must be exhausted after his long shift. He was bound to be asleep the minute his head touched the pillow.

As we lay down, Beck snuggled into me. "Are you a cuddler? If not, we may have a problem. I can't help it. I always end up wrapped around my bedmate."

The truthful answer was, I didn't know. I'd never had a man in my bed. Sure, friends crashed at my place sometimes, but most of the time, they passed out drunk and didn't move until the morning. I certainly never cuddled them. Beck was still waiting for me to answer. "Yeah, cuddling is great." Because to have this man pressed to me all night wasn't going to be a hardship.

He smiled, then yawned enough to crack his jaw. "Sorry, I'm beat."

I opened out my arm, allowing him to snuggle in. When he was all up in my space, his head on my chest, his arm over my stomach, he sighed. "Night, Munro." He turned his head into my chest and pressed a soft kiss on my pec. "So fucking hot," he mumbled as he fell asleep. I followed soon after with—I was damn sure—a huge smile on my face.

I woke up with Beck lying half across me. His legs were tangled between mine, and half his body was on my torso. Oh my god. I'd had sex. I grinned goofily as the night before came flooding back. The feel of him sliding into my body was never going to leave my mind. The whole night had been perfect. I'd dreamt of what I thought it would feel like, and I'd been wrong, so bloody wrong. My imagination was way out. The real thing had been incredible, beyond incredible. I wanted to do it again and again and, hell, again.

But now he was still dead to the world, obviously used to sleeping in late, whereas I'd been getting into work by seven thirty for years now. I'd put every part of me into making the gym work and then keeping it the top choice for gym worshippers for the last four years in a row. What should I do now? I couldn't just post a pic of me with Beck and a **#guesswho'sgay** tagline. Nope, that wouldn't be a great idea. Besides, I might be jumping the gun here. He might wake up and say thanks for last night and wave me goodbye.

Yes, that would be best, but damn, I didn't want to go and not let this happen again. Beck would never join me in my closet. He was the epitome of out and proud. He even had a pride flag tattooed on his left biceps. Should I tell him I wasn't out? Or could I risk hiding? I was sure I could. I could keep my work life and friends separate from my time with him.

But it was a lie.

Maybe he wouldn't ask.

Then it was problem solved.

But I didn't want it to be over. I wanted this with him. I wanted to do this with him over and over again. I wanted to have so much sex with him, to feel him inside me again.

Would he want that too?

Chapter 6

BECK

Waking up was never a slow process. I instantly went from asleep to wide awake. Today was no different. What was different was the naked man in my bed—Munro. I happened to be virtually spreadeagled over him, and as I shifted, he tensed. He was awake, awake and unsure. Why was he still here? I'd expected he would have scuttled out of here the moment I was asleep.

Strangely, I didn't mind that he was still in my bed. In fact, I quite liked it, and maybe he'd be up for round two. I wouldn't mind getting another go at his gorgeous arse. I trailed my hand over his pec, his seriously defined pec, and grazed my thumb over his nipple. It instantly hardened, and a hiss sounded, so I did it again.

A whispered "fuck" escaped his lips, and I smiled. I shifted again, moving my head away until I'd exposed his other nipple. As I brushed his right one again, I licked over the left, then sucked it into my mouth. Munro slipped his hand into my hair and stroked it gently but kept my head in place.

After licking, sucking, and tasting his skin, I wanted more. I pulled free from his grip, slipped off his body, and knelt by his side. "Good morning, this is a surprise." I kissed him.

When I moved away, his eyes were wide, panic written all over his handsome face. "It's a good surprise," I said. "I like it."

"I didn't know what to do. Should I have left?" He swallowed, his Adam's apple bobbing.

"Most do. Do you usually stay after hooking up?" I was missing something here, but I didn't know what. He was acting so unsure.

"I...I don't really do this," he stammered. "Hook up, I mean."

How was that even possible? First, he was drop-dead gorgeous. Second, he was built like a god and must have people throwing themselves at him, and third, he'd have to be in his late twenties, so had he just come out of a relationship?

"Oh." I wanted to say more, to ask more, but it wasn't really any of my business. I wasn't looking for anything more than casual. "Okay, so does that make me your first?" I grinned, waggling my eyebrows suggestively. But he paled, like really just drained-by-a-vampire sort of pale.

He nodded, then seemed to force out a smile, but it wasn't a real one. I got it wrong. He wanted to get out of here. "Hey, Munro, it's cool. I'm going to put the kettle on. I'll make a cup of coffee, and you can come and join me, or you can get dressed and go. There's no right or wrong and certainly no pressure." I touched the back of his hand. "It was fun, Munro. It doesn't have to be anything more than that."

I slipped out of bed, grabbed a pair of briefs from my chest of drawers, and pulled them up my legs and over my bum without looking back. This was his decision. If he wasn't into hookups, then there was no shame in that. Although I had to admit I was curious as to why he'd tried it with me, but again, I wouldn't ask. I left him alone and wandered down to my little kitchen. Unlike Leo, I wasn't a lover of cooking. I was more of an instant-ding-meal kind of person. That was what microwaves were for. Or takeaways. We had just about every type of food available in the city, and I went to restaurants. But I could manage coffee and breakfast, if he was interested. I tried not to listen for the door to open, then close as he left, but I heard nothing. Either he was a ninja, or he was still in my bed.

"Can I have a coffee?" The voice behind me made me jump like a cat spotting the cucumber. He *did* have ninja skills.

"Shit, Munro, don't sneak up on me like that. I haven't shrieked that high or loud since Jaida won Drag Race."

He just looked me up and down, heat flaring in his dark brown eyes. The gold striations flashed, and my body instantly reacted. My dick twitched, and my throat went dry. He was dressed—huge disappointment—but hadn't put his shoes on yet, which gave me a little hope he wasn't rushing away. That thought brought me up short, and I stopped pouring the boiling water into the cups. I wanted him to stay. I'd sworn off trying to make a relationship out of a hookup. They never worked, and I would be left alone again. Which meant I couldn't let this go to my head. I had to play it cool.

"I'm sorry," The smirk on his face didn't back up that apology. "I didn't know men could make a sound quite that high." His grin showed off two dimples I hadn't noticed before. Gah, he was going to kill me.

I ignored that remark and got back to my coffee. "How do you take your coffee? Or would you prefer tea?" I poured the water into my cup.

"Coffee would be great." He gave me a tentative smile that made my stomach flip-flop. He really was beautiful. His hair, which had been styled last night, now hung softly around his face. I preferred it this way. As I stepped past him to the fridge, he brushed his fingers down my forearm.

"I love your tattoos." His voice was a reverent whisper.

The hairs on my arms stood on end, and a shiver rippled through me. *Christ, Beck, get it together.* I grabbed the milk and handed it to him. "I'll let you doctor it."

"Black is fine."

I picked up my cup and strode out of the kitchen, heading back to my bedroom. He followed me. I sat on my bed, my back against the headboard, my legs stretched out in front of me. Munro hovered in the doorway, glancing around for somewhere to sit. I patted the bed, and he sat next to me. His foot bumped against mine, and he hastily shifted his leg. I'd never thought much about the feet of the men I hooked up with, but his were nice. I nudged him with my big toe.

"You have sexy feet," I said. He let out a bubble of laughter. "I'm not into sucking toes or that sort of thing. Not that there's any shame in that, but it's not my thing. I just like the bare feet and jeans combo." Why was I waffling? I needed to stop talking.

"Um, thank you, I think." He had a rosy tint on his cheeks; it suited him. "I don't think anyone has ever said that to me." He sipped his coffee. "I think every part of you is sexy."

"Hmm, maybe you should check it out again," I ran my hand down my chest and abs and over my briefs. My dick was happy with this game and gave a jolt. Munro shook his head and chuckled, deep and carefree. It sounded like he didn't laugh like that very often. "I haven't spent enough time admiring yours." I squeezed his denim-clad thigh. "You're so fit. You must work out all the time."

"A little bit. It kind of comes with the job. I own a gym." More colour bloomed over his face, brighter this time.

"That explains it." I placed my coffee cup on my side table. "I do think I need to inspect all your hard work."

"Sounds good to me." He put his cup down on the floor and whipped his shirt over his head again.

I swung my leg over his hips and straddled him, then kissed him. I stroked over his nipples, remembering how sensitive they were. He twitched as I flicked my nail over the tight nub. His dick also liked it, as it swelled beneath my arse. I got the urge to taste him. Then hopefully, he'd let me fuck him again.

I shimmied down his legs and unbuttoned and unzipped his jeans. His dick sprang free. Hell yeah. He'd gone commando when he dressed. "Can I?" I wrapped my hand around his thick shaft. He raised an eyebrow. "Taste you? I really want to suck your dick. I didn't get much chance last night."

Again, with the long hard swallow. Just how new is all this to him? Never mind. I could debate that later. Right now, I had a dick that needed my full attention.

I moved off him and pulled his jeans off, then nestled between his legs. "Watch." I licked from his balls up the solid length of his dick. Precum nestled in the slit as I reached the crown waiting for me to taste him. As I lapped over the tip, Munro's eyes rolled back in his head. I took him deep into my throat. The thick vein running up his length throbbed on my tongue. He wasn't going to last long. His balls had already drawn up tight inside his body, and his thighs trembled as I continued to bob up and down his length. When he fisted my hair and tugged, I knew he was done.

"Fuck, Beck, I'm gonna come. Pull back." He tightened his grip as he tried to lift me off his cock. Nope, that wasn't going to happen. I wanted him to come in my mouth. I sucked harder. He bucked his hips up and roared out. Thick jets of cum burst onto my tongue. Wow, he was plentiful. I smiled around his dick, and he tasted fucking amazing. He must eat a lot of pineapple.

As he softened, I slowly released him and let his dick slap back down on his stomach. He slung his arm over his eyes, his chest heaving. His abs flexed, each muscle perfectly defined under his tanned skin.

My dick was rock hard, and I really wanted to get back inside him, but as I crawled back up his body, his phone belted out Halsey's 'Bad at Love'. He tensed up, then shifted out from under me.

"I have to get it. That's the gym's ringtone." His face was pale again, the flush of euphoria gone, drained away in an instant. He grabbed his phone from the back pocket of the jeans I'd ripped off him just minutes before.

He answered it with a gruff hello, then used his shoulder to keep the phone to his ear as he pulled on his jeans. A deep frown furrowed his smooth brow. "You have to be kidding me.... Fine, I'm on my way.... That's nothing to do with you. Mind your own business."

He ended the call and stared at the screen for what seemed like an eternity. What was he seeing? When he lifted his eyes to me, I shuddered. He looked...hell, I didn't know. Frustrated, annoyed, angry? No, he looked sad, really sad. "I've got to go." He sounded like a different man, an empty man.

"If I promise not to ghost you, can I have your number?" I asked.

Chapter 7

Munro

I drove away from Beck's, ready to start a fight. The gym hadn't called; it had been Lucie. She was at my place, having a tantrum again. Last night's perfect man wasn't that perfect after all, which was no surprise. She only did it to try to make me jealous. Why she still thought she had a chance, I had no idea. I'd told her from the start there couldn't be anything between us. She wanted the fame she believed Instagram could give her, and I was the one she'd decided to try to get it with.

When I pulled into my drive, her bright red Mini with the Union Jack roof was parked haphazardly. The driver's door was open, and she was sitting sideways, her stilettoed feet on the tarmac. She still wore last night's outfit, her hair all messy and her face a tear-stained mess of dried mascara. I'd seen this too many times for it to affect me.

"I'm so glad you're here, Munro. He only wanted me for sex. He kicked me out after that. I thought he was nice." Sobbing, she threw herself into my arms.

"What did you expect, Luce? You were all over him. That's hardly the right way to find a boyfriend. You can't keep doing this, Lucie. I've told you enough times I'm not here to pick up your pieces. You need to make better decisions." I peeled her off me and held her at arm's length.

She scowled at me, no doubt pissed off that I'd called her out. Then she narrowed her eyes and shook herself free from my loose grip. "You've got love bites on your neck. Now I know why you wouldn't tell me where you were. Who is she? Do I know her?" The accusatory questions fired from her lips. "Where did you meet? I didn't see you with anyone last night. You must have waited till I left. Yeah, thanks."

I tuned out Lucie's ranting and lifted my hand to my neck, a smile breaking free. After we'd both come, Beck had kissed his way to my mouth, one slow inch at a time. I liked that he'd marked my skin, even though I knew it went deeper than that. I was marked all the way to my core, deep in my bone marrow now. I wanted him.

"What I do has fuck all to do with you, Lucie. Just as what you do isn't any of my business. If you want to fuck every guy you meet, then go for it, but if you're doing it for the pathetic reason of trying to make me jealous, then give it up. It'll never work, not because you work for me, but because I don't think of you that way. We won't be anything more than friends." I locked my car and walked up to my house. I loved my home with its sharp, clean edges and large open-plan rooms with floor-to-ceiling windows. The architect who'd designed it had got my ideas spot on. He had even incorporated an underground fitness room and swimming pool.

Normally, I was pretty easy and had an open-door policy. Not today, though. Today, I wanted to be alone and replay every moment of my time with Beck. My first time with a man, the only man I'd ever craved enough to chase. When I walked up the three wide steps to the door, she followed me, her shoes click-clacking on the cement. "Go home, Lucie. I'm not interested in your drama."

She grabbed my arm, forcing me to stop. "You can be a bastard sometimes, Munro. I'll find out who she was."

I didn't reply but shook her off, went inside, threw my keys into the wooden bowl by the door, and flipped the lock on the door. I couldn't deal with anyone dropping by today. I opened my phone, tapped on WhatsApp, and added Beck's number, but I only put the initial B with the number. My phone was secured with face recognition. Not that I left it lying around, but I couldn't be too careful.

The squeal of tyres made it clear Lucie drove away in a huff. But did I care? No. She could go and have a hissy fit with someone else. I'd better go to the gym. I'd told Beck the phone call was a work issue. He didn't know which gym, but it was bad enough to tell him a lie. I could at least get some work done.

Wasn't everything you'd done and said to him a lie? I brushed the words from my snarky arsehole brain aside. I hadn't said anything to him. He didn't know he had been my first or that I wasn't out. He might not even call me. I could've been another notch on his bedpost, for all I knew, but I hoped not.

After a night of very little sleep, I was tired, but I'd take that every night if I could. I needed a shower to wake me up and a change of clothes, then was ready to work.

The gym was buzzing with energy, music pumped loudly, and all traces of weariness left me. A workout would do me good. I went to my office first and switched on my computer. My phone buzzed in my pocket. Groaning, I fished it out. This would no doubt be one of my friends berating me for the way I'd spoken to Lucie. Not that she would've told them the truth. She was a pro at embellishment.

Holy shit, Beck had texted me.

Beck: I hope you got the problem sorted.
Beck: I had a good time with you.
Beck: I'm off work on Wednesday and Friday this week.
Beck: Let me know if you want to get together.
Beck: If you don't, that's cool.

Hell yeah, I wanted a repeat.

Me: I had a great time too.

Me: I'd love to meet up again.
Me: How about dinner on Wednesday?

The three little dots danced on the screen. Then they stopped. And started again. How many ways could he be planning to say no, that he only wanted sex? Not that I would turn that down.

Beck: Sounds good. Let me know when and where. :)

I grinned at the screen. He'd sent a smiley face.

Me: Will do. :)

I put my phone down and opened up my emails, sighing at the amount of them. I spent half an hour answering the important ones, then changed into my gym gear and went to work out. As usual, I started on the treadmill and clocked up five miles, then headed to the weights room. Most stations were already taken. I said hello to the familiar faces and smiled politely at the others. With my earbuds in, I got to work. I checked my movements in the mirror on the wall in front of me, but instead of focusing on my curls, I homed in on the marks on my neck. They were even more pronounced now my skin was flushed and sweaty. I grinned, then ducked my head down.

After my third shower in less than twelve hours, I left the gym and went home.

"Hey, Munro, hold up." A shout came from across the car park.

Ed was jogging towards me, his hair damp and a gym bag in his hand. "Hey. I didn't see you in there."

"I was in the main gym. The volleyball games are brutal." He held up his reddened hand. "Fun, though. Do you fancy getting something to eat? I'm starving and could murder a burger."

My stomach rumbled. "Yeah, I'm up for that. Where shall I meet you?" We agreed on a pub, and I got in my car.

The pub was busy, but I managed to find us a small table while Ed went and got our drinks. When he came back and sat down opposite me, his mouth spread into a broad grin. "Did you bump into a vampire on the way home last night?"

"Something like that, yeah." I nodded, not saying anything else. I wanted to talk about it, tell him I'd met an amazing man and we were going to see each other again, but the knots in my stomach stopped me. I felt like I was betraying Beck by not acknowledging him. And I hated it. This was my fault, my doing, and I didn't know how to change it.

"Soooo," Ed said slowly. "Who is she? I didn't know you'd met someone. Is it new?" He took a long drink of his beer.

"It's new, but I'm going to see how it goes. I had a good time." The words stuck in my throat, but I didn't say anything more and looked down at the menu instead.

Ed got the hint and changed the subject. "Have you heard from Lucie today?" Not what I wanted to think about either, but I filled him in on her mini tantrum this morning. "She's a great girl. We've been friends for a long time and her boss. I'm never going to think of her as anything more than a friend. I don't want to lose her friendship, but she's wasting her time."

"We've all told her, Munro. And maybe now you've got a girlfriend, she'll finally give up. You need to bring her out with us."

I let out a dry chuckle. "I don't think we're at that stage yet." I went and ordered our food. We moved on to other topics, and I relaxed. The thought of Lucie's reaction to me having a girlfriend was bad enough. If she found out it was a guy, she'd go nuclear.

Chapter 8

BECK

Halfway through my shift, while I was still reminiscing over the hours I'd spent with Munro, more specifically the sound of Munro's voice when he came, someone said my name. "Hmm?"

Leo was standing next to me, an amused look on his face. "I only said hello, but now I want to know what has made you smile like that. Or is it who? Perhaps the hot guy from Saturday night?"

It was only Monday, but Saturday seemed a year ago. At least I had Wednesday to look forward to. Would we go back to my place? Or his? I didn't mind either way. "Maaaybe." I drawled out the word. "It was good, like really damn good. He didn't even scarper as soon as I was asleep." I grinned, thinking of the noises he'd made when I sucked his dick.

"Wow! Sounds like a keeper to me. Are you seeing him again?" Leo asked eagerly, clearly hoping I would say yes. All the guys here wanted me to find a good man and be happy.

"We're grabbing a bite to eat on Wednesday." I wanted to shrug it off as if it was no big deal, but little tingles sparked through me. I was definitely not going to look for flaws or ways this could all go wrong. He seemed into me. Hell, he'd persisted enough.

"A date, *niiiice.*" Leo gave a low whistle. Then he got all silly. "Where are you going? Have you told anyone else? How much do you like him?" He tapped a little drumroll on the bar.

"Leo, babe, I love you, but please calm down. We haven't decided where we're going. You're the first person to ask, and I like him enough to see him again." I really wanted to tell him I'd had the best time, that I really liked Munro and wanted it to go further. But I'd done that before, and every time I'd ended up being the one dumped, ghosted, or shown up when the man I'd been with came in with someone else.

Leo squealed for a good ten seconds, then calmed down and gave me a hug. "I have a good feeling about him, Beck. He went out of his way to see you, and you had a great time in bed. I can't wait to tell Bruno."

I inwardly groaned and left him to go and serve a customer. Hopefully, he'd moved on to something else when I got back to him. Monday nights were never too busy, which meant it always gave us time to catch up. I loved hearing about him and Bruno. The chance of finding your one, your forever man, was so slim that their story always warmed my heart. They showed that love could conquer everything, that if he was your person, then nothing would keep you apart. I didn't need rich or famous. In fact, after seeing the hassle Leo and Bruno went through, I'd happily settle for fun and faithful. And Munro and I'd got off to a good start. He seemed as much into me as I was into him. Still, there had been a few awkward moments when Munro acted a little weird. But I'd never got the feeling he didn't want to be with me. If his phone hadn't rung, we would've carried on and got naked again. Would he have wanted to fuck me? He's got a nice dick, not quite as long as mine, but his girth would cause a delicious burn.

I could send him a message, couldn't I? Just something funny, not too gushy or enthusiastic. I didn't want to look too eager. The truth was I was seriously into him. I grabbed my phone from the till and opened WhatsApp.

Me: Hey, just thought I'd say hi.
Me: I'm looking forward to Wednesday.
Me: Have you thought about where to go?

I didn't expect him to get back to me immediately, but instead of putting my phone back on the counter, I stuffed it into my pocket. If he did reply, the vibrations would alert me.

The evening dragged by, and Munro still hadn't replied. Dammit. Maybe I'd come across too keen after all. Not a lot I could do about it now. Closing time arrived—thank god that was at eleven tonight—and I shut the doors after the last patrons with a heavy sigh.

Leo was already closing down the tills, and it took another twenty minutes before we'd finished. "I've got Bruno's car. I can give you a lift home if you'd like?" Leo asked when we stepped out of the door. Leo's boyfriend had an Audi R8, and I always jumped at the chance at a ride in it.

"Hell, yeah. Thanks." I elbowed him. "What did you have to do to get his car?"

"Wouldn't you like to know?" He waggled his eyebrows. "Anyway, I don't think you need me. You've already got a ride." Leo gestured across the road.

I swivelled around. Munro was leaning against his BMW, his arms folded over his chest and his legs crossed at his ankles. He smiled, and my stomach did its flip-floppy thing as excitement fluttered through me.

"I'll see you later, Beck. Don't do anything I wouldn't do." Leo laughed and patted my back, then unlocked his car.

I wandered to the man who had distracted me far too much tonight. He uncrossed his arms and straightened, looking a little wary now.

"Hi," he said quietly. "Sorry I didn't reply to your text. I thought I'd come and speak to you in person."

I slowly perused his body, then smiled. "I like this way much better." I stepped a little closer until we were almost chest to chest. I brushed my lips over his. He stiffened, but when I repeated it, he relaxed.

"Can I drive you home?" Munro asked, his voice low.

"Yes, please."

Munro opened the passenger door, and I got in. When we were both settled, our seat belts buckled, he started the engine.

"Your friend drives a nice car. I wouldn't have put him and that car together," he said almost too casually as he pulled onto the empty road. What did he mean by that?

I chuckled. "Yeah, he does. The car belongs to his boyfriend, Bruno."

His eyebrows shot up into his hairline. "Bruno Alderton? I should've guessed. There aren't many of those cars around here."

"You know him?" I asked. How would he know him? I thought he ran a gym.

"I do. He's helped me out from time to time when I needed some promo work. Mainly when I first started." He shook his head. "I hadn't put two and two together that his boyfriend worked with you. He's mentioned him."

"What a small world we live in." I joked, but he didn't smile.

When we reached my place, Munro switched off the engine but didn't move. He kept his hands on the steering wheel. When I covered one with my own, he flinched but looked at me, his eyes full of worry.

"You're coming in, right? You didn't just turn up at my work to act as a taxi, did you?"

He nodded, and a small smile appeared. It was tight and not the easy-going one from ten minutes ago. "Yeah, I'd like to. If that's okay."

Something was going on, and I didn't like not knowing what. Why had he had a panicked look on his face when I mentioned Bruno? Maybe this wasn't a good idea after all. He didn't seem enthusiastic about it. "You don't have to, Munro. We can get together on Wednesday."

That seemed to shake him out of his melancholy. "No, I want to. I really do." His smile was better this time, warmer, more genuine, and finally reached his eyes. "I haven't been able to get you out of my mind."

"Then maybe we should go and give you something more to think about. I haven't tasted enough of you yet." In the low glow from the streetlight, the blush on his cheeks was cute. "Get your arse indoors. I want my mouth on it."

"Christ, Beck, you can't just say that."

"Oh, I can, and much more. I want you screaming tonight."

Chapter 9

Munro

With a muted thud, my head hit the pillow as my legs stiffened and my balls tightened. Beck's throat constricted around my cock as he swallowed. Grunts and groans I didn't recognise filled the room until I realised I was making them. I'd never imagined an orgasm could totally consume me, but as I fired cum into his mouth, my vision blurred and went black.

The tight, wet heat surrounding my dick slackened as Beck lapped up my softening length, then released me. He kissed up my body until he reached my mouth and pressed his lips to mine.

"Told you I could make you scream." His lazy smile turned into a full-blown grin. He flopped down next to me. "I'll give you a few minutes to catch your breath."

"Okay. And what happens then?"

"Then I'm going to get my tongue in your arse, and maybe if you can last, I'll fuck you too." He waggled his eyebrows, the gleam in his eyes wicked and dangerous. My dick throbbed. It knew what it wanted, and more orgasms were definitely at the top of the list. The thought of his mouth on my hole was scary, forbidden, embarrassing, but god, I wanted it. I'd spent too many hours wanking as I watched rimming scenes on PornHub, wondering what it would feel like and if I'd want to do that. But after seeing and feeling Beck's arse, I knew I wanted to try it.

"Only if I get a chance to taste you too." I leant closer and kissed him. He opened his mouth, and I slipped my tongue inside to stroke his. I wasn't going to need any more time. My dick was rock hard again. I rolled on top of him so our dicks touched, and rocked my hips, rubbing us together.

Beck broke the kiss. "Fuck."

"Yes, please." I stared down at him. "Fuck me now." The rimming would have to wait. I grabbed the lube from the middle of the bed, where he'd thrown it and a condom before we got naked. I straddled his waist.

"You just keep getting hotter," Beck growled and tore the condom open with his teeth. He skilfully reached between my legs and rolled the condom down his length. I ran my lubed hand down his cock, then lined him up to my opening. I knew from all my time with my dildos that I loved the burn of being stretched, and I lazily lowered down.

I groaned as he split me. I slowly took him all, the delicious heat scorching my channel. "So good, so fucking good," I crooned. Beck slid his hands up my thighs, rubbing his thumbs over the crease. I'd never thought of it as an erogenous zone, but damn, it felt good when he stroked me there.

I relaxed into the intense feeling and let my body take over. I rocked my hips slowly back and forth, which made Beck's cock rub my prostate. Sparks shot through my body. I always thought of sex being frantic, fast, a clash of two bodies racing to climax, but this, this was so different. No rush, no hurry. It was more than I'd ever thought I'd be able to have. I didn't want to give this up.

"You're squeezing me so tight, Munro. It's incredible. Ride me, baby."

I found my rhythm and knew I wouldn't last long. I leant over Beck's body and captured his mouth. I fucked into his mouth as he pounded into my arse. My orgasm burst from me, spraying Beck's stomach. I arched my back, crying out his name. As Beck stiffened beneath me, he dug his fingers in my thighs. His dick thickened and swelled as he fired his load into the condom. My arms gave way, and I flopped down onto Beck. He didn't seem to mind and wrapped his arms around me.

"It's never been as good as it is with you," he murmured into my hair, his breath warm on my ear. "I'm getting addicted to you. I haven't been able to get you out of my head."

"I feel the same," I spoke quietly. It was true. I lifted my head. "I really like you, Beck."

"Can you stay tonight?"

I nodded. No way was I going to leave this perfect place. "Yeah, I'd like that." I kissed him. "And maybe a shower?"

Lying in bed with Beck was like a dream. We fitted together. We talked softly, nothing too serious, just a bit about our lives, films we liked, books we'd read. I didn't share anything about my life that would tell him too much. He hadn't recognised me, and I wasn't going to be the one who would burst this bubble. That would mean I had to tell him I hadn't been honest about who I was. He curled his body around mine, and I fell asleep with him breathing softly on my neck.

I woke after only a few hours' sleep. I always did. The result of years of going running before school, then college and now as part of my business. I had to stay in shape and needed to always look at the peak of fitness for all my posts and blogs. I kissed him, then slid out of bed and pulled on my clothes. I'd seen a notepad on the front of the fridge, so I went in and left him a message.

Off to work. See you tomorrow. I'll pick you up at 7.30 x

After closing the front door, I got in my car and smiled, a smile that filled my heart with joy. The drive to the gym was quiet. I liked this time of day. And today was going to be different. It was time to work out a plan to come out. I needed to check all my sponsor contracts, maybe speak to some of the bigger ones. They already had gay influencers on the books. The idea of having Beck in my pictures thrilled me. I wanted him to be my boyfriend, but I needed to get this all done first.

I pulled into my parking space. The familiar black R8 was parked in the far corner. Bruno was here. This had to be a coincidence, surely. Leo hadn't seemed to recognise me. And I'd never seen the beautiful blond man here with Bruno.

I grabbed my bag from the passenger footwell and went inside. Bright lights lit up the staff entrance. The morning shift started at six a.m., ready to supervise the early-morning members. Ignoring the stairwell that led upstairs to the offices, I walked straight into the changing rooms. Music thumped from the main gym. Someone was into Ed Sheeran this morning.

Bruno was running hard on the treadmill, and judging by his sweat-soaked vest, he had been here for a while. I weaved through the machines to him. He gave me a wink through the mirror but didn't stop. I doubted he knew anything, and the tension in my chest dissipated. I started my warm-up run and slowly increased the speed. As I ran, my head was full of images from last night—glimpses of the sheen of sweat on Beck's body, the curve of his jawline, and the bright ink that covered his arms, his chest, just about all of his torso. If I clenched my bum, it ached deliciously, as if he was still inside me.

"You must have had a good night." He laughed.

"You might just be right." I wanted to ask him about his coming out. His fame was reaching its peak, and he'd managed to raise his profile by admitting his sexuality. I was nowhere near as well known as him, so why was I still worried?

"Good for you, Munro." He was slowing down. "Beck's a great guy."

My feet stumbled, and I grabbed the rail to keep upright. Without looking in the mirror wall, I knew I must have a terrified expression on my face. Bruno stopped his machine and looked at me as if he were reading every thought in my head. I stopped my treadmill and slowly turned to him.

"Shit, sorry. Have I fucked up? You're not seeing him?"

I checked the rest of the room. It was empty except for a woman on a rowing machine and a man working his glutes and thighs on the stepper. Neither was close enough to hear me. "Um, it's complicated."

"I can see that. I've gotta say, mate, I never knew you were gay, or is it bi? Or maybe I should shut up and mind my own business."

"I..." I had no words. My head was a jumble of panic and the need to tell him, to talk about it. "I-I'm gay, but I'm not out. No one knows. The whole thing is new to me, and I don't know what to do." Wow, had I just come out to my friend? "This is the first time I've admitted that out loud."

He froze. Then a hardened look crossed his face. "You'd better not fuck Beck around. That group of friends is like nothing I've seen before. They protect each other fiercely. I know from personal experience they will shut you down the moment you hurt him."

"I know that." I choked up again. "It's a fucking mess, and I don't know how to change it."

"If you're serious about him, then you have to be honest. Tell Beck, talk to him, explain everything. I've got to say I don't think Beck will ever go back in the closet for anyone. Coming out cost him a lot. You're going to have to decide if you want it to go further. But I'm here for you if you need to talk. I know coming out is hard, and I'd never push anyone to do it, but if you can't, then leave him alone until you're ready."

I nodded. Chains of guilt and fear wrapped around my body again. Locking me straight back in the closet. I wanted Beck, but I was scared. The positivity I'd felt when I left him had gone. My secret wasn't so secret anymore. How many more of Beck's friends had recognised me? How many of their partners now knew? The walls around me were starting to crumble, and I didn't know what to do.

"Beck doesn't know who you are, does he?"

"No, he hasn't recognised me." I let out a dry chuckle. "I wasn't sure whether to be disappointed or relieved."

"I'm not sure whether Leo will tell him. I can't ask him not to, not without going deeper into why. I don't keep secrets from my boyfriend, Munro, but unless he asks me outright, I'll keep this conversation private." Bruno wiped down his machine, and with a pat on my shoulder, he was gone.

His words stayed in my head. *I know coming out is hard, and I'd never push anyone to do it, but if you can't, then leave him alone until you're ready.*

Am I ready, or do I need more time?

BECK

The floaty feeling I had didn't go away. I spent my day off lazily, not wanting to get the images of Munro out of my head.

Until I received his message.

Munro: Hey, Beck, I'm sorry, but I'm going to have to cancel tonight. Something has come up at work.

Well, shit. That was a brush-off if ever I'd heard one. Disappointment rolled through me, which was crazy. We'd only hooked up twice. Why had I put him in a different category than that? It was just that. He'd hung around after work for me both times. Neither encounter had been a date.

I wasn't sure what to do for the rest of my day off. As I ran the work rota through my head, I worked out that Sawyer was off tonight. It would be good to catch up with him. He probably had plans with Devon, but it was worth asking if he was up for a pint. I had to reply to Munro first, though. I pushed the hurt away.

Me: No worries. See you around.

The dots blinked as he wrote a reply, then stopped, and the screen went blank. Then they were back. It happened another three times, but his reply never came.

I shot a new message to Sawyer.

Me: Hey, are you free for a drink tonight, maybe pizza?
Sawyer: Yeah, sounds good. 7.30 at the bar? We can go on
from there.
Me: Yeah, great. See you there.

At least I'd salvaged my day. Except all my warm fuzzy feelings were now replaced with disappointment and sadness. Another chance at happiness gone. When would I ever learn?

When I walked into the bar, Sawyer was already there. He was talking to Max and Jonas.

"Hey, what's this? A mother's meeting?" I chuckled.

Jonas gave me a searching look. I hated when he read me like this. He always could get me to tell him exactly what I was feeling. Maybe we should talk again and see if we could get things to work for us this time around.

Max answered me. "We're discussing employing a new bartender. Gus isn't able to commit to the hours anymore. His teaching job at the university is consuming enough of his time. I don't want him taking on too much."

I nodded. I knew Gus was stretched thin. He'd already cut his hours down. "Have you got anyone in mind? You must have had inquiries since the new uni year has started."

"We have, and there are a few that look promising," Jonas said. "I'm calling them in for an interview."

Leo joined the conversation after finishing an order. "I thought you were getting all loved up this evening. What happened?"

Crap, I really didn't want to talk about it, not in front of them all. I'd planned to get Sawyer's thoughts on it. I didn't think he knew or had anything to do with Munro, whereas Leo could get Bruno involved.

"Nah, it fell through. He had something come up." I shrugged it off. "Shall we go?" I said to Sawyer.

He nodded, and we said our goodbyes, but I could feel all their eyes on my back. It was a short walk to the pizza place, which was a favourite of ours. It wasn't a high street chain, but they made pizzas that were to die for. We knew the owners, and eating there always resulted in having a good evening.

We were seated quickly, and after ordering a drink, Sawyer pinned me with a 'don't mess with me' look. "Spill the beans. What's going on?"

I gave him the short version, not wanting to go into too much detail. "So I think I was just an itch he needed to scratch. He'd said he'd never done this sort of thing, so I guess I was an easy pickup."

"No way. He's been watching you for weeks, months even. Hell, Beck, he was one step from being a stalker." He shook his head. "Maybe something really had come up. Did you ask him?"

"No, because it's a classic brush-off. If he'd meant it, he would've called or tried to make another date work." I got my phone out and showed him the message.

Sawyer frowned as he read it. "I think you pretty much closed the door on it going any further."

"Yeah, I did. I'm not someone's fuck toy or experiment. For all I know, his girlfriend has forgiven him for whatever happened, and they've got back together."

Sawyer grimaced but didn't contradict me. "Yeah, maybe. But it might be worth you speaking to him when he gets back in touch."

"If he gets in touch again." I wasn't holding my breath.

We moved on to safer subjects, like our friends' love lives, and discussed who would be our new bartender. The food was great as always. We'd had a few beers so that by the time we were ready to leave, I had a nice buzz going on.

"Where to next?" I asked Sawyer when we got outside. "Will Devon have finished by now?"

"Yeah, but he's probably knackered and will want to go home." We walked back towards BAR 28.

Leo banged the till closed and wiped the counter so hard the glasses rattled. He was spitting fire. If looks could kill, there'd be bodies everywhere.

What had happened? The evening had seemed normal, not too busy, just a regular Wednesday night.

"What's up?" I asked.

He startled, and his eyes flickered over, but the throng of people blocked my view. "Nothing, sorry. Just a pain-in-the-arse customer. How was your pizza? Did you put the world to rights?"

"Yeah, it was good. I'm not stopping long, but you know how it is. I just can't stay away from you." I laughed and nudged Sawyer, but he was looking in the same direction as Leo. The group of girls in front of me moved, giving me a view of the corner.

And Munro.

He was with the same girl again. With them were two other guys, who I recognised too from earlier visits. Before Sawyer or Leo could say anything, I walked up to them. All I could think of was how fucking gorgeous Munro looked. He wore a tight black V-neck T-shirt that showed off his muscular chest and arms. The colour made him look even more tanned. He was laughing. He glanced up, and his smile fell away. All the colour drained from his face, and his eyes went wide. Yep, caught you out, arsehole.

Then the girl saw me. "Oh hey, I'm glad you're here. Can we have another round of drinks, please?" She gathered the empty glasses and handed them to me. "You're a star."

I stared at Munro, waiting for him to speak, to say anything. Maybe introduce me to his friends, but he didn't. He looked away and said something to another man.

Well, didn't that just put me in my place?

Chapter 11

Munro

Bruno had been right that I had to get my head straight and my life in order before I could be out, openly gay, and with Beck.

But how did I do that? How did I tell Beck that I was a closet case? That I couldn't be out, open, and honest with him because I was afraid I'd lose my friends, my followers, and possibly my sponsors. Maybe not because I was gay, but because I'd been lying to everyone, even if it was by omission.

I'd pored over the contracts with my sponsors, and while they all read as inclusive, all mentioned morality clauses. Situations that would embarrass the company, tarnishing the company's reputation. If only I could hand it all over to my lawyer, but that would be telling him why, and the hole I'd dug myself into would keep getting bigger.

My phone rang, jolting me from my daze. "Hey, Ed."

"Hi, Munro, how's your week going? Cause mine is a shitshow. I could do with your advice. Do you fancy a couple of drinks tonight?"

Shit.

"Um, I had something planned, but I can cancel." How could I dismiss my date with Beck so casually?

"Awesome. Bros before hoes, right?" He chuckled. Mine, in return, was weak and felt like it was choking me. "Can you make eight o'clock?"

My mind was screaming at me to take it back. To tell him I couldn't cancel, that my plans were too important to miss.

I checked the time. It was past lunchtime, which meant letting Beck down at such short notice was a shitty thing to do. "Yeah, sure."

"Thanks, mate. Is The White Hart, okay?"

"Yeah, see you there." God, I was a fucking coward.

Ed said a cheery goodbye. I couldn't find my voice to respond. After dropping my phone, I bent over and knocked my forehead against the cold wood of my desk over and over. What the fuck had I done?

Slowly sitting upright again, I grabbed my phone and opened my messages with Beck, trying to think of a way to cancel. Finally, I came up with a lame excuse.

Me: Hey, Beck, I'm sorry, but I'm going to have to cancel tonight. Something has come up at work.

Then I waited for his reply. When it came, I wanted to cry. It was a terse dismissal. I knew it was over, but what could I expect? I didn't even have the balls to call him, to organise another time. I clenched my eyes tight, forcing the tears to stay locked down. When I'd got myself back in control, I shut my work down and went home.

At eight o'clock, I walked into the pub and scanned the room for Ed. He sat in the corner. I gave him a wave and gestured to the bar I'd get a drink. I wasn't in the mood for alcohol and ordered a Coke, then went to Ed's table.

"Thanks for coming, Munro," Ed said as I sat down and placed my drink on the highly polished, round wood table.

"No worries. What's up?"

He rattled on about all the details of his bad day, and while I tried to offer some advice, I knew it was lacking and not very helpful.

"You okay, Munro?" He slapped his hand on his forehead. "I really did stop you from seeing your secret girlfriend, didn't I?"

"I told you it was okay. Don't worry about it." I hated myself for being such a coward not only to Ed but to Beck as well. After all the effort I'd put in, I was the one to dismiss it so quickly. I would never get another chance, and I deserved to be alone.

We chatted about other things, the gym, my latest products to promote. "You should come in, join my workout. Grab some free kit for a couple of photographs."

"Yeah? Okay. Unless it's bright orange." We both groaned at the memory of a hideous set of gym wear one of our would-be sponsors had sent.

A shrill voice called our names. I set my Coke down with such force the liquid sloshed over the rim onto my hand and the table. "What's Lucie doing here? You know she's got worse about me lately."

"Yeah, she called. I told her we'd be here. It's not a big deal. She was okay when I spoke to her." Ed didn't even look the slightest bit remorseful.

"Great, thanks a lot, Ed." Lucie was the last person I wanted to see, especially not after her rage the other day. "If she starts on me, I'm going home. I'm sick and fed up with her clingy bullshit."

"She's always been like that. It's only now that it's bothering you. Is it because you've met someone?"

Did I really want to have this conversation? No, because there was no point. Not after the stupid message I'd sent. Lucie strutted through the room, swishing her long, blonde, and perfectly straight hair over her shoulder. I got an image of the bitchy girl from that Netflix programme, *Selling Sunset*, in my head. I had to hold back the laugh but snorted as she reached us and bent down to air-kiss my cheek.

"What has you making animal noises?" She simpered, her voice like saccharine. "No hot date tonight, Munro?"

"No, not tonight," I muttered. Any hint of laughter had evaporated.

"Well, I can't wait to hear all about her. Spill the beans, sweetie." She sat next to me and plastered another fake smile on her face. Her eyes flicked to my neck and the still obvious bruises.

"Nothing to tell. I don't think it'll be happening again." I fiddled with my glass of Coke, trailing the beads of water gathered on the glass with my fingers. If only I had ordered vodka.

"Well, never mind. We can cheer you up. Can't we, Ed? Anyway, I said we'd all meet Will at BAR 28, so chop, chop." She stood up again.

What the fuck? I couldn't go there. It might be Beck's night off, but his friends would still be there. Another of Bruno's warnings came back to my mind. That they all protect each other fiercely. "I think I'll head home."

Lucie gave me the evil eye. "Don't be stupid, Munro. It's early still."

"I'm not going to BAR 28 tonight, Lucie. You can go and do what you like."

"What's wrong with you? You like it there. I want to go and stare at hot bartenders for a couple of hours."

"You know they're all gay, right?" My voice got higher and louder as panic flowed through me.

Both Ed and Lucie stared at me. "I know that, but they are all so pretty. Do you have a problem with them being gay? I've never thought of you as a homophobe, Munro. Shame on you. I'll protect you from them." Then she stroked my chest and patted it.

"What? Of course, I'm not. Stop being a bitch, Lucie." I checked my watch. "We'd better go, or Will will think we've deserted him."

Lucie preened, glowing as if she'd won a prize. She smoothed her hand down her skintight and extremely short dress and strode past me.

The whole night had now gone to shit. I glared at Ed. "Thanks, mate, thanks a fucking bunch."

"Yeah, okay, I'm sorry. She really does seem to have it in for you. I don't know if she loves or hates you."

"I'd rather she didn't think anything about me."

We followed her, and five minutes later, we were at BAR 28, and I wanted to shrink into a corner and hide away from all eyes. Yeah, great idea, apart from Leo instantly spotting me. He smiled, then scowled as he saw who I was with, or maybe it was who I wasn't with.

I managed to avoid sitting next to Lucie, who was already spouting off her order to a server. But I loved Ed and Will and chuckled at something Will said.

Then, of course, it all went catastrophically wrong.

Beck was here. Marching towards me, but before either of us could speak, Lucie ordered another round of drinks. I wanted the ground to open up and swallow me into the fiery pits of hell as she handed him all our empty glasses.

Beck looked at her like she was an alien, then glanced at me. I wanted to say something, anything to make all this go away, but nothing came out. With one slow blink, Beck turned away from me. The hurt on his beautiful face cut me to the quick. I shot out of my seat and rushed up to him.

As I reached him, he was placing the used glasses on the bar top. Leo was glaring at me as he said something to Beck.

"Beck, I'm sorry. Please can we talk?" I tried to touch him, but he stepped away. "I'm sorry Lucie did that. It was wrong of her."

"Is that it? That's all you're sorry for, Munro?" His voice was so sharp he could've slashed me open. "Go back to your friends and leave me alone."

"I don't want to. I want you, Beck. I fucked up, I know I did, but please let me explain," I pleaded with him.

"What's taking so long?" Lucie stepped next to me, her hand on my shoulder. I shrugged her hand off.

"Go away, Lucie. Just leave me the fuck alone. I've told you enough times," I snapped. She stared at me, then at Beck.

"Why aren't you sorting our drinks?" She swept her hair over her shoulder.

"Lucie," I snarled. "Go away, right this fucking minute."

I looked back to Beck. "Please, Beck?"

Chapter 12

BECK

This was ridiculous. Why hadn't I turned away, left him standing, and gone home? Leo looked like he was about to call Steve, one of the doormen, to get them all out of here. Sawyer put his hand on my shoulder and gave it a squeeze.

Munro stood in front of me, staring, imploring me to stay, to listen. He clenched his hands in and out of fists as he seemed to hold himself back from touching me. I ached to do the same, but there was more going on here, something that was beginning to make sense.

The blonde, Lucie, was watching us, her eyes narrowed. Whether she would decipher what was going on depended on if Munro could get her to leave us alone.

"Lucie, go and sit down." Munro looked over his shoulder at his friends. One of them stood up and walked over to us. "Ed, I need a minute to talk to Beck. Take Lucie, please."

"How do you know his name?" Lucie glared. Then it was like a cartoon, and a lightbulb went on over her head. "Munro, you've got to be kidding me? Him? He's who you've been with? Him? A man?" Her words came out in a high-pitched screech. Munro looked terrified, frozen to the spot as if he were waiting for the world to collapse around him.

The new guy gave me a look of understanding. He didn't seem surprised, and with a weak smile, he took hold of Lucie's wrist. "Enough, Luce. C'mon, leave Munro to talk."

Sawyer broke the silence. "Go out the back, Beck. You can talk it out with Munro there."

I nodded, not sure if this was a good idea. Munro had gone pale, his eyes wide with what looked like terror. "Okay, yeah. Come this way." I gestured to the back of the bar and stepped around him. He didn't move, so I brushed his hand. "Munro?"

My touch seemed to stir him out of his trance, and after a brief look to the table with his friends, he followed me.

The corridor felt a mile long as I led him to the break room. I let Munro walk in first, then closed the door behind us. I leant against it, although I knew no one would come in.

"What just happened, Munro?" I snapped

He stayed silent, looking everywhere but at me. I said his name again, softer this time.

"Christ, I can't believe I'm going to say this," he mumbled under his breath, so quietly I wasn't sure if I was meant to hear him. Then he lifted his head. He looked terrified, one step away from running away. He blew out a shaky, stuttering breath. "I'm not out. I'm twenty-eight and, until you, a closeted virgin."

What the fuck? How? What? Shit.

Before I could speak, Munro put up his hand. "Please, Beck, just wait. Let me explain."

Yes, an explanation would be great right about now.

"My name is Munro Sylvester. I run and own Well Fit, a company with six gyms in major cities. I'm kind of popular on Instagram. I never meant to leave it so long, but the more popular I became, the scarier it got and the easier it became to stay hidden. I have so many sponsors who pay me to advertise and promote their goods I was frightened to see what would happen to my company if they found out after this long."

Oh, god. How had I not recognised him? I should've realised when Bruno mentioned helping him out with some promotions. But I would never have contemplated having a celebrity who would like me and wanted to be with me. Why hadn't Leo told me who he was?

A huge lump grew in my throat, and I had to swallow several times to clear it. "You should've told me," I blurted out. "Christ, Munro, why? Why didn't you say anything?"

"What? You're kidding me, right? What would you have done when I was naked in your bed and I said, 'Oh, by the way, I'm really well known on social media. I'm not out, and also I'm a virgin'? I'll tell you what would've happened. You would have kicked me out of your bed and your home in ten seconds flat."

The images of that night flooded my brain: his hesitancy in the car, the shake in his voice, the trembling hands as he stripped off. The signs had been there, but I hadn't paid attention to them. Would I have stopped it? I wasn't sure. What I was certain of was that I wanted him, and he was eager, desperate even, to be with me. The rabbit-in-the-headlights face was back. "No, I don't think I would've made you leave. But I probably wouldn't have taken it so far. Kept it to hand or blow jobs and talked through anything else."

"Yeah? You say that now." He paused. What else was on his mind? "I didn't want to take it slow. I wanted you so much. I still want you so much. I've been watching you for months now, and I know you've noticed me. I had to take the chance. I knew you weren't ever going to call me, so I waited. And, Beck, it was the best night of my life. You made it the greatest night. I wanted to tell you, wanted you to know how special it was to be with you. I could've met someone on Grindr, let a stranger fuck me, then leave, never to be seen again. But I couldn't. I wanted my first time to be with someone I felt a strong attraction to, a connection I thought could lead to something further than a one-night stand."

I was speechless. He was telling the truth. It had been a great night, one of the best I'd had, and I wanted more. "Oh, Munro," I said sadly. "It was a great night, but still, you should've told me."

"Why? Do you ask every guy you take to your bed if they've done it before? Of course, you don't. If you both went willingly to your bed, then it's a moot point."

"That's not the main issue, Munro. My issue isn't with your virginity. I'm thrilled that you loved what we did because I did too. The fact that you're not out is my bone of contention. That is what would've stopped me from going further that night, and that still stands. You're a great man, but I won't be—can't be—with someone who isn't honest about who he is. I'm not going to be your secret. I've been that before, and I swore never to be it again. Since I came out, I've had to give up a lot of things, and however hard that was at the time, I'm glad I did it. I love who I am. I love being an out and proud gay man. Staying single is a price I'm happy to pay to live my life genuinely."

Munro stayed quiet, and I hated it. I wanted to pull him into my arms, to feel him against me, because I really liked this man. I hated that we'd had all we could have.

"I'm sorry, Munro, so fucking sorry." My voice broke. My eyes burnt with unshed tears I rapidly blinked back.

He slumped back against the arm of the sofa, his shoulders dropping as if every hope he had for us evaporated. "It's me who should be apologising. I'm so sorry. I don't want this to be the end of us. I doubt anyone will ever beat you. We have the chance of something special. I think you know that too. Do you really want to throw that chance away?"

"No. No, I don't. So here's the thing. You need to go and work out your life. You have to decide what risks you're prepared to take to be true to yourself and be out and proud. You may decide the risks aren't worth taking and that you can't change your life. Then that's fine. It's your decision to make. But if you do come out, and you still want to take a chance of happiness with a tattooed man who's only a bartender, then come and find me."

Munro nodded. His eyes glistened with tears. He chewed on the corner of his mouth, and one tear slipped free and slid slowly down his cheek. Fuck, this was killing me. I stepped up to him and did what I'd wanted to do since we'd started this conversation: I wrapped my arms around him and held him close. He slipped his arms around my waist, and we stayed silently in the bittersweet embrace for a few minutes. Then I kissed his forehead and released him.

"I'd better go," he whispered. I nodded and moved aside.

When he reached the door, his hand on the handle, he looked back. "Thanks, Beck. Thank you for everything. I need to sort things out, but I'll come back to you, and if you're still interested in me, then maybe we can see how good we could be together." He stepped into the corridor, and I counted his footsteps until they were gone.

"I'll wait," I said to the empty room. Hopefully, it wouldn't be for too long.

I waited for my friends to come and find me, to tell me it would all be okay. Sawyer was the first to come looking for me and gave me a hug. "You okay?"

I shrugged. "No, not really, but I will be. I always get back up again, you know that."

"If it makes you feel any better, he looked as wrecked as you."

"I'm not sure how that's going to make me feel better, but thank you." My chuckle sounded more like a snotty hiccup. "I'm going home."

"D'you want me to come with you?"

"No, I'll be okay." I wiped my hand over my face, pulling myself together. "I know I shouldn't feel like this. We've only got together a couple of times. But I thought we were at the start of something good."

"It's okay to feel like this, Beck. It will all work out in the end. He's your person, and he'll get it sorted. You just need to give him some time."

I wanted to scoff, to deny Sawyer, but I couldn't. And that was because I believed him. I was supposed to be with Munro. Hell, I had no idea how I knew, but I was as certain of it as I was of my own   name.

"Yeah, I know."

Chapter 13

Munro

I pressed the button on my ridiculously expensive coffee maker, a total pointless indulgence, considering I take my coffee black. After a night of fitful sleep and dreams full of Beck walking away with another man, I felt like utter shite. Last night, I hadn't bothered going back to the table where my friends had been waiting. Instead, I'd walked out of the bar and towards the taxis waiting just up the road.

The last person I'd wanted to see was Lucie. None of this would've happened if she hadn't made me come to BAR 28. The way she had treated Beck made my blood boil, not just because it was to the man I was falling for, but because no one should be so rude and disrespectful. She never used to be like this. When had she changed? One thing I did know was that I was done with her.

As I picked up my full coffee cup, the doorbell rang. Groaning, I walked to the panel on the wall by the door and looked at the screen. Bruno was standing on my doorstep. No surprise there. And by the scowl on his face, he was about to kick my arse. He had warned me, but it hadn't been all my fault. I hadn't expected to see Beck last night. Yep, a totally pathetic and weak excuse. I deserved whatever Bruno had to say.

I opened the door and stepped aside, letting him enter. Was Leo with him? The car was empty. Thank god he'd come alone. Leo had looked like he was ready to throw a punch last night.

Bruno smirked as I closed the door. "I left my little Rottweiler at home. Trust me, it's safer for you."

"I know. I thought he was going to kick me out." It was easier to get all this out of the way before I asked him for help. "Coffee?"

Bruno nodded, and I went back to the kitchen. The coffee didn't take long, and with mugs in hand, I led him through to my living room.

"Go on then. Let me have it." I sighed as I sank into my squishy sofa.

Bruno looked down at his coffee, taking his time. He shook his head. "You fucking idiot. I warned you not to mess around with him. So what the fuck happened?"

"I did what you said. I cancelled my date with him and was going to leave him alone. I wanted to look into what coming out could mean to me professionally and get my lawyer to check through all the contracts I have. To reach out to other influencers who had come out and ask for their advice." I put my mug down on the wood-and-resin coffee table and flopped back, resting my head on the back cushion as I stared at the ceiling.

"Then what the hell were you doing in his place of work?" Bruno shifted sideways and tucked his bent knee up on the seat.

"I wasn't supposed to be, and I sure as shit didn't want to go." I filled him in on Lucie's behaviour and her calling me a homophobe, then what had happened in the bar. Bruno knew what Lucie was like. She knew Bruno's sister.

"Bloody Lucie, so she's guessed, then," Bruno said.

"I dunno. I haven't spoken to her." I shrugged. The first thing I'd done when I got in the cab was switch my phone off. "I don't want to be anywhere near any of my friends right now."

He nodded. The sympathetic look on his face nearly broke me. "Leo said you spoke to Beck, but since you're alone here, I'm guessing it didn't go well."

The swell of tears built up again. I picked up my coffee, just for something to do. "Honestly, Bruno, it went better than I expected it to. But no, he's not here, and until I'm ready to come out, he won't be."

"He gave you an ultimatum? That doesn't sound like Beck."

"No, he didn't. But he explained he wasn't ever going to hide who he was or be someone's secret. I get it, and I don't blame him. But he told me to find him if I get myself sorted," I chuckled a dry laugh. "He said if I was still interested in him, a tattooed man who's only a bartender, that is."

"Yeah, Beck doesn't have a high opinion of himself. He judges himself on his failures and the successes of those around him. He shouldn't because he's one of the nicest men I've met. He's true and honest to himself and his friends."

"Yeah, I know that. I only hope no one else sweeps him off his feet before I get a chance."

"I don't think you need to worry about that. Beck's your person. He'll wait for you." Bruno drank his coffee, then stood up. "You shouldn't leave it too long, though, Munro. Not if you really want him. I'm here if you need to talk and if you need any advice about coming out. My lawyer is brilliant at this sort of thing. I can get in touch with him if yours doesn't give you what you need in terms of advice and support."

At the front door, Bruno gave me a hug, something he hadn't done before, but I appreciated it. "You've got to want to do this, Munro. Don't do it just for Beck. Do it for you. If you want anything, give me a call. That does mean turning your phone on, though." He clapped me on the shoulder, then left.

He was right. I had to want this for me. The first thing I had to do was call my PA to let her know I wasn't going to be in for a couple of days. I went to my office and picked up my phone from the counter, where I'd left it last night.

Erin was surprised. And I couldn't blame her. I rarely took time off, but she agreed to rearrange my meetings. Which left me staring at the screen and the number of missed calls, voicemails, and messages. Now wasn't the time for them. I needed to get the legal aspects of my coming out started.

I waited for the call to connect, my knee bouncing with nerves.

"Hobson, Whitworth, and Mortimer, how can I help you?" the receptionist said.

I rubbed my free hand down my leg, wiping my sweaty palm dry. I coughed, clearing the boulder that seemed lodged in my throat. "I'd like to speak to Martin Hobson, please. It's Munro Sylvester."

The line went quiet.

"Munro, great to hear from you. How are you? What amazing deal have you been offered now?" Martin said. He was a great guy, not much older than me.

My laugh was hollow, and the boulder was back again. "No, not this time. Look, this is an incredibly difficult thing to say, and I'm hoping you can help me." I hesitated. "Okay, here goes. I'm gay."

Silence. Then Martin sighed softly. "Thank you for telling me, Munro. I hope it feels good to say it out loud. I've always wondered if you were."

Huh? I sat down with a thunk into my chair. "What? How? I mean, I don't understand." My breathing got harder, heavier as I tried to drag air into my lungs.

"Munro, take it easy. I've known you for nearly a decade, and in all that time, you've never mentioned a partner of any gender. You could be ace or demi, but my inner gaydar always went with gay."

"I can't believe it. Why have you never said anything?"

He chuckled. "For many reasons. First, it would have been highly unprofessional of me. Second, it's not any of my business, and third, it's your life and your journey. Now, how about you tell me what you need me to do? Because I'm certain you didn't only want to come out to me."

I let out a long, low breath. Then I laughed. The relief flooding through me was exhilarating and totally unexpected. "Yes, I mean no. That's not why I called. I've met someone, and I don't want to hide anymore. How are my contracts going to fare? Is my coming out going to cause problems? Can they drop me?"

"They can't cancel the agreement because of your sexuality. That breaks far too many laws, but they are within their rights to pull the endorsements at the end of the contracts. They would also be able to cancel if you broke any morality clause."

"I've read the contracts and noticed that, but what exactly does it mean?"

"It means if you were found to be doing something illegal or improper that could lead to harming the brand in any way, the company could withdraw their sponsorship."

"That won't be a problem." I couldn't imagine being brave enough to do anything more than hold Beck's hand in public. I was hardly going to blow him in the toilets of BAR 28.

"Munro, I made sure your contracts are watertight and in your favour, but the problem could lie with someone taking photographs of you in a private moment. Have you shared your news with your closest friends? Is there anyone who could or will take the news negatively? Because I'm sorry to say that these breaches of confidentiality and privacy are often performed by disgruntled relatives or friends."

Lucie and the horrified look on her face as she'd worked it out came to mind. "My friend Lucie questioned me last night. I haven't seen or spoken to her since. I turned my phone off after I'd spoken to Beck. By the way, he's the man I want to be with."

"Perhaps we can leave her for a moment. The first thing to do is decide when you want to contact your sponsors. If one of your friends could cause a problem, then maybe sooner rather than later. If you're ready now, I can put together a notification for you to approve. Then I can get it to them. Unless we hear anything negative, when and how you make it public is up to you."

My heart was pounding so hard it was as if I had a troupe of Taiko drummers in my chest. My knee was jittering again, as were my hands. Was I ready to do this, to be an out man? Could I be a proud gay man who had a boyfriend? Martin said my name. I took another breath in. "Sorry, I freaked out for a moment."

"Munro, don't do anything you don't want to. Make sure you're ready, talk to your friends, maybe explain what it's been like hiding who you are and why you did it. Ask for their help and support."

"What if they don't like it?" Shit, what would Will and Ed say?

"Then they aren't the friends you thought they were, and you don't need them in this new part of your life." His voice held a harsh tone but one of sadness too.

"You sound like you know what you're talking about."

"I do." He went quiet for a moment. "Munro, you have my support. Have a think about what you would like to do and let me know."

This was it, make or break time. "Put the notification letter together, please. I'm not hiding any longer. I've got a chance with the best man I know. I'm not going to lose him."

"Okay, then. I'll have something for you by the end of the day," Martin said.

"Thank you, thank you so much."

We ended the call, and I leant back in my leather office chair. This was it. With shaking hands, I scrolled through the messages, ignoring Lucie's—I'd had enough of her—and opened Ed's first.

What?

Chapter 14

BECK

It had been over a week since I'd spoken to Munro and he'd walked away. I hadn't expected to feel so lonely after he'd left. We were hardly an item. We had only had a couple of nights of great sex. But he'd felt so right. Everything we'd done and shared had been so easy as if we'd known each other for years. Yet it was so excitingly new. His need for me, for more, was matched by my own for him. I needed him to make the right decision, to choose being out and being with me. But it wasn't up to me. Sawyer had kept me company when I wasn't at work, and everyone here has been great. I'd had boyfriends for longer and not felt this unhappy. Maybe it had been my fault. I should know by now that finding someone right for me wasn't going to happen.

"Beck." Gus laid his hand on mine. "Are you okay?"

I jumped at the contact. Damn, I'd been out of it. What could I say? Yeah, no worries, or did I say that I felt like I'd the rug pulled out from under me and I was falling?

"Yeah, of course. Just lost in my thoughts." I smiled and listened to the conversation again. We were looking through some of the application forms for the new bartender. Gus had finally decided he needed to quit. His workload at the university had got too heavy for him to keep working here. He didn't need the extra money and late nights anymore.

Max and Jonas had been through them first and rejected the ones who weren't suitable. Now they wanted our opinions. We had to be the ones to work with them, so we should get a look, Jonas told us.

"What about this one?" Sawyer handed me a couple of A4 pages stapled together. "He seems good."

"Haydn Cooper," I read his name, then continued down the page. He was twenty-four and had worked in bars before. He seemed okay. "Yeah, he looks good."

Gus nodded and put him on the yes pile. "I've seen him. He hand-delivered his CV. He's cute. He wore black-framed glasses and an old Libertines T-shirt and had a trendy-geek vibe going on."

He was the last of the choices. Thank god. I wanted to get home and hide for a day or two. My friends had been brilliant, so supportive, but being the single guy again was chafing my nerves.

"Have you heard anything?" Leo asked. Did he know something I didn't? Bruno was Munro's friend. I was certain he would've been in touch with him.

"No, I don't think I will be. He's too locked down. He may want to be out, but that's not the same as coming out. We all know that. I think you probably know more about how he is than I do."

Leo shook his head. "No, I don't. Bruno hasn't said anything. I told you he went around there the morning after you spoke, but he hasn't told me anything. I'm not going to ask either. This isn't my business, Beck."

"Thank you. I know it's dumb, but I have to get used to knowing that it has stopped before it even started." I hadn't told them I was prepared to wait, as I wasn't sure how well that would be received. I did believe Munro was the one, that he was my person, and I wasn't giving up on him yet. Not until he told me he was staying in the closet. "I'm off, guys. I'll catch up with you later."

When I stepped outside, cold wind whipped into my face. I shivered and wrapped my coat tighter around my body. With my head down, I hurried toward my flat.

"Hey, you! Beck!"

I stopped and turned around. Who had called my name? A woman strode up to me. The woman who had set all of this off. What was her name? Lucie. Munro had called her Lucie. Her face was a mask of fury. I didn't need that right now. Ignoring her, I carried on walking. Until she grasped my arm.

"Get your hand off me," I hissed at her. Mid-afternoon was always a busy time, the pavement filled with shoppers or people leaving the bars and restaurants after lunch. I wasn't going to have any kind of confrontation with her.

She tightened her hand around my forearm, effectively stopping me. "What do you want?" I didn't give a damn that I sounded rude.

"You're kidding me, right?" She sneered. "What I want is for you to leave my friend alone. I don't know what you did to him, but he's not gay. I've been his friend, his best friend, for years. I'd know if he was."

I gaped at her. Was she for real? Did she really think that she knew him better than he knew himself?

"He won't speak to me. He's not answering his calls or his messages. This is all your fault." She poked her finger in my chest.

I gently pushed her hand away. "You don't know anything about me, and it seems that you don't know your best friend. Just go away. Leave me alone. You need to take this up with him."

"I told you he won't talk to me. He won't even open his door." Her eyes flared.

"That's your problem, not mine."

"Fuck you. You know who he is, don't you? What do you think his followers would think and say about him if they thought he was gay? If he was with someone who looked like you? He'd be ruined. His whole business would collapse. And it would be your fault. Any rumour would be the end of him. You wouldn't want that, now would you?"

"You're crazy. No one will give a shit. You're the only one who hates the idea, and that's because he's never wanted you. However many times you've thrown yourself at him, he's turned you down." I stepped back and walked away, leaving her fuming on the pavement.

As I walked home, her words wouldn't leave my mind, though. That he could be ruined, lose everything he'd worked for if it got out that he was gay. I knew she was wrong. Bruno coming out hadn't damaged him. If anything, his popularity had grown. But he was in love with Leo and had him by his side when he'd told the world. Then it struck me what was going to happen. Lucie was going to out Munro and spread rumours about him. She wanted him to get hurt, to be damaged. I needed to warn him.

As soon as I got home, I pulled my phone out and brought up his messages. The last one still hurt, but I needed to move past it.

Me: Can we talk?

Would he reply? A few seconds later, the three dots appeared. I held my breath, but they disappeared again. I slumped back against the hallway wall. Dammit, he didn't want to talk to me. Then my phone vibrated and rang out. He'd called me.

"Hi." My voice wasn't much above a whisper. My stomach clenched. I had no clue what he was going to say.

"Beck? I can't believe you called. God, I've missed you." He sounded as breathless, as cautious, as me.

"Yeah, I've missed you too. Listen, I think you're going to be outed." I explained what had happened with Lucie and that it sounded like she would do something.

"God, that bloody woman," he snapped. "Okay, thank you, Beck. I appreciate it." He was quiet for long enough I checked if he'd ended the call, but it was still connected.

"Munro, are you okay?" What was going on? Did he have more to say? Was he going to tell me not to call or speak to him again?

"No, not really. I hate this. I hate that you're not here, not with me while I go through all this." The pain and hurt in his voice were palpable, and I felt the same.

"I hate it too, but, Munro, we agreed for you to do this in your own time. It's only been a few days. I can't force you to do anything. That would make me as bad as her."

"My lawyer is going to contact all my sponsors with a statement, and then I will know where I stand. And like he said, if they don't want to continue to support me, then they aren't the sponsors I want or need. The contracts only mention a morality clause, but as we haven't even been photographed together, let alone in a compromising position, they can't use that to break a contract. I'm serious, Beck. I'm doing this because you are more important to me than Instagram. My business won't collapse because I'm gay, I promise you."

My head was spinning. He was really doing it. He was choosing me. "No one has ever chosen me before," I croaked out, my throat thick, my eyes burning.

"I won't let anyone come between us. For as long as you want me, Beck, I'm yours."

I sniffed as the weight of my loneliness without him came crashing down. "I'm yours too."

"Then come to me, Beck. I'll send you my address."

"Okay. Now? Shall I come now?" I laughed through my sniffles. "I'm a bit of a mess."

"Now, and I don't care. I want all of you, even the messy parts." I heard the smile in his voice and managed to find one too.

"Send me your address, then."

"Oh, and, Beck, I can't believe you called. I was about to fall apart."

We said goodbye, and a couple of seconds later, his address came through.

I followed the satnav directions, then let out a low whistle. Not only was his house huge but so cool. A brand-new build that could only have been independently designed, a commission. I pulled my modest car up next to his BMW, and before I'd turned the engine off, the wide, black glossy front door opened. Munro stood there looking gorgeous. I had my door open in a split second, and then I was rushing up the wide steps to him.

He dragged me inside, then pushed the door shut and me up against it. He crashed his mouth onto mine. The desperation was in every fibre of him, in his eyes, his touch, his taste. He needed me as much as I needed him. I groaned as he slid his tongue over mine. I pulled him to me while he tangled his hands in my hair. He pressed his body to mine. Every hard ridge of his torso seemed to ripple as our kiss deepened. I never wanted this to end. I wanted to feel this need for him to stay with me forever. Eventually, as oxygen became an issue, we pulled apart. Munro's lips were deep red, puffy from the force of our kiss and totally beautiful.

He shuddered as he rested his forehead against mine. "I've missed you so fucking much, babe. I've never felt so lost. I didn't know what to do without you. Does that sound crazy? I wanted to drive past your flat, but I knew I would've stopped and begged you to come back with me."

"I would've come," I said, meaning every word. Now that I was closer, I could see the toll the last few days had had on him. The dark shadows under his tired, red-rimmed eyes gave him away.

His phone rang. "It's Martin, my lawyer. I left a message after you called." He answered, and even though he stepped back, he didn't leave me to talk privately.

His conversation gave me the chance to look around the downstairs of this gorgeous home. The wide-open wooden staircase to my left seemed to float up between two separate living areas to the upstairs. His kitchen was at the back and took up nearly three-quarters of the width of the house. It had warm cherry wood cabinets with creamy countertops that looked like some kind of composite or resin. The material was so inviting I wanted to run my fingertips over the smooth surface.

"Yes, Beck is here now."

Munro had told his lawyer about me already? The man moved fast when he'd set his mind to it.

Chapter 15

Munro

"Yes, Beck is here now. It seemed pointless for us to be apart, since we both want to be together." I winked at him. He smiled shyly, his cheeks pinking up adoringly.

I struggled to hear what Martin was saying. Beck was too much of a distraction. I held out my hand, needing to touch him again. As soon as our fingers brushed, I could focus again. "Thank you, and yes, he's wonderful. Okay, and I'm so pleased with the reaction. Now I need to decide how to post my status on my social media."

"Perhaps it could just be as simple as a picture of the two of you as you introduce him. No need for a fanfare or a long-written piece. Make it as easy and as natural as you want. Be yourself and be happy. I'll deal with Ms Enderby if she causes you any trouble."

"Thank you, Martin. I appreciate your help and advice." I said goodbye and tapped my phone against my chin.

"That's a happy smile. Did he give you some good news?"

"He did. Every company were fine with me being gay, saying that it made no difference to our contracts. He did suggest that I let my followers know and to do it my way." I pulled Beck close, then planted a kiss on his cheek and snapped a photograph. "That should do it. Now to upload it to my sites."

"Hey, hold on!" Beck grabbed my phone.

Oh, dammit, I should have asked him if he wanted to have his picture taken.

But he smiled. "What if I don't look good?"

"You always look good. You're gorgeous." I kissed him again and took a few more pics, letting him see them before we chose the one we liked the most. After a quick message to go with the image, I sent it to my social media sites. Then I held my breath, my eyes locked on Beck as he opened his phone and went to his Insta account.

"It's there." He turned his phone around and showed me.

Seconds later, my phone rang. "It's Bruno," I said and answered it.

"You're a fucking legend, my man," Bruno shouted. "I'm so bloody proud of you. Leo wants us to get together later to celebrate."

I grinned at his enthusiasm and shot Beck a wink. "I'll need to check with my boyfriend." His smile set my heart alight. Then it faded away, and I went cold.

"I'm working tonight," Beck groaned.

"No, he isn't," Bruno said. "Leo said Max has seen the photo and that he doesn't need to work tonight. We'll pick you up at eight. That should give you enough time to reacquaint yourselves."

"If you think five hours is long enough, then I pity Leo. See you later, and thank you, Bruno, for everything."

After pocketing my phone again, I took Beck's hand. "Come with me." I walked him to the stairs. Hopefully, he'd be good with where we were going. "We're going to spend the next five hours before Bruno is here in bed. And FYI, you'd better not be in the mood for a quickie."

He grinned. "You'd better hurry up, then. We're wasting precious time."

When we reached the top of the stairs, we all but ran to my bedroom. I was stripping out of my clothes before we'd even shut the door. A good thing I hadn't bothered with shoes and socks. I shoved my jeans down my legs.

Beck pushed his jeans over his arse, his naked arse. "Commando? I like it," I teased as the last piece of his clothing hit the floor. "I need you inside me so fucking much." I opened a drawer and threw a condom and a bottle of lube onto the bed.

I left him to wriggle out of his incredibly skinny jeans, clambered up onto my bed, and grabbed the lube. After slicking up my fingers, I got on my knees and reached back to prep myself.

"Fuck, Munro, you're the hottest man on earth. I could stand and watch you do that all day." He strutted up to me and swatted my arse. "Not that I'm going to. I need to be inside you too fucking much."

I pulled my fingers free and waved my hand. "Get busy," I demanded.

I watched him over my shoulder as he knelt behind me and squeezed lube onto his fingers. As he kissed each cheek, I let my head fall back onto the pillow. I shivered at the cold gel and the soft pressure of his fingers circling my hole. One, then two fingers pumped inside me, scissoring and stretching. It wasn't long after the third digit entered me that I'd had enough. "Enough, I'm ready."

As soon as the condom was on, he was pushing inside me. It burnt, but it was a good burn, a great burn, a 'why did I leave it so long' burn. "Fuck, yeah! God, that's sooooo good." I swayed my hips, adjusting to the welcome intrusion.

Beck leant over my back and kissed between my shoulder blades. "You ready, babe?"

"I've been ready since the first night I saw you, so just fuck me." I needed him moving inside me.

Slowly Beck pulled back. When the blunt head of his cock dragged over my prostate, I squeezed around him. He pushed back in, only to withdraw again. "Just fuck me," I cursed.

"I am. I'm just taking my time. We've got five hours, remember?" He kissed my shoulder again, his mouth curled up in a smile. His hips undulated as he stretched his arms forward, stroking down my arms and knitting his fingers with mine. I'd never felt so cherished as in this moment when Beck's mouth left open-mouthed kisses across my shoulders and nape, his fingers squeezed my own, and his body rocked inside me. This wasn't fucking; this was worshipping. This was making love. I never wanted it to end.

And soon, the familiar tingle, the spark of electricity, fizzled down my spine to my balls. "I'm close, babe, but I never want this to stop." I sighed as he thrust a little harder.

"I want to see you." Beck pulled out and flipped me over to lie on my back. I opened my legs, and he slid back inside him.

"Touch yourself," he whispered. "Beautiful." Still keeping the rhythm slow and steady, he took me higher.

This was the best sex. I couldn't even imagine it being like this—slow, intense, and just fucking perfect. "I'm going to come."

"Yes, come for me. Let go, Munro." He changed tempo and pushed my thighs up as he pumped into me. My cum flew from my dick, coating my abs and chest. Beck shuddered, his body stiffening as he also came. I loved watching him let go, to be the man who has made him feel this good.

I reached up and was about to cup his face, then saw the state of my hand and, grimacing, dropped it. "Too much spunk," I said and kissed him.

Beck lay on top of me as our tongues tangled, the kiss as sweet as the lovemaking. My heart constricted. If I weren't careful, I would fall for Beck. No, I couldn't. It was too soon. I was too inexperienced, but he was all I wanted and had been for the past six months. Beck pulled back. Had he noticed my confusion?

"Hey, you okay? Did I do something wrong?"

"No, it was perfect. It was intimate in a way I never thought sex could be. Hot and intense and the way you moved inside me...Oh god, shut me up." My cheeks heated. Could it be any more embarrassing gushing on about it?

With a sweet smile, he pecked my lips. He rolled to the side and dealt with the condom, then grew serious. "We both know that was a bit more than just sex, but it was the best I've ever had. Every time with you has been the best, Munro. I have to be careful around you." He eyed me cautiously.

I frowned. What was wrong? "What? Why? I don't understand. I thought we were on the same page. It sure felt like it."

"We are at the moment, Munro, but I can see me losing my heart to you. And that scares me. This is new to you, and you'll realise I'm not enough for you. Not the type of guy you should have by your side."

I flinched like he'd just struck me, but he continued. "Please don't be hurt. It's just that I like you so much, and my immediate impulse is to believe it'll never work. That if I fall in love with you, you'll leave me."

A little piece of me wanted to be angry with him, but the biggest part of me hurt for him. That he believed he wasn't worth loving. "Then I'll have to prove you wrong because you're everything I've ever wanted. No one has ever made me want to be this brave, to be strong enough to weather any backlash and any haters. You're the man I've been waiting to give it all to. As scary as all this is, it's worth it because I have you. I've already lost my heart to you, Beck, I'm trusting you to look after it, and I'm prepared to wait until you trust me enough to give me yours."

I drew in a jagged breath as he stared at me. What was he thinking? Had I made a huge mistake? No, even if he walked away now, I'd done the right thing.

He kissed me, tentatively at first, but as I parted my lips for him, his tongue dove in, dominating me as he devoured my mouth. He rolled back on top of me, and as our groins touched, my dick came back to life again. I groaned as he rocked his hips into mine. His cock pulsed and thickened against mine.

My groan broke our kiss. Beck reached between us and grasped both our shafts. Even without any additional lube, the sensation of the drag of satin-smooth skin and the twist of his hand was exquisite. I thrust hard up into his fist. Beck's eyes were locked on mine as he slid his thumb over the crown of my cock, smearing my precum over both of the heads.

"Fuck, Beck. Don't stop," I gasped

"Wasn't planning to." He grinned.

I tangled my fingers in his hair and pressed my lips to his. It was my turn to take as I slipped my tongue in and possessed his mouth. Beck's hold on our dicks intensified as his strokes sped up. The embers of my last orgasm flamed again, igniting at the base of my spine. As the flames licked higher, my balls tightened. I was going to come a second time.

"Gonna come." I tore my mouth away. My balls fired, and intense pleasure exploded through me. My cum splashed onto my stomach. Beck let out a groan so deep it reverberated in my chest. He stroked us with less fervour as our dicks softened, but he seemed determined to wring every drop out of me. "Enough." I squirmed as the sensitivity became too much.

Beck knelt up and sat on my thighs. He brought his fist up to his mouth and licked the cum from his fingers and palm, then bent over me and kissed me. As I opened for him, he let our cum drip into my mouth. It was the dirtiest, sexiest thing ever, and I loved it. I'd tasted my cum after having sex with him before, but this was a fantasy come true. I sucked greedily on his tongue, making him moan this time, and I cleaned every drop from him. With a sigh, he collapsed onto me again.

"Is this squashing me going to become a habit? I'm gonna need to add extra bench presses to my workout." I chuckled and roamed my hands lazily up and down his back and over his arse. I dipped a finger into his crack. "Would you let me fuck you?"

Beck lifted his head from the crook of my neck, his eyes dark, smouldering as he nodded. "I thought you'd never ask."

I laughed, relaxed in the moment. "I'm not sure I've got it in me right this minute, but I'd like to someday. I've always imagined being at the receiving end, but now that I know how that feels, I can't help wondering how good it must feel for you, pushing inside me."

"Shit, Ro, you're going make me hard again."

I stared at him. He'd shortened my name. I liked it. It felt natural coming from him.

"What?" he said.

"Nothing. You shortened my name."

"Is that a good or a bad thing?"

"It's good. I like it. No one has ever done it before. Not my friends, not my pa—" My parents. "Shit!"

"What? What's wrong."

"I haven't told my parents. The news will have got to them by now. I need to call them." Not something I was looking forward to.

Beck swung his leg over mine and sat up. "Will it be a problem?"

"I guess I'm about to find out." I moved and got out of bed. The remnants of cum had dried now, leaving a crusty mess. "Maybe a shower first." I held out my hand. "I think you'll like my shower."

BECK

Munro had been correct. His shower was awesome. We took turns soaping each other, and Munro took his time tracing my tattoos through the bubbles.

"I love these," he said as he twirled his finger around the tribal ink around my nipple. "Do they hurt?" He kissed my shoulder over the edge of a pink lotus flower.

"Not as much as you'd think. I wouldn't have so many if it hurt. Have you ever thought of getting one? My guy is a genius with ink."

He shook his head. "Never seriously. I haven't found anything I'd want on my body forever."

"Good for you. You shouldn't ever have something you might regret." I looked down at a patch on my wrist. It had taken a lot of ink to cover the name of a man who had no right to be remembered. "Ready to get out?"

Munro's eyes darkened as they roamed over my body. "Nope, I'm going to spend the afternoon running my hands over your wet, painted skin." He slid his hands down my back and cupped my arse. "Or I could get on my knees and blow you."

My breath caught in my throat as he sank to his knees. My dick had been semi-hard all the time he'd been touching me, but as his mouth closed over the head and slipped down my length, I went to rock hard. What Munro lacked in skills, he made up for in enthusiasm, and god, his mouth felt incredible. He struggled a little working out what to do with the beads, but he got there. Would I manage to come again after the two orgasms I'd already had? As he worked me with his mouth and hands, my balls drew up high, and I cried out. Munro swallowed, then pulled off, letting the last spurts hit his face.

Hot.

As.

Fuck.

I hauled him up and cleaned his face with my tongue, licking the last drop away. "You're a fucking demon."

He blushed, the tips of his ears turning pink as his cheeks flamed. "No, I just have a lot of fantasies to try."

"I can't wait, Ro" I kissed his nose. "But neither can your parents."

"I know. Will you stay with me when I call them?" He bit his lip. All the confidence of this afternoon had gone.

"I'll do whatever you want. I told you I'm here for you, and that includes difficult moments."

Munro switched off the shower, which seemed to have endless hot water, and stepped out. He grabbed two pristine white towels and handed the first to me. I watched as he wiped the water drops from his muscled chest and over his defined six-pack. My throat tightened as I swallowed heavily. I was falling for him. It was too soon. Was it, though? He was a good man, and I believed him that he wanted me just as much. I was still not sure I deserved him, but I wanted him with everything I had.

He had stopped scrubbing his hair and was eyeing me. "What?"

"Nothing. I should visit your gym. I'm a weakling compared to you." Not that I was unfit. I walked nearly everywhere, was on my feet all the time at the bar, but that kept me fit, not muscly.

"You look perfect. But if you want to come along, then I'd be honoured to show you around. Leo too. Maybe you could buddy up with him." He smiled, which morphed into a wide grin. "I'll give all of you at the bar a lifetime membership. Then you could all come together."

I chuckled. "You don't need to do that. You'll be giving too much."

I rubbed my hair dry when Munro stepped up to me. He pressed his chest to mine and dropped a kiss on my lips. "It's not too much, and I want to." His breath ghosted over my lips. He stared at me until I nodded.

"Okay, they'll love it."

"And their partners, although I think it's only Sawyer who dates outside of your circle."

"You remembered that?" That took me by surprise. We had talked about it on our first night together—one of the many topics we'd spoken about in the early hours that night—and he hadn't forgotten.

"I remember everything you said." He sighed. "They're your family."

With another peck on my lips, he walked out of the bathroom. I had no qualms about ogling his tight arse. It truly was a work of art. A living proof that squats worked.

We went downstairs and into his office. Munro was back to being nervous. He turned his phone in his hand over and over. I wrapped my arms around his waist, pressed my chest to his back, and kissed his nape. "It'll be okay." Hopefully, I was telling the truth.

He nodded and opened his screen to his contacts. After scrolling through them, he brought up the number, took a deep breath, and pressed Call. It rang a few times. Then it was answered.

"Mum, it's me." His voice trembled a bit, but he ploughed on. "I've got some news." Another deep breath in. "I've met someone. His name is Beck."

Wow, I hadn't seen that coming. He'd announced me rather than said he was gay.

"Is it the handsome young man in the picture you put up?" his mum asked, so casually I couldn't believe it. Was it this simple?

"Yes, he's amazing, Mum. Are you okay with it? That I'm gay?"

I sat down on the large, black leather chair and pulled Munro onto my lap. He gave me a grateful smile, then put his phone on speaker.

"Oh, Munro, of course it is. You're my son, and I love you. You've been alone for so long. Is this why?"

"Um, yeah, I backed myself into a corner by not coming out sooner. I was worried about work and all my sponsors. Martin dealt with all that, and they're all okay with it." He leant against me, and I tightened my grip around his waist. "Beck's here. Would you like to say hello?"

He nudged me. "Um, hi, Mrs Sylvester." I croaked.

"Well, hello there, Beck. Thank you for helping my Munro find himself." Her words were so sincere my eyes prickled. Why couldn't every coming out conversation be like this one?

"You're welcome, I think." My cheeks were burning. Munro shook his head and silently laughed.

"You've made him go bright red, Mum. Is Dad there? Has he said anything?"

"He is, but he's out in the garden. Did you want to speak to him?"

"No, it's okay. I know what he's like when he's out there. But has he seen the photo? Is he going to be okay with it?" He ran a hand through his hair.

His mum let out a tinkle of laughter. "He is. He said it was about time you got yourself settled with someone. He wants you both to come to dinner on Sunday. Would that be okay? Beck, would you like to come? We don't want to pressure you, but we'd like to meet the man who has made Munro smile so brightly as he is in the photograph."

I was at a loss for words. They wanted to meet me? Me, the tattooed bartender? I had met the parents of previous boyfriends— the few who were open-minded enough—but all those meetings had been a catastrophe. "Y-yes, okay. Thank you."

"Excellent, we'll see you at two. And, Munro, I'm so happy for you."

"I love you, Mum." Munro was choked up.

"We love you too. Now go and be proud of who you are."

The call ended, and we sat in silence.

"That was incredible, Munro. Did you expect that?"

He buried his head in my neck. It was only a second before his tears wetted my skin. As he cried quietly, I kept my arms around him, holding him close as he dealt with it all.

After a couple of minutes, he lifted his head. His eyes were red, but he still looked beautiful to me. He tried to smile through his emotions, but it wobbled. "I never thought that would happen. I know that they love me, but that was, god, I don't know what it was. It was incredible. So easy."

"That's how it should be, Ro. Everyone should be accepted for who they are. You're a very lucky man." I kissed him. "Maybe you should have done it years ago."

"No, I'm glad it was now. I wouldn't want them to meet someone who wasn't important to me. You're the man I want them to know, to love as much as I do." His eyes went wide when he realised what he'd said. "I mean, like, that they like you as much as me." He stumbled and stammered over the words.

"It's all good, babe. I know what you mean, and I feel the same." Yes, it was true. I loved him. It didn't matter it was too soon. It was right.

We stayed sitting close for a little while longer. Until his stomach rumbled loudly, and we both laughed. Munro stood up from my lap, then held out his hand for me and pulled me upright.

"We should eat something. We burnt off too many calories this afternoon."

Together, we walked to the kitchen. A knock on the front door startled us. Munro froze. "Let me check who it is."

He walked over to a screen on the wall I hadn't noticed before. He frowned, and I went to him. "Who is it?"

"My friends, Ed and Will." He pressed a button, and the latch clicked and unlocked but didn't open. Munro opened the door, his posture rigid. Then he relaxed, and a choked laugh broke free from him. When he smiled at me, my body lost its tension too. They talked quietly. Munro looked over at me, and I winked.

"Ed, Will, I'd like you to meet Beck, my boyfriend."

God, I was so fucking proud of him.

Chapter 17

Munro

I'd never dreaded opening my door the way I did then. Just seeing my best friends on the other side made my blood run cold. With my hand on the door, I took a deep breath. It felt like that was all I'd been doing lately. I was surprised I hadn't passed out after holding it for so long. I wanted Beck to be behind me, his hand on my back for support.

When I opened the door, they grinned at me. Ed held up a bottle of champagne. "We saw your Insta and wanted to come over to, like, celebrate with you."

"Unless he's here and tied naked to your bed. Then we can come back later." Will winked.

"I can't believe you're here like this." My eyes burnt as tears threatened again. "Beck is here, and he's not tied up." I looked over, and Beck winked at me. "Come in." Beck walked up and put his arm around my waist. "Ed, Will, I'd like you to meet Beck, my boyfriend."

"Hey, it's good to meet you. We thought he'd never get his head out of his arse." Ed laughed as he shook Beck's hand.

"This day just keeps getting weirder," I said as Will said hi to Beck. I wandered to the kitchen and put the bottle on the island.

"What's wrong?" Beck asked and kissed my temple.

Will had opened the cupboard where I kept the glasses. He knew my house and was comfortable enough to help himself. We'd been friends for years. We'd met on the first day of secondary school and just clicked. We'd hung out together ever since. When we were at college, Ed arrived and seamlessly fitted in.

Ed stood on the other side of the island and glared at me. Tension radiated off him. He was going to let me have it any moment now. Will picked up the bottle and went to open it but paused when Ed spoke.

Ed looked at the glass, then at me. "How could you, Munro? How could you hide this from us or doubt that we'd accept it? We've been friends for fucking years. You didn't even answer the message I sent you. Did you really think so little of us, of our friendship?"

Beck bristled next to me. I put my hand over his. "Shh, it's okay. He's allowed to say this to get it off his chest," I murmured, then turned back to Ed. "I'm sorry. I never meant it to go on for so long. There was always something else happening. I had to get the business running, and then I gave it my everything. I wasn't admitting it to myself for long enough. It was easier to not think about it, to not date and to pretend. And... and I was shit scared."

Will looked as if he was about to cry.

"It's been fucking hard and fucking lonely. The deeper I hid, the worse it got, and I'm so sorry. I should've trusted you. You've been with me from the beginning, and I'm sorry."

The tears were dripping down my face, my nose was running, and I couldn't stop it. I wiped my eyes with the heels of my hands, but it wasn't working. Arms came around me, and they weren't Beck's. These belonged to my best friends. We stood in a huddle until I stopped snivelling.

"Thank you," I said to them both, then looked for Beck. He was still here, and he smiled, just the tiniest lift of the corners of his mouth. I went to him, and he opened his arms and hugged me into his body. "Thank you."

"Nothing to thank me for. You needed your friends, not me. But I won't ever be far away." He wiped my eyes for me, and I half sobbed, half laughed. "You'd better not be."

The pop of a cork broke us apart. Will filled the glasses and handed them out. "To Munro, for finally getting his cherry popped."

I blushed but laughed and lifted the glass to my lips. Beck threw his arm over my shoulder and tapped his glass to mine. "To cherry popping." He took a sip.

"What's Lucie said?" Ed asked.

Both Beck and I stilled. Beck kissed my temple and whispered, "Shall I tell them what happened?" I nodded, and he continued. "Lucie approached me this afternoon. She wasn't happy, going on about what had I done to Munro, stupid shit like she'd have known if he were gay. She's furious that Munro hasn't spoken to her."

I took over. "She said any rumours would ruin me and that Beck wouldn't want that."

"It sounded like she was going to be the one to spread those rumours," Beck said. "She was crazy, her eyes blazing as she ranted. That's why I called Ro. I needed to warn him."

Will grinned, and Ed quirked his eyebrow. They'd take the piss out of me later. They knew not to shorten my name.

"Yeah, so I called Martin, my lawyer, and he said the sponsors were all fine with it and if I wanted to do something, it was okay. And here we are." I kissed Beck's cheek.

Will shook his head. "She really is breathing fire. She blew up my phone about you ignoring her. She'd have done it, Munro. You did the right thing telling the world before she could." He sipped his drink. "I did wonder about you. Not that I gave it much thought, but at school, then at college, you were never interested in girls. I put it down to how dedicated you were about Well Fit and why you needed to make it a success."

"To be honest with you, I was fine. It took me a long time to work it out. I'd always been so focused on sport at school, then on getting my degree. Which morphed into starting Well Fit. I've worked solidly for over ten years. It wasn't until I moved into this place that I realised I was lonely. This house has been designed as a home for a family, not for just one man. That's when it hit me. Well, that and a Cocky Boys subscription." I grinned when Beck snorted and whispered Carter Dane in my ear. "Then I saw Beck. He seemed to be everywhere we went, and the more I saw him, the more I knew I wanted him."

Beck moved his arm from my shoulder and wrapped it around my waist. "I'm so glad you were a persistent fucker." He gave me a squeeze. "Where and how did Lucie come into this? I can see you're good mates, but she's not a low-maintenance friend."

Will and Ed snorted a laugh, gesturing for me to answer. "She works for me and has done for years. She runs a lot of the classes. They're very popular, and she's good. Then she just kind of joined us. Whenever we were going out, she came along. She's good fun, likes a laugh, but she became very clingy. It was as if she'd decided we were best friends, and I had to put up with all her drama."

"I thought you were together. She was all over you the first night you left your number. That's why I didn't call," Beck said. "She wants you, Munro. As more than a friend. You should've seen her this afternoon. She was livid."

"It doesn't matter what she wants. I've never led her on or encouraged her into thinking there would ever be more than friendship between us." Memories of all the times we'd spent together as friends popped into my head. The Sunday morning brunches, late-night movies and popcorn, her sleeping over in one of the guest rooms. Had I given her the wrong idea after all? To me, she was just a friend.

"You were really close, Munro. At first, we had wondered if you had a friends-with-benefits kind of relationship, but you turned her down so many times it soon became obvious you weren't interested," Will said. "She would flirt and mess around with other guys to make you jealous, but you never were. She would end up going home with whoever she found, then turn up the next morning with a sob story, didn't she?"

"Yes, and I told her I'd had enough, that she was responsible for her actions and had to own up to her mistakes. I wasn't going to pick her up and dust her off anymore. I don't know what will happen now. Whether she'll want to work or if I can trust her to act professionally."

"I suppose that only time will tell," Beck said. I was more than happy to leave it at that.

The conversation shifted to easier topics, and I watched Beck as he became friends with mine. They were laughing as he talked about his work and friends. It was strange seeing the three of them together, a sight I hadn't ever envisioned because I'd never thought I could be out and still be with my best friends. Beck was so relaxed with them, which I supposed could be because he was used to talking to people he didn't know. It didn't feel like that, though. His eyes were bright as he chuckled at Will's tale of our school antics. It felt genuine.

I'd underestimated my friends, and I should've known better. Shame washed over me to have doubted them, but fear of losing them had kept me back. I needed to apologise properly to them.

A hand touched my arm, startling me out of my thoughts. Beck's lips were turned up in an amused smirk. "You still with us, babe?"

"Sorry, I tuned out for a moment. Today has been a bit of a mindfuck."

"Will and Ed are going to come out with us."

"Yeah, sounds like it's going to be a good night." Ed grinned. "I'm going to see if Mel wants to come."

Will rolled his eyes. "They're getting serious now, even if he won't admit it."

"Good for you, Ed," I said as I gave Will a light-hearted punch on his shoulder. "Serious is a good thing."

I sent Beck a smile that probably made me look goofy, but I was way past caring. I was crazy for him, and he knew it.

BECK

As I walked into the bar with Munro holding my hand, I beamed like a damn lighthouse. At least it felt like that with the way my mouth stretched so wide and everything inside me lit up. Munro wasn't as comfortable, though; his hand was slightly clammy in mine. "It's okay, Ro. This is a safe place."

"I know, but it's still nerve-racking. It feels like everyone is watching," he whispered.

Bruno chuckled. "Munro, chill. It's going to be great."

"They're probably looking at you anyway."

I squeezed his hand and kissed his cheek. "Bruno's got nothing on you, babe."

Max, Gus, and Jonas were behind the bar, and they all grinned at us. "Good to see you both." Max held his hand out to Munro. "Welcome to the family."

Jonas greeted Munro with a smile, although a little sadness clouded his eyes. I doubted anyone had noticed but me. I knew the reason why. It wasn't that we hadn't made it—we both knew it had been the best solution to break it off—but he was the only man alone now. We had to find someone for him.

"Thanks, it's pretty bloody terrifying right now," Munro said, his voice shaky.

"We've got the corner set up for you. Go on over. We'll bring you some drinks." Gus winked.

I slid into the booth and pulled Munro down, then captured his face in my hands and kissed him. "You are amazing, and you've got this."

"Yeah, I'm okay. It felt good, Beck, holding your hand with everyone around. Thank you."

I stared at him. Why did he feel the need to thank me? To be honest, I was nervous too. I didn't want my face all over social media. But this was my place, my family, and I trusted them to have my back. "I don't know what you need to thank me for, Ro. We're in this together. It's new ground for both of us."

The corner was soon full of our friends, both mine and Munro's, congratulating us. Munro hadn't stopped smiling and laughing. It was a relaxed side of him that I'd only seen in my bed. The times I'd seen him out with his friends before he'd been tenser, or maybe that was because he had been trying not to be caught looking at me. Now he had his hand on my thigh or was holding mine, not leaving my side. I was more than happy to let him touch me, just like I trailed my fingers under his shirt as he leant back in the seat.

The empty glasses and bottles piled up on the table, Munro was enjoying himself, but was still being careful. I wanted a clear head for when we got back to his place. Or mine. I didn't care where we ended up. He probably wanted to make sure he wasn't caught drunk on camera by someone from outside our group. Leo and Bruno had no such qualms and were happily drinking champagne and cocktails all night, but this only made them funnier as they regaled us with stories of being papped after Bruno had come out. Munro tightened his hand on my leg as the stories got sillier. The idea seemed to terrify him.

"I need to pee," he whispered and stood. Everybody shuffled to let him get out from behind the table. As he crossed the floor to the bathrooms, my stomach did flip-flops. I didn't know where the feeling came from all of a sudden, but a shiver crept down my spine. Bruno must have sensed my unease. He leant over the table. "I'll go."

I nodded, grateful that he understood my concern.

Sawyer slipped into Munro's seat and gave me a drunken grin. "You don't make life easy for yourself, do you." It wasn't a question.

"Where's the fun in that?" I joked back. Not that I cared. I'd walk through fire for Munro.

"He's a really nice guy, Beck. I'm happy for you. We all are. You deserve someone good, someone who will put you first."

"Thanks, Sawyer. I hope it all works out for him and for us." It wouldn't be as simple as it had been today. I was waiting for the other shoe to drop and the shit to fall down around us, for the rumours and lies to start. I doubted we'd seen or heard the last from Lucie, and that troubled me.

"It will. Have faith. It was your turn." He patted my shoulder, then moved out of the booth and went back to Devon, sat down on his knee, and wrapped his arms around his neck. Devon smiled and whispered something to him. Whatever it was made Sawyer blush and nod. They were both larger than life, with Devon a little taller at six five. It still boggled my mind that Sawyer called Devon Daddy when they were in private.

Munro sat back down next to me, his face paler than when he'd left, and Bruno was nowhere to be seen. "What happened?" I pushed his hair from his forehead.

"Lucie is here with a group of girls." He gestured to the busy bar.

"Did she say anything?" I was ready to have her chucked out when Bruno came back.

"What happened?" I asked Bruno, but he gave a tiny shake of his head.

Munro answered. "Just some shit. She didn't say it to me, only to her friends, loud enough for me to hear. It was bound to happen."

"Do you want to go?"

Munro was already shaking his head. "No, she's not going to ruin tonight for me." He moved closer and pressed a kiss on my mouth. It was firm, possessive, and went straight to my dick.

I hummed as his tongue slipped between my lips, but before I could deepen the kiss, he pulled away. His eyes sparkled in the dim light. "Tease," I chastised him.

"You like it." He smirked.

"You two are just so cute together." Gus laughed as he cleared the table. "We're closing soon, but you don't have to leave."

The bar closed earlier on a weekday than at the weekend, but keeping the licence the same made it easier than asking for an extension every time it was needed.

"They may have more important things to do. Like each other." Will waggled his eyebrows.

"And comments like that shows why you're still single." Ed elbowed him in his side.

Will groaned. "I'm single because I like it. I keep telling you that."

"Leave him alone," Munro told Ed. "He's waiting for Mrs or Mr Right." He grinned, but Will's eyes widened as he swallowed hard. He flushed when he saw me watching him and ducked his head. There was more to Will than his friends knew.

While Ed and Munro continued to tease their friend, I turned to Leo. "Thank you for this. It's exactly what he needed. I'm not sure what's going to happen over the next couple of days and weeks, but having the support of his friends will help."

"Hey, no worries. I've been where you are. I know what it's like to suddenly have all eyes on you."

I scoffed. "I think Bruno is way more in the public eye than Munro."

"Don't underestimate the power of social media, Beck. It'll be all over you. Trust me that the first time you're followed when you're only getting a coffee, your face will be on Twitter and everywhere else. Or when you're caught scratching your arse or tripping up in the street, it will be captured. You have to develop a thick skin and ignore it all. It'll take a while for you to adjust, but it'll all be worth it. You've found your person, and that's all you have to remember."

As I looked back to Munro, I caught him gazing at me. "Are you okay?"

I nodded. Because Leo was spot on. Munro was my person. "Yeah, I'm good. You ready to get out of here?"

Munro pressed his mouth to mine, then with only an inch between our lips, he slurred in what I assumed was meant to be a whisper, "I'm ready to ride you."

Everyone either groaned or howled with laughter. But all it did to me was make my dick instantly hard. I pressed the heel of my palm to my crotch in an attempt to make it behave. "Let's go."

I stood up and grabbed Munro's hand. "Say goodnight to the boys and girls, babe."

All our friends grinned and catcalled as we stepped past them all.

"Be good and play safe!" Will called out, and Munro flipped his middle finger. I went to the bar to thank Max and Jonas for a great night. Munro asked to settle the tab, but Max shook his head.

"This is on us. We're delighted Beck has found his one," Jonas said. His eyes flickered to mine, and he smiled. "Beck deserves the best. Be good to him."

"I will. He's my one too."

Chapter 19

Munro

Beck seemed to be a lot soberer than me. "Haven't you been drinking? I mean, I saw you drink, but you're not even the slightest bit tipsy. I feel like I've got my shoelaces tied together, and I'm walking on ice."

"I like you relaxed like this. It's different, a new version of you." He pulled me to him and kissed me. I tensed. I couldn't help it. We were outside, on the street. Where anyone could see us. But it was okay. This was Beck, my boyfriend.

The kiss ended. "I'm sorry I froze. I'm not used to being kissed out in the open."

"Hey, it's okay. I didn't think. We should grab a cab."

"We could walk to your place. It should sober me up a bit." I needed to have a clear head to enjoy what I wanted to do to him.

"You sure? You remember how your bed is way more comfortable than mine," Beck said.

"Fine, but if I fall asleep before I've had your dick inside me, then it's your fault." I headed for the cabs waiting outside the bars that line the street.

I scowled, which only made Beck laugh. "You are just the funniest. I promise I'll make sure you don't go to sleep unsatisfied."

I dragged him to the taxi at the front of the queue. Once we had both sat down, I told the driver my address. He grinned at me over his shoulder. "Congrats on coming out, man. Nicely done."

I gaped at him, my mouth slack. Beck gave my hand a squeeze. "It's okay, babe," he whispered.

I let out a long breath. "I know. It caught me by surprise, is all."

"Hey, I'm sorry if I said something I shouldn't. But my son's gay and has struggled with his friends accepting him. He was well chuffed when he saw your post. He's a huge fan," the cabbie said.

Wow! That was awesome. "That's great. You should bring him to the gym. I'll show him around."

The cabbie nodded and grinned at me through the rear-view mirror.

When we got to my place, I pulled a business card out of my wallet and handed it to him along with the fare. "Give that to the reception. I'll let them know I'm expecting you."

Coming out had been the best decision and not because of myself. It had made a boy happy. Beck was chuckling. "That made you feel good, didn't it?"

"Yeah, really good." I drank him in. "I can't believe you're mine. Today has been crazy but in a brilliant way. All because of you, because you want me."

I grabbed his hand and pulled him closer until we were almost chest to chest. The dirty blond hair was now all tousled after running his hands through it too many times. The stubble on his chin and jaw made him look older. I breathed in deeply, the faint aroma of my shower gel on his body tickling my nostrils. I admired the bright colours of the ink on his neck, which was so flawless, so incredible. His eyes were dark, dilated pools of obsidian. For me. "Take me to bed," I croaked, my voice husky and deep with want.

Beck's mouth on mine was brief but full of promise. Then we rushed up the stairs, racing each other as we tried to get there first. I cheered, throwing my arms up. "I won."

Beck laughed and pushed me back onto the bed. "I think I'm the winner here."

His next kiss had me melting into the mattress as I wrapped my arms around his neck. As our tongues danced together, I slipped my hands under the hem of his shirt, needing to feel the heat of his bare skin. He sucked on my tongue, and I pushed my hips up to his. Our erections, hard and trapped in denim, throbbed.

"Fuck!" Beck burst out the curse. "We need to be naked."

As he stood up, I pulled my shirt over my head, too eager to undo the buttons, but I got trapped. My head and arms were well and truly stuck. "Help." I laughed. His fingers worked the buttons open until I could wriggle free.

I flopped back down. "That never happens in porn."

"Who cares about that? This is real. I like you like this. Now strip." He waggled his eyebrows at me. "You said you wanted to ride me." Beck was out of his clothes in no time, leaving on a pair of tight black briefs, then climbed onto the bed and lay flat on his back. His rock-hard dick strained against the fabric, his precum forming a damp patch.

The condoms and lube were still on the bedside table, ready for me to grab. As soon as I was naked, I crawled up to him and straddled his thighs. "What's with the underwear?" I rubbed my hand over his length and gave it a squeeze. Beck moaned as he pushed into my grip.

"Something for you to unwrap."

"Hmm, I like unwrapping presents." I squeezed him again, then shuffled farther down his legs. When I was far enough back, I leant down and nuzzled his groin. God, he smelled divine. The clean scent of his skin mingled with the musk of his arousal. As I mouthed over the head of his cock, the sweet saltiness of his precum bloomed on my tongue.

How had I gone so long without this?

As much as I wanted to be on top, doing the riding, I still wanted Beck to lead the way. After way too short mutual blow jobs, Beck called a halt and got me prepped and on top of him. I loved looking down on his tight body, the amazing ink that rippled and shone under the sheen of sweat that covered his chest, down to his hips. He wasn't gym ripped, but there wasn't an ounce of excess fat on him.

"Christ, you're so deep," I moaned as I ground down. "I'm close already."

"Me too, babe. Stroke yourself." He put his feet flat on the mattress and lifted his arse up. He instantly took over and pummelled into me. Each stroke hit my prostate, and stars exploded. A whole galaxy of them fired bright behind my eyelids.

My orgasm burst from me like a rocket, pelting Beck's chest like fireworks as they lit up the sky. With his hands on my hips, Beck fucked up into me. The pleasure coursing through me as he nudged my spot sent another spurt of cum from me. Then he stilled, his teeth gritted and the tendons in his neck stiffening, and he cried out. The heat of his orgasm filled the condom. What would sex feel like without a barrier?

Once we were showered, the congealed cum rinsed away, we climbed back into bed. I was tucked under Beck's arm with my head on his shoulder.

"You surprised me tonight." He tipped his head down as I lifted mine up.

"It was a great night, and we were with our friends. I wasn't worried."

"Well, yeah, there is that. And you were amazing, but that's not what I was talking about."

"What are you talking about, then?"

He chuckled and kissed my nose. "Your spectacular orgasm without once touching your dick. Of course, I'm going to take the credit, but I was impressed."

"Oh, now that you mentioned it. I hadn't realised." I grinned. "That was quite impressive, wasn't it? And of course I'll let you gloat over your stunning sexual prowess." I yawned and snuggled back down, closing my eyes on my first day as an out and proud gay man.

"I want to know what happened with Lucie. Can we talk about it tomorrow?"

I mumbled my agreement, then fell deeply asleep.

Chapter 20

BECK

We slept in late, and then after a breathtaking frottage session that got us hot, sweaty, and sticky, we needed another shower before we made it downstairs.

"Can we talk about Lucie?" I asked Munro as we sat at the island in the kitchen. I'd made coffee with a machine that was more sophisticated than the one I used at work.

"Hmm, you need to be here to make my coffee every morning. This is better than I manage to make," he said, totally ignoring my question and not quite meeting my eyes.

"Stop deflecting, babe. But I have to agree. It's damn good coffee."

"Fine." He placed his No 1 Son mug down on the polished worktop, then shoved his hand through his damp hair. "She said I was stupid for coming out and wrecking my career for a man who wouldn't hang around. She said you were nothing but a man whore who fucked his way through the customers in the bar and was after my money." He took a few wobbly breaths in and looked down at his mug. "She said that it wouldn't be long before I was nobody, with nothing but a bad memory and no friends."

He lifted his eyes, and the hurt and vulnerability in them pierced my heart. She'd rattled him, and even though it wasn't true, he couldn't be a hundred per cent sure. I got off my stool and moved around the island to him. Then swivelled his stool around so he faced me, and slotted between his parted legs.

"She's wrong, Ro. We already know that your coming out is helping people. The taxi driver last night was so grateful for giving his son more confidence. Your friends are still with you. There's no way Will and Ed will turn against you. My friends like you too." I pressed a kiss to his forehead. "And I'm not going anywhere, not until you tell me to leave."

He snorted. "I don't think I'll ever have enough of you, Beck. You're stuck with me."

"The best way to deal with her is to ignore her. She's jealous because she wants you. You've rebuked her every advance. You've never led her on, so this is on her. Whatever claim she thinks she has on you is all in her head."

He nodded, but he still looked wary. "I don't know what will happen at work, if she'll even show up. She has classes she needs to teach. She has a contract with Well Fit."

"Honestly? I don't think she'll turn up."

Munro's shoulders slumped. "Yeah, me either." His voice was flat, distant even. "Why couldn't she have just been like my other friends? Why is she acting like I've cheated on her? She was my friend, Beck, and it's sad that she's become like this."

If only I could answer him, but I didn't know her. Yes, she'd behaved like she was his girlfriend, but she's also been a flirt, and I'd seen her with other men too. So it wasn't like she really believed she and Munro were more than friends. I didn't want to think bunny boiler. I totally believed that however someone labelled themselves—male, female, trans, NB, gender-fluid, straight, gay or any other classification they chose to go by—they should be allowed to live their life. But for Lucie to be this strung up or angry wasn't right. This was nobody else's issue. Whatever she had going on in her head was because she'd put it there.

"I don't know, babe. If she doesn't come into work, then she's shown her hand and isn't coming back. But please, Ro, don't contact her. Go through your company's policy and let someone else deal with it. You've got an HR person. Let them handle it."

Again, Munro nodded. He wrapped his arms around my waist and laid his head on my chest. With one of my hands around him and the other stroking through his hair, we stayed still and quiet until the alarm on his phone broke us apart. With a kiss on the top of his head, I let him go.

"I have to go to work." He finished his coffee. "What time are you working today?"

"I'm doing twelve till seven." It would be a busy shift. We had happy hour and half-price cocktails for two hours, starting at five.

"I'll come and pick you up. We can grab some dinner together."

"Sure."

He picked up his bag, which was a basic gym bag—nothing flashy about my man. Well, apart from his really cool car and designer house.

"Come here."

When he got close again, I pulled him up to my body and proceeded to kiss the breath out of him. When we separated, his skin was flushed pink and his lips were swollen.

"Something for you to think about today." I winked.

"Like I ever have you off my mind," he said drily. "See you tonight."

After he'd left, I tidied up the kitchen, making sure it was all neat for when he came home, then walked back upstairs, made the bed, gathered my clothes together, and went to my place.

My flat seemed tiny, but I liked it here. It was my space, and I'd worked hard to get it. This morning I had plenty of mundane chores to do before work. I got my first load of laundry running, made a list of groceries I needed, changed the sheets on my bed, and vacuumed throughout.

By the time I had to leave, I'd finished it all. As Munro was coming to get me tonight, it seemed pointless to drive, so I walked to the bar.

Jonas's door was shut. Odd. Something he never did when he was at work. And he was always at work. I pondered about it while I continued to the break room, where Leo was putting his stuff into his locker. For some reason, he was wearing sunglasses.

"What happened?" I pointed to his face. He was paler than he usually was. "Are you okay?"

He took off the glasses, showing me a pair of bloodshot, puffy eyes. "You did this," he grumbled.

What the hell was he talking about? "Me? What did I do?"

"You met a really great guy, who happens to be a friend of Bruno's. 'Let's have a party', Bruno said. And this is the result of the party. Too many tequila shots and enough vodka to drown in." He growled like a lion, or rather an adorable cub. Leo was such a cute twinky guy he was crap at pulling off being angry.

"You mean, you stayed way too long and ended up getting into a shots competition with Sawyer." This wasn't a new game, and everyone knew nobody could outdrink Sawyer. The man was a goliath and could drink alcohol as if it were water.

"Maybe," he grumbled. "I'm still blaming you."

"You need hair of the dog. Shame you can't because you're working." I gloated because I'd had the sense to take my man home before it turned into a mess.

"Fuck off," he lamely protested, then slipped his sunglasses back on.

Changing the subject might be a good idea right now. "Why's Jonas's door closed?"

"Interview. The cute guy—Haydn something or other. We were talking about it yesterday." Leo opened a bottle of Red Bull and chugged it down. He grimaced and let out a huge belch, then quickly covered his mouth.

"Jesus, Leo. Why don't you go home? You're two deep breaths away from vomiting." I shook my head and grabbed my apron. "You're useless like this. We can cover for you."

He nodded, dug his phone out of his pocket, and swiped it open. "Bru, baby. Come and get me. I'm dying." Whatever Bruno said to him had Leo scowling. "Fine, I'll get a cab. Oh, okay, thank you. I love you so, so much."

He ended the call and looked at me sheepishly. "He was at the gym, but he's gonna come and get me."

Next in the room was Sawyer. He took one look at Leo and laughed until I thought he was going to pee himself. I thumped his arm. "Hey, this was your doing, so we're now a barman down. I'm going to make sure it's you who does double the work."

Sawyer just shook his head and gave Leo a hug. Then it was time to open the doors and serve drinks for the next seven hours.

Leo sat in the same corner we had taken over last night while he waited for his boyfriend. It was another thirty minutes before Bruno arrived. Instead of getting to his boyfriend, he made his way to me.

"What's up?" My stomach churned. Was he going to say something about Munro? "Has something happened to Munro?"

"Stop panicking, Beck. God, it's a good job you don't play poker. Munro is fine. He just wanted to let you know that Lucie turned up." My eyes went wide, but Bruno held up his hand. "She resigned, then cleared out her belongings and stuff and left."

"Oh, okay. Thanks for telling me." I gestured over to the corner. "Go and get your sorry-arsed man home."

Bruno laughed. "I told him to call in. But you know Leo. He's a stubborn arse."

Once they'd both left, I got to work. The time passed quickly thanks to bottomless Prosecco lunches and then happy hour.

Despite the busy crowd, I watched the door like a hawk, waiting for Munro. At ten to seven, he finally walked in. He'd changed from this morning's smart casual trousers and a short-sleeved button-down shirt to a pair of well-worn jeans and a Well Fit T-shirt so faded it looked vintage. His hair was styled but still messy from his hands fiddling with it. He looked fucking edible.

"Well, hello there, handsome. What can I get you? Beer, wine, a cocktail, or today's special—me." I grinned when he barked out a laugh.

"I'll take the special, please. It looks delicious." He leant forward and licked his lips. Oh yeah, I was getting a taste of him. I met him halfway and pressed our mouths together. It was way too chaste and over with far too quickly.

Chapter 21

Munro

The feeling as I walked through the doors of BAR 28 was so different now. These were my people in here. My boyfriend and his friends. The men who had embraced me into the tight-knit group that was their family. I looked over to the bar, my eyes homing in on Beck as if he were a magnet.

He studied me in a lazy 'I know what you look like naked' way. Then slowly a smile broke out, lighting up his whole face.

God, I was so totally in love with this man. But it was way too soon to tell him. The bar was crowded tonight, and I had to weave through a throng of people to reach the bar.

His greeting had me laughing and wanting to kiss him. So I did. Although it probably was more him kissing me, but who cared? I was kissing my boyfriend.

"I've got ten more minutes. Do you want a drink while you wait?" he asked.

"No, I'm good. I'll just ogle the hot barman in front of me." I winked at him, and he might have blushed a tiny bit.

"Okay, it's just that Leo had too much of a hangover to work, so it's just me and Sawyer."

"It's fine."

He moved down the bar to serve someone, and I turned and scanned the room. What sort of people came here at this time of day? When I'd been here before, I'd been too worried that I'd be noticed staring at Beck to register what was going on around me. They had a surprisingly diverse clientele, ranging from college kids to people still in suits coming straight from work and people dressed up and ready to have a night out. And the great part was that nobody was paying anyone any attention. It was inclusive, a safe place.

A nudge on the shoulder jostled me. The man, in his late thirties, was tall and well built under his button-down shirt.

"Sorry," he said, then gawped at me. "Oh! You're Munro Sylvester."

"I am, yes." Great, what was he going to say next?

"Awesome, I've followed you for years. Your fitness and training routines are the best. I'm Warren." He enthused, then motioned to someone else. "Cole. Come here."

The next thing I knew, I was shaking hands with his friend and a couple of others.

"We saw your coming out post. Well done, mate." Warren patted my shoulder and stared behind the bar. "That's your boyfriend? The guy from the post. Good for you."

Beck walked up to us. "Everything okay here, gentlemen?"

Warren thrust his hand to Beck and introduced himself. "Your man is the best."

Beck chuckled. "I think so too." Then he turned to me. "I'm done. I'll go and grab my jacket."

While he did that, I talked to the men about my work and how I devised the programmes. They seemed to be good guys. And another piece of my past life fell away. The man who hid in full view of the world was gone.

When Beck got back, we said our goodbyes and left the bar. Beck took hold of my hand, and we discussed where we wanted to go to eat.

"I don't want to go to another bar. How about Indian?" He pointed to a restaurant a few doors down. Then shook his head. "Probably not the best choice, not with what I want to do to your arse later."

I burst out laughing as my cheeks burnt. "Jesus, you can't say that out loud. Mexican is a no-go as well, then."

"You're right. There's a good steakhouse not far from here. How's that?"

"Lead the way."

Once we were seated and had a drink in front of us, Beck spoke. "Tell me what happened with Lucie. Bruno gave me a very brief rundown."

I took a sip of my wine and sighed. "It was nothing. She came into my office and handed me her resignation."

"Is that all that happened?"

"No, not really. It was crappy. I tried to tell her that it didn't have to be like this. That we'd only ever been friends and I didn't want it to end this way. But she wouldn't let it go and tried to make me see how great she and I would be together."

"She really is obsessed with you, Ro."

"I know. But I can't help that. I don't know why she doesn't see that I've never led her on. In her head, we were already a couple. I'd had enough of her by then and told her she was in breach of her contract, that I could sue. Then with a final 'fuck you' from her, she stormed away. And that's it. She left."

"Will you sue her?"

"God, no. I'm not like that. It's for the best if she just leaves. Yes, it'll be difficult for a while without her, but I can take her classes until we find someone to replace her."

The waiter arrived to take our order. We both ordered steak, but where Beck ordered chips, I had a salad.

Beck was smirking when the man left. "A salad? You can't have that with steak. It's, like, against the law."

"You'll have to share your chips, then."

"Er, no. That's not how it works. If you wanted chips, you should've ordered them." Beck was shaking his head while his eyes were sparkling with humour.

"But it's part of the boyfriend code. I read that all boyfriends must share their food." This was fun, being out in the open with the sexiest man alive, just messing about.

"You must have the old version. That bit was taken out." He grinned.

After only a couple more minutes, our food arrived. I groaned at the sight of Beck's chips and caved. "Can I have an order of chips too, please? It seems that I missed the memo that boyfriends don't share."

The waiter laughed, giving Beck a mock frown, then said he'd be right back.

The rest of the meal carried on in the same manner. It was perfect.

Beck put his cutlery down and smiled softly. "Y'know, this is our first real date."

"God, that fucking awful night feels like years ago, not just over a week. My life has become so very different."

"But in a good way, right? You're not having any regrets?" How could Beck still be nervous about this? "You see, it's normally at about this time that my previous boyfriends have broken up with me. Too many tattoos to take me home or to meet his friends. Or work too many anti-social hours. Pretty much any and every excuse that can be made has been."

"Beck, baby, the feelings I have for you are off the charts. You're the most gorgeous man I've ever seen. I love your tattoos and have no qualms about taking you home to meet my parents. I'm not going to ever break up with you." I reached over the table and stroked the back of his hand, and when he flipped it over, I held on to it. "You've brought me alive. Turned my black-and-white life into full-on technicolour. I only had my work and a few close friends before you. You've shared your life and your family with me, and that makes me so bloody happy."

I sat quietly while he digested my words. When he finally spoke, his voice was gruff, husky, full of emotion. "Thank you."

"Let's go home." We settled the bill, and I took his hand when we got outside. When we reached my car, I led him to the passenger side. Instead of opening the door, I pressed him against it and crowded him with my body. "Everything that has happened has been about me. I haven't paid enough attention to how this has affected you. When we get home, I'm going to show just how I feel about you and everything you've given me."

And that was exactly what I did. Everything Beck had done to me, I did back. I kissed every inch of his colourful body. Licked and sucked places that had him squirming and crying out for more. And finally, when he begged me, I entered him.

The feeling of being inside the man I loved was...I didn't even have the words for how wonderful it was. As we gazed into each other's eyes, I slowly moved, rocking my hips, grinding into him. Then he begged for more, for harder, for it to never end.

But when it did, it was everything and so much more.

I collapsed down onto him, and he kissed me. "I've fallen in love with you, Ro." The gruffness from earlier was back again. "I know it's probably too early to say the words, but I can't hold them back anymore."

I pushed his sweaty hair back from his forehead and kissed him there. Then his nose, his cheeks, and finally his lips. "I love you too. I've been holding on to those words, scared that you'd be running for the hills if I said them out loud."

We stayed in our embrace until my flaccid cock reminded me that I needed to ditch the condom and get us cleaned up. After that was all done, we lay with me resting my head on his chest. I was back to following the lines of black ink with my fingertips while his heartbeat thumped steadily under my ear.

"How do you feel about me getting tested?" he asked, breaking the comfortable silence. "I mean, I get tested regularly, and I'm always clear. But I'd like to get it done again for us."

My fingers stilled. I hadn't expected that. "Really? You want to do that? I mean, yes. If that's what you'd want. I'm assuming you don't want to use condoms. Is that why? I'll get mine done too."

"Babe, I'm the only person you've ever had sex with. I'm sure you don't have any STIs."

"That's true, but it's not just for that. I've travelled a lot, been all over the world. I need to be clear of any of the other transmittable diseases."

"Of course. I'm sorry. So is that a yes?" Beck grinned.

"It's a yes."

BECK

It was no surprise that Jonas and Max offered Haydn the job. He was so nervous at first, trying to stay quiet and out of the way of the rest of us. But as always, we embraced him into our family, and he started to come out of his shell. I'd noticed Jonas hovering around him, spending more time behind the bar than he usually did. I thought he was keen on him, and that made me smile. Jonas should have the chance to find his person. And the looks Haydn gave Jonas when he thought no one would see gave away his attraction. No one else noticed, but maybe because they didn't know Jonas as well as I did. Haydn had been here about three weeks now and was really sweet. He fitted in easily and didn't even care when we protected him from dick patrons who thought he was easy pickings.

"What's wrong? You look like the world is about to end," Haydn asked.

"What? No nothing. Well, not really nothing. Munro is taking me for Sunday lunch at his parents'," I told him and went back to chewing my thumbnail. The fear of being rejected by his parents was stuck in my mind.

"That's a good thing, right? I mean, you and Munro are so cool together." He was rather starstruck by Munro and Bruno.

"Parents don't normally like me. Not even my own. Especially my own." Why had I added that? I shouldn't talk about them at work. It never left me in a good mood.

"I don't think they would've invited you if they thought that," Haydn said kindly. I gave him a small smile because Haydn never said a mean word.

"Thought what?" Leo asked.

"Parents," I said. "I'm going to meet Munro's parents on Sunday." We'd had to put off the lunch for a few weeks because of my shifts. The guys knew how my parents thought about me. They didn't know just how deep their hateful words and actions had sunk into me. My stomach churned at the thought of them. Other parents had looked at me with derision yet smiled falsely. Any chance I'd had at a relationship with their son had disappeared faster than the snow under the sun.

"Have you told Munro how you feel?" Leo asked.

I frowned. Had I? No, not really. He knew I was nervous, but not why. "Um, no. Well, a little bit, maybe."

"That's all very vague, Beck. You should tell him. He'll understand. He's head over heels for you. He's not going to throw you to the lions."

He was right. I needed to get it off my chest before Sunday, or I'd be a wreck by the time we had to leave. We'd made plans to meet up later this evening because he had a games night with his friends—Playstation and Call of Duty. Everyone would have left by the time I got to his place tonight. "Yeah, okay."

We both stayed quiet while Haydn bounced up to the bar, pushed his glasses up his nose, and spoke to a customer. "He's a happy little fucker." I laughed.

"He's exhausting, but I like him. He kinda reminds me of Gus when he first started here." Leo chuckled.

The night was busy, and I was exhausted, and for the first time in three weeks, I wanted my own bed, my own space. Munro's house was gorgeous, and I loved being there with him, but tonight, after having my parents on my mind, I wanted to be on my own.

As I walked to my car, I pulled my phone out and called him. It rang a few times before Munro answered with a laugh. "Hi, babe, are you on your way?" Before I could answer, he shouted something about Ed being crap at shooting. It sounded like they weren't wrapping up anytime soon. I waited for him to come back to me. "Sorry."

"Yeah, I'm going to go back to my place tonight. I'm knackered." I sighed when he muttered something else not meant for me.

"Don't do that, please, Beck. Come home. I'll chuck these losers out."

"No, carry on. I'll see you tomorrow."

"Beck, please?"

"See you tomorrow." I ended the call and pressed my key fob to unlock my car.

The drive home took less than half the time to drive to Munro's, and the need to sleep washed over me in waves. I had to park a couple of doors up from my place, but I was indoors in seconds. I shut the door and locked it, then threw my keys onto the small table in the hall and stumbled down to my bedroom, where I stripped off and collapsed face first into my pillows. After a little wriggling, I tugged the covers over me and was out for the count.

I dreamt of my parents, of them chasing me out of the house. I couldn't hear what they were shouting, but they looked so angry. My sister, Katherine, stood there with my clothes in her arms. She sneered at me and threw them at me. Then just laughed at me, pointing as I ran. Just as my father was going to catch me, I woke up gasping, out of breath, and covered in a clammy sheen of cooling sweat.

Fuck!

That was what talking about families did to me. I was over everything my family had done, and I didn't give a shit what they were doing now. It was the thought of having to get to meet people who might have an immediate bad opinion of me that had caused this. I grabbed my phone and checked the time. Crap, nearly seven. I hadn't had anywhere near enough sleep. I shoved the tangle of quilt off my legs and swung them over the edge. I sat there with my head in my hands as I pulled myself together.

First order of business was a shower, so I pushed upright and headed into the bathroom. As soon as the hot water pounded over my head, I felt better. The water washed away the demons, along with the sweat and the stale smell of the bar. After soaping myself, I stood with my head bent, my hands on the tiles, and let the water hit my neck and down my back until it cooled down. I dried off and went back to my bedroom. I quickly straightened and tidied the tangled sheets and bedding, then climbed back in and closed my eyes.

A shrill sound broke through my sleep-fogged head, and I reached out to find the culprit. My phone vibrated under my palm, and I dragged it to my ear. "Wha?" I mumbled.

"It's me. Can you let me in?" Munro's soft voice came down the line.

"Whattimeisit?" My tongue seemed to be stuck to the roof of my mouth. I licked my lips and tried again. "What time is it?"

"Nearly one o'clock. I was getting a little worried." His voice was laced with concern. I hated that I had him worried.

"Shit, yeah. Hold on." I got out of bed and padded down the hallway to the door.

I opened the door a couple of inches and peered out. It was just Munro. I stepped back behind the door and let him come in. He grinned and looked me up and down. "Do you always answer your door naked?"

"That's why I only opened it a little bit, you plonker." I walked back down to my bedroom. "And stop ogling my arse." I sat on the edge of my bed and rested my hands on my knees, my head bowed.

Munro broke into a peal of laughter that made my heart sing. I'd needed the night alone, but I was so happy now he was here. "Beck, baby. You have the hottest arse in the world. I'm gonna stare at it whenever I can."

The door closed, footsteps got closer, and Munro stopped in front of me. He caressed my cheek. "What's wrong?" His hand stilled, then fell away. "You're breaking up with me?"

"What? No, of course not. I'd hardly open the door naked if I was breaking up with you." I lifted my head.

"Then what? I've been shitting myself all night, and then you haven't called all morning, and..." He gulped. "What else would I think? I've never done this before, and I have an overactive imagination. It's been a really tough twelve hours."

"Oh, Ro, I'm sorry." I stood. Damn, he was right. I *was* naked and exposed. I went to a drawer and pulled out a pair of old grey sweatpants. I was going to have to talk about my fears and explain why I'd had a freak-out last night.

"Don't get dressed on my account. I like you naked." The little humour that had crept into his voice settled me.

"I can't have this conversation with my tackle out." I pulled the soft fabric up my legs and tucked myself in, aware that Munro was watching my every move.

"That sounds ominous. Something has happened I'm unaware of, and that makes me nervous."

Now that I had some clothes on, I approached him and placed my hands on his hips. "We're good, babe. I'm not breaking up with you. I love you, and I take us seriously. And, Ro, I've never said those words to anyone else."

"I love you too."

"I need coffee. C'mon, I'll put the kettle on."

It was time to face the music.

Chapter 23

Munro

I hadn't been kidding when I said I'd spent the time since Beck announced he wasn't coming to me in a panic. The fun I'd been having with Ed and Will had evaporated, stopping me from getting back in the game. When I explained what had happened, they were cool about it, both saying to not read too much into it. But I couldn't help it. Every scenario ran on a reel. He'd met someone else at work and had taken them back to his place. He'd realised how boring I was, that there was nothing special about me, or that he didn't want to be part of a life that seemed to run on Instagram. It went on and on. The worst was thinking of him in bed with another man, kissing him, touching him, fucking him. What he'd said to him. Had he told him how good he felt, used the same words he'd said to me? Oh, fuck.

And now here I was, watching him, unable to take my eyes off his bare torso. What was I looking for? Evidence of another man's hands on him. Christ, stop it. He loved me. We were not breaking up. There was no evidence of any sex. I trusted him.

"Munro? Where'd you go?" Beck's soft question took me out of my nightmarish thoughts.

"I thought you might've brought someone home with you. That you didn't want me anymore."

Beck reeled back like I'd slapped him. His pale face had two pink spots on his cheeks, and anger flashed in his eyes. "You think I'd cheat on you?" His voice was barely a whisper.

"No, no, I don't. I trust you, Beck. With everything I have, I trust you. But I told you I have an overactive imagination. I've never done this before, and I'm failing at it. I'm crazy in love with you, and I couldn't bear to be without you. I'm sorry. Please forgive me."

The kettle clicked off, and Beck turned away from me and made two mugs of instant coffee. When he was done, he placed them both on the little table. He pulled one of the chairs out and sat down. I copied him and sat facing him.

He had his hands wrapped around the mug, staring at the black liquid and the bubble still swirling on the top until it burst. "I'm sorry too. I'd never cheat on you, Munro. And you're not failing, not at all. It's a really stupid thing. You're not going to believe how dumb I'm being. But I'm terrified of meeting your parents."

I stared at him, the wariness and fragility showing in every aspect of his face. He was scared, really scared. "Why? What do you think will happen? Beck, they're so excited to meet you. I know they'll love you."

"You don't know that, not really. Look, I have an issue with parents, or more specifically, my parents." When he picked up his coffee, his hands were shaking. "They were good people. I had a great childhood. They're both teachers, so our holidays were long and full of days on the beach or travelling through France, Italy, or Spain. It all stopped when I was fifteen and realised I was gay. I'd never wanted to be with a girl. Sure, I liked them. I had lots of girls in my group of friends, but I knew that would be all they ever were." He sipped his drink, then put the cup down.

"Yeah, I was the same."

"I thought that because my parents were teachers that they would be open-minded, understanding of LGBTQ+ kids. I knew I wasn't the only one in my school, so I assumed it would be the same in the school they worked in. It wasn't. In fact, it was the complete opposite. They went bonkers, totally flipped, shouting that I was looking for attention, that it was a stupid phase I'd grow out of. The crux of it was that they didn't care about the sexuality of other kids. They could do whatever they wanted. But not their child."

"What did they do?" Did I really want to know? Was he chucked out and had to live on the streets?

"They told my brother and sister that I was a disgusting pervert. I lived there and had to put up with all the jibes and the hate speech. I was called every name you can think of and probably some you don't know. The worst part was they carried on with their lives outside of the house as if nothing had changed. That was when I started to get tattoos. I wasn't old enough to get them, but I had a friend, Craig, who was really good at art. He wanted to be a tattooist, and I let him practice on me." He chuckled a little, but it caught in his throat.

"The first few weren't very good." He pointed at a patch on the inside of his arm. I thought it was an amazing tribal symbol, circular and intricate.

"That looks good to me."

"Yeah, it is now, but you should've seen what was underneath it. Anyway, my mum and dad saw them and had another reason to hate me. 'I was ruining my chances of ever getting a job. No one would want me,' they said. All that did was make me get more. Craig got better and better, and it became addictive. Whenever it got really bad at home, I'd get another one. It became a vicious circle."

"I love your tattoos. They're beautiful, captivating. I could stare at them for hours. They are who you are. They're bright, bold, interesting, and deep. Some look so intense, almost painful, and sad. They are you, Beck. They tell the story of who you are. And you are all the things I see in them. You are an amazing man, with so much love and kindness in you."

Beck swallowed hard, and a tear slipped free. Instinctively, I wiped it away. He gave me a sad smile. "It seemed that from then on, every time I met someone, had a boyfriend who was serious enough to take me home, it would go wrong. Their parents would hate me on sight, judge my ink rather than get to know the man behind them. The boyfriends never lasted after that."

I got up from my chair and knelt between his legs. As I rubbed my hands up his thighs, I kissed his chest, over the ink that covered most of his torso. A couple of inches square over his heart was a blank space. I'd seen it before but never really thought about it.

"Why's this part empty?"

Beck wiped his hands over his face, sweeping any remaining tears away. "It's waiting for my forever man, the man I want to spend the rest of my life with. It will be inked very soon."

"Me?" I squeaked. "What? I mean, really?"

All Beck did was shrug, but a cute, quirky smile played on his lips. He bent his head and pressed a firm, possessive kiss to my mouth. As I parted my lips, the tip of his tongue slipped in and touched my own.

"Bedroom," I said as he pulled back. His eyes were already inky black when he nodded.

The fact that I had on way more clothes than Mr Sweatpants meant nothing. I was soon naked before him. Then I was on my back with my legs spread and a hand on my very hard dick. He smiled down at me. He had a bottle of lube in one hand and a condom in the other. He silently questioned me. We'd only just had our test results back and were both clear. I grinned and pointed to the lube.

Beck threw the condom over his shoulder and had his sweatpants off before I could blink. His dick was a sight to behold. Long and thick, it stood upright, the head glistening with the slick of his precum, the metal beads shining. I licked my lips, and of course, Beck saw it and chuckled. "Something you want to taste, babe?"

I crooked my finger at him. "Just get here." I bent my legs and opened them wider, showing him my hole. Nothing turned me on more than having him look at me like he was now. I grabbed the lube, squirted some onto my fingers, and reached between my legs. I was an exhibitionist in my daily life, but I'd never expected to be so brazen, so confident to do the things I knew Beck loved. And he loved seeing my fingers in my arse.

When he knelt between my thighs, he took the lube and slipped a slick finger in alongside my own.

"Fuck, that feels good." I pulled mine free and gave him a nod. "I'm ready."

He spread more lube over his bare cock and pressed at my entrance. God, it felt different without the latex, hotter, smoother, and *soooo* much better.

Beck grunted as he slid in farther. "Jesus, this is going to be over embarrassingly quickly. Nothing has ever felt this good."

"Uh-huh." Was all I could manage. As inexperienced as I was, I knew that nothing could beat this feeling, this moment.

Beck leant over me, his head in the crook of my neck, licking, sucking, marking me as he thrust inside me. Over and over, he pegged my prostate, and soon, my orgasm was barrelling through me. I tightened the grip on my cock and cried out my release. Beck followed, the heat of his cum filling me as his orgasm poured inside me.

We lay together, Beck panting into my neck as I stroked my hand up and down his back. Both of us were quiet; no words were needed.

It wasn't until we were under the spray of the shower that I spoke. "We don't need to see my parents, Beck."

"No,   it's   okay.   I   trust   you."

BECK

Today it was happening. Munro had spent the last few days filling me in on everything about his parents and his childhood. In the end, I had to tell him to stop. He was worrying more than I was. He'd turned my whole concerns upside down and was now scared I wouldn't like his parents.

"Munro, please, just stop. I'm fine about meeting them, and I'm sure we're all going to get on perfectly. I love you, so there's no reason why I won't like them. And you love me, so again, there should be no reason they won't love me too."

"When did you become rational? I thought I'd be having to drag you up the driveway." He sighed.

I laughed and gave his thigh a squeeze. "Nope, I said I trusted you. And your mum does sound a lot of fun." Over the three weeks we'd been together, Munro must've spoken to her about three or four times a week. To say I was envious of the relationship he had with them was an understatement. And since our conversation after I'd bugged out for the night, the conversations had ended up being on speaker. I was more confident, happier even.

They lived about an hour away, out in the countryside, and we'd been driving for nearly that long now. "And here we are," Munro announced. My breath hitched in my throat, and my palms got sweaty.

I couldn't see a house, yet he'd come to a halt. "Why have you stopped?"

"So I could do this." He reached over the centre console, cupped my face in his hands, and pressed his lips to mine. It was firm, and with only a flick of his tongue, I opened for him and let him in. As our tongues stroked together, I relaxed again. It was a blissful kiss, unhurried and perfect. When he moved back into his seat, Munro smiled and thumbed his bottom lip. "Feel better?"

"As long as my hard-on goes down before your parents open the door, I'm good."

Munro let out a hearty laugh, but he palmed his dick. He put the car back in gear and pulled away again. A few minutes later, a house came into view. It was a cream stone cottage set in a large garden that surrounded it. Someone was a keen gardener. Huge flower beds burst with colour, even at this time of year. But before I could ask him, the front door opened, and two people came out. His mother was a short, slim woman who smiled so wide I couldn't help but smile back. His father looked like Munro, only twenty-eight years older.

"At least I know what you're going to look like in the future. You're the image of him." I nudged him with my elbow. "Still going to be hot."

"I'm pleased to hear it. No lusting after him." He grinned.

"You're safe. I'm not looking for a Daddy."

"Oh god, no. I'm not having that image in my head. Come on. My mum will be dragging you out of your seat otherwise." With the engine switched off, we unclicked our seat belts and got out. I collected the bouquet of flowers and bottle of wine I'd brought. Munro said that bribery was cheating, but I didn't care. I called it being polite. I was glad when Munro took hold of my free hand and gave it a squeeze.

"Hi, Mum," Munro said, a slight edge of nervousness in his voice, which I was sure his parents heard too. "This is Beck, my boyfriend. Beck, this is my mum, Emma, and my dad, Michael."

"Oh, look at you, Beck. So handsome, so colourful. Oh, Munro, you did well, my boy." Warmth spread up my neck and over my cheeks, but then his mother pulled me into a hug.

"Muuuum!" Munro groaned.

His dad sighed. "Emma, let the poor man breathe."

When she released me, I was smiling but a little choked up. She just *hugged* me. I seriously couldn't remember the last time my own mother had hugged me. Probably about fifteen years. When I hit puberty, she stopped. My eyes burnt, prickling with the threat of tears. I blinked, rapidly halting them from tipping over.

Munro was immediately in front of me and cupped my face again. "You okay?"

I nodded, not sure if my voice would work. I swallowed the lump in my throat. "Yeah, I am. Surprised, but I'm good."

A hand squeezed my shoulder, and when Munro stepped back, his father was there with a kind, understanding smile. "It's good to meet you, son. I'm glad you're here."

Son? Okay, that was it. I gave a sniffle and wiped my nose with the back of my hand as I chuckled pathetically. "I'm sorry. I'm not usually like this. It's been a while for me."

"A while since what, Beck?" Emma asked. Munro shook his head, telling her to stop. I took his hand and held on tight.

"Since any parent has been nice to me. My parents...well, they just don't." I shrugged. "Never mind. It's lovely to meet you."

We finally—post my mini breakdown—made it indoors, which wasn't what I'd expected. Instead of small rooms, it had an open-plan space with stairs on the left to the upstairs. The rest of the ground floor was made up of a huge kitchen with sleek dark green cupboards and solid wood countertops. An island about two metres long had the same wooden top, and tall stools stood along one side. Each one was different, but they coordinated. Copper pans hung overhead, gleaming in the sunlight. I imagined them still glowing warmly when the lights were on.

"This is amazing." The room looked cosy with soft, comfortable sofas and a packed bookcase. Another sofa farther down faced a wall with a TV mounted to it. More seating and a large dining table looked out over floor-to-ceiling glass windows, which, I assumed, opened up to the patio and garden beyond.

"Thank you, Beck. We're very happy here."

Not long later, a cup of coffee was placed in front of Munro and me. Then his mum and dad got busy cooking. They basted a large piece of beef and put it back in the oven, then prepared the veg while they all chatted. I was happy to listen as they teased each other and talked about everything that was happening in their lives.

"Beck, how long have you worked in the bar?" his dad asked.

"A while now. At eighteen, I started to work there when it was just a pub. A few years ago, Max and Jonas bought the place, and luckily, they wanted me to stay. Sawyer started at the same time as me. We've all been friends a long time."

"It's great to see them all together. They've become family to each other and have been really good to me, welcoming me with open arms," Munro said. "It's been a huge scary rollercoaster ride for me."

Both of his parents gave him a sad smile. "We wish you'd told us, Munro," his dad said. "It must have been a confusing and lonely time for you."

"It wasn't like that, Dad. I mean, maybe a little, but I needed to focus on work, which was more important to me." He gave me a wicked grin and bumped my shoulder with his. "It's all his doing. One look at him and I knew it was him I wanted."

Heat burnt on my cheeks, and I ducked my head.

"He turned me down a few times." Munro laughed. "I ended up accosting him after work."

And he'd been determined, but I didn't regret giving in to him. He was perfect. "I'm glad he did."

The conversation flowed easily. Munro would fill in gaps for me or explain who everyone was. The love in this family was obvious. Not just in the way they laughed and teased each other but also in the photographs of Munro at every age hanging everywhere. He was an incredibly lucky man.

During dinner, an awkward moment happened when Emma mentioned Lucie.

"I never liked her," Emma said. "She had her sights set on you and your money from the moment she met you."

"Well, it doesn't matter now. She left, and I doubt I'll hear from her again." Munro effectively ended the topic. I wasn't so sure we'd seen the last of her, but I held back my comment. The saying 'hell hath no fury like a woman scorned' came to mind. Lucie wasn't going to give up.

By the time we left, I was stuffed full of delicious food. I hadn't had a day like this for such a long time. If ever.

Emma hugged me again. "It's been such a pleasure to meet you, Beck. I've never seen Munro so happy. Thank you for allowing him to be the man he's supposed to be."

"Thank you for having me here today. I've had a lovely time. You've been very kind to me." She squeezed me one more time, then turned to her son.

Michael shook my hand. "Welcome to the family, Beck. It's been a pleasure to meet you."

"Thank you. I've had a great time."

When we were back on the main road and heading into town, Munro let out a long sigh. "Please tell me that was okay. That my mum wasn't too overbearing. I don't think I want to know what she whispered to you."

Chapter 25

Munro

Beck was quiet on the journey home, not uncomfortably, more pensive. His hand rested on my thigh, his finger stroking up and down my inseam. Had something gone wrong? I ran through the afternoon in my head. He'd laughed and joked, told stories of his own, some about us, others about his friends and work. He'd looked through photographs and listened with interest to my dad talking about the garden and the plants in it. There was nothing I could put my finger on.

"Your place or mine?" I asked as we got closer to town.

"Hmm." He looked at me as if he was still deep in thoughts. Then he shook his head.

"Oh, sorry, Ro. Your place if that's okay." He squeezed my leg.

I took the turning, and fifteen minutes later, we were home. Beck wandered down to the kitchen, where he took two bottles of beer out of the fridge and held one out to me. I nodded. He uncapped them, but instead of giving one to me, he put both bottles down on the island and came to me. He slid his hands up my chest and over my shoulder, and the tension I'd experienced since we left disappeared. As he fingered the hair at my nape, I gripped his waist and pulled him against me.

"Talk to me," I said. He stared into my eyes as if he was searching for something, and I met his gaze with all the love I felt for him. Whatever it was he'd been looking, he seemed to have found it as he relaxed.

"I had a great time today." He tightened his hold on my neck for a second. "I'd forgotten what family life could be like. What being spoken to kindly felt like. Your mum hugged me, and I realised I hadn't been hugged like that, by a parent, for well over a decade. I wasn't expecting it and had no idea how to deal with it."

My heart broke for him. I snaked my arms around his back and held him close. Our foreheads touched, and his breath was warm on my lips. I sensed he had more to say and stayed quiet.

"You told me it would be okay, and I trusted you. But I still had my doubts, although they were about me more than you. I expected to do or say something that would turn them against me. But when we left, your mum thanked me. She thanked me for making you happy and for letting you be you. The real you."

"I knew she'd said something embarrassing."

"That's just it. It wasn't. It was heartfelt and genuine. She loves you with everything she has. And I'm angry that you'll never get the same welcome from my parents. They won't get to know how amazing you are. How happy you make me. They will never welcome you into their house, let alone the family. And I'm so sorry." His voice broke, and his eyes glistened.

"Hey, no. No, don't do that. Don't blame yourself for their shitty actions. You are so much better than them. They don't deserve you, and you don't need them. We don't need them, babe." I pressed my mouth to his, and when he parted his lips, I licked inside his mouth, flicking my tongue to his, coaxing him to kiss me back. It didn't take him long to join me. He curled his fingers up into my hair and tugged on the strands. Pleasure shot through me, and I knew he needed this, needed to take from me. Take control.

His hands were everywhere, pulling at my clothes. I tugged at his with the same frenzy. When we were naked from the waist down, he dropped to his knees and took me deep into his mouth. He sucked and swirled his tongue over every inch of my cock until I was a panting, gibbering mess. He swallowed around the head, and it was game over. I cried out as I poured my release down his throat.

My head was still spinning as he let go of my dick and turned me around. He bent me over the island, my face pressed against the smooth surface. Something rustled behind me. Then the cold slick of gel on his fingers as he probed my hole.

"I'm good," I growled after he'd pumped two fingers inside me. "Fuck me, baby. Fuck me hard."

And oh my god, did he ever. His need matched my own, and soon I was crying out again as he hit my prostate. He gripped my hips tightly, shuddered, then paused. His dick swelled, and the heat of his cum filled my arse. I pushed back, wanting him deeper, as far as he could go. Buried inside me forever.

Together we slumped to the floor, me on Beck's thighs. His dick slid free, and his cum dripped from my hole. I tucked my head into his neck as he wrapped his arms around my waist.

I laughed. "Bloody hell, I wasn't expecting that."

"Too much?" Beck pressed his lips to my hair.

"No. Never. It was fucking hot. We're definitely going to do that again." I lifted my head and grinned. "But maybe a towel on the floor for the drops?"

Beck chuckled, the heaviness in his eyes gone. My boyfriend was back. "Maybe you can fuck me next time?"

I shifted off his legs, grabbed my jeans, and pulled them on, not bothering with my underwear. "I'm going to get cleaned up."

"Does that mean I have to wash the floor? Great, thanks, babe." Beck tugged on his jeans and gathered up our briefs.

After our shower, we wanted to do nothing more than lie around on the couch, neither of us having an appetite. As usual, my mum had served up way too much food, but it had been so delicious we'd taken seconds. I was lying between Beck's legs, my back on his chest and his arms around me. It was perfect.

"I think I'll come to the gym with you tomorrow," Beck said. "I need to run off that sponge pudding your mum made."

"Great, you should take one of my classes too. I think you'd enjoy it." I tipped my head up. "It's a kickboxing class, one of the beginner ones. It's only been running a couple of weeks."

"I've always liked the idea of that but been too nervous to try. All the people doing it are crazy fit." He wriggled to sit up straighter, and I shifted so we were sitting next to each other, then laughed as he pouted at me for moving off him.

"I promise you it's not like that in my classes. I've got people of all ages and sizes. One lady is in her fifties and is killing the classes. It's empowering and will leave you feeling so good afterwards."

He thought for a moment, then grabbed his phone. "What time does it start? I'll ask Leo if he wants to come. Maybe Sawyer too."

The guys from the bar all had a membership to the gym, and I'd seen all of them there at some time. Even Gus, who Max had to coax to come, but now said—with a smile—he doesn't hate it.

"I've put it in the group chat. I'm sure someone will want to come with me. Now back to cuddling, please." He pulled me back into position.

The next morning, as I set up the gym room with mats and punch bags, the attendants arrived. I greeted them with a smile that grew as Sawyer, Leo, Beck, and the latest member of the bar and their family, Haydn, came in, laughing and joking with each other.

After introducing myself and welcoming the new members, I had to control my urge to kiss Beck. He looked hot in a tanktop, which displayed all his tattoos. He gave me a wink. The fucker knew I liked him dressed like this.

"Okay, warm-up time."

The lesson was fun and fast-paced, and I led them straight into jabs, hooks, and kicks. I kept the reps short but powerful. Beck and his friends seemed to enjoy it and even showed some potential to be good at it.

When the class finished and the other members had said their goodbyes, I went over to Beck. "So what did you think?"

"It was great, a really good workout. My legs are going to be feeling it tomorrow," Sawyer said as he stretched out his hamstrings.

"Beck?"

He grinned and gave me a crushing kiss.

"Yeah, I'll come again. The instructor is hot." He slapped my arse and winked. "See you later, hot stuff."

BECK

We'd been together nearly four months now, and it just kept getting better. Munro had had to travel for a few days for some promotion work. He'd hated going alone and phoned me the whole time. And honestly, I hated it too.

Generally, our life-work balance worked, but after my late shifts, I went home to my place. My flat was cold and empty without him, but I loathed waking Munro up at three thirty when he had to be at his work at seven. I had the feeling he was going to ask me to make it official and move in with him, and as much as I'd like to, I worried it was too soon and he'd get fed up with me. I was sure of him. He was the one for me, but I'd been wrong before. Admittedly, no one had ever loved me or said he loved me as much as Munro did. So for as long as he wanted me, I was here, and he said he wanted me forever.

"Beck, babe?" Munro called me from his office. He'd had some work to organise, and I'd left him to it and was now watching Supernatural. Jensen Ackles on Munro's humungous TV was like the best thing ever.

I paused the programme and went to him. "Yeah?" He had a look that was half excitement, half nervousness. Hopefully, he wasn't going away again unless it was to Bali or somewhere equally exotic and he could take me.

"I've got a promo day with one of my sponsors on Wednesday. Would you come with me? They'd like to meet you."

I frowned. "Why would they want that? I'm no fitness god like you."

He cocked his eyebrow, and a dimple appeared on his left cheek. "I'm a god, am I? I like that." He flexed his biceps, then cracked up laughing.

"Fuck off, cocky twat. You know what I mean." He was never going to drop that now. It was true, though. The more I got to know him, the more impressed I was with his enthusiasm and commitment. He really did love his work. I'd been to the gym with him plenty of times now, not just for the kickboxing class, and I saw a difference in my body. It would never be like his, but that was fine by me.

"Anyway, putting my deity to the side"—his chocolate-brown eyes flashed—"they said they were interested in having you in a couple of the shots."

My mouth dropped open. "No thanks. Not really my scene. That's your gig." God, the thought of them taking photos of me. I wanted to run and hide. I'd be too self-conscious, wondering if they'd be judging me by my tattoos. And what if they didn't like me? Would it damage Munro's relationship with them?

"I thought you'd say that, and that's fine, but would you still come with me? I'd like to show you this side of my work."

I wasn't working on Wednesday, so I had no valid reason to turn him down. And it would be interesting. "Um, I don't—"

"Think of it as a good free lunch."

"I was going to say yes, Ro. You don't need to keep selling it to me. Although now I know there will be free food, I'm up for it for sure."

Munro jumped up from his chair behind his desk. He wrapped his arms around me and kissed me. "Awesome, thank you. You'll enjoy it. They're good people, one of the first to approach me."

Now I was standing in a huge conference room of a posh hotel, watching Munro schmooze with some sharply dressed men and women.

"What do you think of it all?" a pretty, young woman beside me asked. She was dressed casually in a pair of faded black skinny jeans and an old Guns and Roses T-shirt with the arms ripped off at the shoulder. She oozed confidence in who she was and didn't seem to care that everyone else was in business attire.

"It's different. This is a side of Munro I didn't know about. He's good at all this. Not that I should be surprised. He has the ability to fit in with everyone."

Her gaze traced the tattoos on my arms and neck. "He is. He's very photogenic and totally in love with you." Her candidness was surprising but refreshing, and I smiled, secretly loving that it was so obvious how much we loved each other. "You have some beautiful ink on you. The detail is incredible."

Another surprise. I'd intended to cover them up by wearing a long-sleeved button-down shirt, but Munro had stopped me. He'd wanted me to be me, not a person I thought he needed me to be. "Thank you, and yes, my friend is a genius with a needle and ink."

"Would you let me photograph them?" She blushed. "I'm sorry. I should've introduced myself. I'm Lizbeth, the photographer for today. Which has nothing to do with why I'd like to take some shots of your ink. I have a show coming up about diversity and inclusivity. How people are perceived against who they really are. It's about acceptance and beauty in the unusual. You're perfect for it."

I raised my eyebrow. "You think I'm unusual? I'm not sure that's a compliment or not." The concept of her show appealed to me, but did she want to photograph my tattoos for the right reason?

"It was absolutely a compliment. You remind me of Stephen James, only more colourful." She dug in the pocket of her jeans. "Take my card. Have a look at my website and the other work I've done. You can call me if you're interested. I'm paying, by the way."

I took the card and slid it into my back pocket. "Do you know Munro well? Have you worked with him a lot?"

She chuckled. "I've been taking pictures of your boyfriend for years. I've watched him grow, become more and more confident, but never as much as he is now. You finding each other and him having the strength to come out has changed him. There's a sparkle in his eyes I haven't seen before."

I knew exactly what she was talking about. The Munro who'd approached me for the first time was long gone. "They asked me to take part today." Why did I tell her that?

"I know. I asked them to. I hope you'd reconsider. I'd love to take pictures of the two of you together. You're so different from him, and the contrast works. You're stunning together."

Before I could reply, Munro slipped his arm around my waist and kissed my cheek. "Hi, Lizbeth. I hope you're not putting any pressure on my boyfriend."

"You caught me. I was just about to." At least she had the decency to blush. "Please reconsider, Beck."

I looked at Munro. Should I say yes or use him as a shield and stay in the background?

He shrugged. "It's up to you. I'd love to have some professional shots of us together, but I'm not going to force you."

"How about some candid shots?" Lizbeth asked. "Not for the campaign, but some photos that would look great on your social media."

I liked the idea of that more than posing for them. "Okay. But I want to be able to veto if I don't like them."

She practically bounced with enthusiasm. "Absolutely. I promise they'll be discreet and perfect for you both."

So that was what happened. For the next two hours, I laughed at Munro when he did something goofy, and I relaxed so much. Instead of staying glued to the wall, watching, I was with him between the official shots, totally forgetting about Lizbeth until she called that she had everything she needed.

After that, Munro, Lizbeth, the guy in charge—Chris—and the sponsors gathered around the laptop screen and looked over the shots. At one point, Munro glanced over at me, his eyes blazing with love. I shivered. What had he seen? I pushed myself up from the sofa and walked to the table.

Munro's jaw was tight, the muscle in his cheek pulsing. Uh-oh, he had something on his mind.

"What's wrong?" I asked.

"The best photo of the day is one of us both. When we were messing around with the bottle. You were doing your cocktail moves with it."

I knew exactly which moment he meant. He'd stood behind me, his arms around my waist and his chin resting on my shoulder as I twirled the bottle. We'd both been laughing, and he'd kissed my neck.

"That's great." Where was he going with this?

"Not really, because you don't have a contract with these people, and it's you holding the product. *Annnd* you said you didn't want any images of you to be used."

How good could this pic be if they were that serious? "Can I see it?" When I looked at the laptop screen, I smiled. It was really an amazing photograph. Lizbeth clicked through the other pictures. I understood why they wanted that one. It was the best of the bunch. I looked different...happy. And I finally saw what Gus and the other guys had been on about. The way Munro looked at me was how their boyfriends looked at them, something I'd always been envious of. "Okay, you can use it."

Apparently, it wasn't that easy, and by the time the day was over, I'd signed my name about a gazillion times and was wishing I'd stayed at home. But I had earned considerably more money than in one day at the bar, so that was one positive.

We were back at Munro's place. Munro was quiet, probably tired. It had been a packed day, but I'd seen him in his element, and being included had been more fun than I'd expected. We were sprawled out on his large sofa, staring at some bland action movie on the TV, but neither of us was watching. "Are you okay, Ro?"

Munro turned to me and yawned. "Sorry. I'm exhausted."

"We can go to bed. There's no rule on what time you have to stay up."

He nodded, then pushed me down on my back. "Are there any rules about making out on the sofa with the best boyfriend in the world?" He draped himself over my body. I parted my legs to let him lie between them. His arms were on either side of my head, holding the bulk of his weight off my chest.

"There are." I smiled. "In fact, it's compulsory after the best boyfriend in the world let someone take photographs of him."

"Did I push you into it?"

"What? No. It was fun, and I enjoyed it much more than I thought I would. And of course, you needed me to make the best shot of the day."

Chapter 27

Munro

We were sitting together on the sofa, enjoying a couple of beers and devouring a pizza. "Did I push you too far today?" I asked.

He twisted around, his knee bent up on the sofa, frowning. "What makes you think that? Is this why you've been so quiet?" When he shifted, I scooted closer so he could swing his other leg up over mine. "When do I do anything I don't want to?"

He shook his head. "Today was fun. I loved watching you. You're good at it. It all comes so naturally to you. I know you've been doing it a long time now, but I was impressed."

"But you got caught up in it, even after you said you didn't want to. I didn't mean it to happen, so I'm sorry. And the contract has a cooling-off period. You can call and cancel it tomorrow if you've changed your mind. Lizbeth will understand if you don't want her to photograph your tattoos. I know they are all so meaningful to you."

Beck moved so fast and had me on my back before I could even blink. Our bodies weren't touching, but he pinned me with his eyes, which burnt with an intensity I hadn't seen before. "Stop talking. Stop saying you're sorry. I'm good with everything that happened today. The project with Lizbeth is exciting, and I know that the contract is only for today. I don't want to do what you do, babe. But I'm happy to come with you when you have another photo shoot. Okay?" He lowered his hips onto mine. "Ro, do you understand?"

He rolled his hips, and I lost all cognitive thinking. "Uh-huh."

"Good." Then his mouth touched mine, and my worries were gone. A few minutes later, our clothes were too. God, the things this man did to me. When he entered my body, I was soaring.

A week later, Chris called that the ad was due to release on the following Monday. He gave me the go-ahead to talk about it on my social media as long as I didn't publish the official pic of Beck and me.

"That's great. Beck had such a good time. He's going to be in Lizbeth's exhibition, which surprised me. He doesn't like to be in the spotlight."

"We'd love to have him back again, so we'll keep in touch." Chris ended the call.

How would Beck feel about that? Hopefully, his confidence would grow under all the positive reactions. I hated that he had such a low opinion of himself. The man he showed the customers in the bar was so different from the one he was with his friends and with me. His biological family had done so much damage to his mental health. I would happily string them up on the highest tree. Luckily, my mother adored him and often phoned him—not me— just to ask how his day had been. He always glowed after speaking with her.

I didn't have time to call him now, as I had a spin class to teach. Lucie's position got filled quickly, and the new instructor, Vicky, was doing a great job. She might be even better than Lucie.

Everybody loved her. I gave her a wave as she encouraged her class to hold a lunge position.

My spin class was waiting for me, talking among themselves.

"Ready to suffer, guys?" I clapped my hands. "We're going for endurance today. Remember to breathe."

They all groaned, but they loved being pushed hard. "Sadistic bastard," one of them grumbled.

"I heard that, Lewis."

Forty-five minutes later, the class was finished, and the groans and moans made me laugh. "If you can still talk, you haven't been working hard enough," I joked. "See you all next week."

I slapped a few on the back as I made my way to my office and my private shower. For the remainder of the day, I had video call meetings and admin work. A necessary evil. I loved teaching all kinds of classes, but I could do without all the paperwork.

My thoughts drifted to Beck. I couldn't wait to see him tonight. I'd never been unhappy, but now I knew what being truly happy felt like. However busy my days and nights had been, I'd been lonely. Something had been missing. Or rather, *someone* had been missing.

At last, my desk was clear, and I closed down my laptop. Erin had left a couple of hours ago, but the gym was still buzzing and would be until ten o'clock. After saying goodnight to the instructors working this evening, I walked out to the car park. The wind whipped around me, chilling me, as I hustled towards my car. The drive into the city, which should've been a quick ten-minute drive, took over half an hour. Roadworks and a diversion made me late to pick up Beck.

When I finally made it inside the busy bar, I didn't spot Beck. Instead, Sawyer and Leo were behind the bar. "Hi, guys," I greeted them.

"Good to see you, Munro," Sawyer said and bobbed his head in the direction of a table in the corner. "He's over there. A woman came looking for him."

A woman? I spun around. Beck was laughing at something Lizbeth said. "That's Lizbeth, a photographer. In fact, she's an excellent photographer. Have they been talking long?"

"About twenty minutes. Do you know what she wants from him?" Leo said.

"Yeah, I do." I turned back to the guys. "He hasn't told you?" Why had he kept quiet about the exhibition? He'd been enthusiastic about it, looking forward to her taking the photographs.

"No, what's he up to?" Sawyer looked intrigued now.

"I'm sure he'll tell you soon enough." I tapped the bar, then wandered over to the two in the corner. "Can I join the conversation, or is it private? If you're trying to poach my boyfriend, Lizzie, you've got no chance."

Beck stood and kissed me. "You're late. Everything okay?"

"There were roadworks all over the south side, and it took for-bloody-ever to get here." I leant down and kissed Lizbeth's cheek. "It's good to see you again, Lizzie."

I sat down next to Beck, who immediately put his hand on my thigh. I loved how tactile he was and wanted to touch me whenever he was near me.

"Lizzie wanted to make a date for the photo session. I can do it next Wednesday. Are you free then?"

"I am now. This is too good to miss. Is that okay with you?" I checked with Lizzie.

"Of course. Maybe I'll take a couple of photos with you two together, just some body shots. I love the contrast of his colourful tattoos and your smooth, clear skin."

I agreed, and we chatted for a few more minutes. Then Lizzie said goodbye. "Do you want to grab something to eat?" I was starving and could eat a horse.

"I don't want to eat out, but we can get some takeaway," Beck said as we stood. We waved at the guys and left. "Jeez, it's cold. When did this happen?"

We decided on Chinese, and I called in the order to collect. "Chris called today. The campaign goes live on Monday."

Beck was quiet, not the reaction I had been expecting. "Beck, you okay?"

"Nervous, I think. Don't get me wrong. I had a fun afternoon, but it doesn't feel real that a photo of me will be part of a nationwide ad campaign that will be published in magazines and on the internet. It's weird."

"It's going to be okay, babe. The public are going to love it. Have you forgotten how hot you look in it?" I joked, hoping to lighten the mood. Beck laughed, the tension dissipating.

"I think that's you." He rolled his eyes.

We left it at that and moved on to other topics.

When we got home, I carried the bag of food into the kitchen. Beck veered off to the stairs. "I'm going to grab a shower."

As much as I wanted to join him, I refrained. We'd never get to eat otherwise. But before I had collected the plates and cutlery, Beck was calling out. "Put that in the oven and get your arse up here!"

Not going to say no to that. Nope, no chance.

Chapter 28

BECK

The release of the ad was gratefully unclimactic. Everyone at work loved it, and of course they took the piss out of me, but their ribbing was all in jest and supportive. But now it was time for the photo session. Only it felt more as if my tattoos were being dissected. Munro had to deal with an emergency and would be joining me as soon as he had it sorted. I was standing in Lizbeth's studio, a large room, empty except for a few pieces of furniture. Brilliant sunlight shone in from the three tall windows on the south side.

"You're nervous," Lizbeth said. "Are you having second thoughts?" She looked a little panicked, which surprised me. I doubted my ink was that important to the show.

"Yes, I'm not used to having my body scrutinised. I know plenty of my tattoos are always visible, but usually, if someone's looking this closely, it's to criticise them and me, not to admire them." I shrugged, feigning my concerns about being judged.

"Beck, I promise you that even you will see them in a different light by the time I've finished. You're a walking work of art. The time, effort, and I can imagine some pain that went into every tattoo is worth celebrating." Her earnest enthusiasm told me she was being honest with me. She really did love them. "Can you tell me about them, the meaning or reason you have them? Not every one of them, but maybe some of the ones I want to focus the most on?"

I scoffed. "Be prepared to be bored. Some I had done just because they're beautiful. Others are to cover some major mistakes."

Her smile broadened, and her eyes lit up. "That's exactly what I want to know. Are you ready to start, or do you want to wait for Munro?"

"I don't know how long he's going to be. We'd best start." Hopefully, he wouldn't be too long. I needed him here.

"Great. One more question. How much of your body is covered?"

"Most of it. My torso. And my legs have plenty, but they're not completely covered like my arms. I have some on my, um, my arse, but not for any specific reason. And before you ask. No, I haven't got any on my dick."

Lizzie laughed as her cheeks pinked. Ha, she was totally going to ask me that. "Guilty."

We got down to business. First up were my arms. It was fascinating to see her focus on ones I'd not thought about for a long time. Craig had started on my arms, and he'd inked a couple of messy ones that I hadn't had covered up later.

"Tell me about this one. The white rose."

"That was one of Craig's first attempts at a flower. He's been begging me to let him cover or rework it, but I won't."

"Why? It's not as good as the other flowers." The camera kept clicking away.

"You're probably going to laugh. One of the meanings of a white rose is a new start, a new beginning. I was in a really tough phase and had to rethink my life and where it was going to go. Which is why I won't let him redo it. It holds a lot of painful memories that are worth remembering every now and again. If only to give me the strength to live my life the way I want to." My voice shook. "Sorry, I didn't mean to get so deep."

"No. Don't apologise. It was beautiful. I knew you'd have a story to tell the moment I saw you. There's a lot more to you than people see or perceive, Beck."

We carried on chatting about anything. I liked her, she was easy to talk to, and I could see us becoming friends.

"Ready to take your T-shirt off?"

"Yep, but you'd better have the heating on in here."

Lizbeth started with the most recognisable: my Pride flag. "It's incredible," she said as she aimed her camera at it.

"I love it. I love the way it looks like it's rippling in a breeze when I move. Craig had improved plenty by now. The reason I have it is obvious. I am out and proud, and I will never hide or deny who I am."

She clicked away and asked more questions about my tattoos. "I notice you have an empty patch over your heart. Can I ask the reason behind it?"

"It's waiting for the right person to fill it."

"And that's not Munro?"

"Oh, it's for him. I'm waiting for Craig to have a free moment to ink it. Munro is my person, my love, my life, my forever. He makes me a better person. He sees me, the real me, and still loves me." Shoes scuffled at the other side of the room, and I looked up. Munro stared at me, a shocked look on his face. Why was that? I told him I loved him all the time.

"Talk of the devil." I gave him a wink.

"Perfect timing, Munro. I'd like to take some pictures of both of you on there." She pointed to the large brass-framed bed in the corner. The sheets were pure white. "It won't be full-body shots, only pieces of you. Can you strip to your underwear?"

"What if I'm commando?" Munro greeted her with a hug, then kissed me. "You're my everything too," he whispered.

"If you're going to be naked, then make sure your bits behave," Lizbeth said.

"I'm only kidding," Munro said with a throaty chuckle, then turned to me. "Only you get to see my junk."

"Damn right." I grabbed his hand and dragged him to the bed.

For another hour, we messed around on the bed with Lizbeth shouting out instructions from up a ladder or kneeling on the mattress.

"Okay, gentlemen. That's it." She grinned wildly. "I think I've got some amazing shots."

I collapsed back onto the crisp, white pillows, tugging Munro with me. "Hmm," I purred and snuggled into his neck. I like you here." I clamped my legs around his, holding him down.

"Let go of me." He wriggled around. "If I get a boner in front of Lizzie, I'll make you pay for it."

"Yeah? And how are you going to manage that?" I squeezed him tighter and sucked on his neck.

"Kickboxing class. I'll have you on the mat in three seconds flat." Laughing, he struggled to get free.

I pulled him close again, and with my hands cupping his face, I kissed him. "Thank you for being here today."

"You don't have to thank me. But we can't lie here all day. I do need to get back to work."

I frowned. He'd been rushed off his feet lately, often being the first in and the last out. "Is everything okay?"

"Yeah, but there's a problem at one of the other gyms. I may need to go over there for a few days." Munro sounded concerned.

"Which one?"

"Leeds. I'm trying to sort it without having to be there in person."

We both got dressed and walked over to Lizbeth. She was loading the images onto her computer, and by the look on her face, she was pleased with them.

"Will you let me know when the show opens? I'd like to see what you've done," I asked.

"Beck, baby." She smiled as if I'd said something funny. "You'll be getting an invite to the opening night."

"You don't need to do that." Why on earth would she do that? When would I ever go to a swanky art gallery? I doubted they'd even let me in. It was kind of her to say it, though.

She and Munro seemed to have some sort of silent conversation, where Munro ended up smiling but shaking his head. "Come on, let's get out of here."

When we were out on the street, I stopped him. "What was all that about?"

"You're the main focus of the show, babe. Or rather, your tattoos are. Lizzie wants you to be there. You're her muse if you like." I didn't like the smirk on his face. It came across as condescending, as if he was patronising me.

I stood stock-still and glared at him. "I hardly think I warrant that. We've only just met. Anyway, I thought the whole point of the show was the tattoos, not the owner."

"It is, but you have the most amazing artwork, Beck. People will want to meet you." He looked like he was a heartbeat away from rolling his eyes.

Damn, I should've thought more about this. Of course, I'd considered it was going to be a big thing. Lizbeth was a world-renowned photographer, and it was bound to be a high-profile show. But how did I feel about it now? I wouldn't be going. I wasn't a circus sideshow.

"We'll make a night of it. Get all your friends to come along." Munro said as if that made it better.

"I don't want them gawping at my arse," I snapped back. Not a great excuse, but it would do for now.

"It's a bit too late now, Beck. You read through the contract. We both did. Martin approved it before you signed it." Now Munro sounded annoyed with me, and that pissed me off even more.

"I'm not bothered about that or her showing off my body. I just don't want to be at the show. I'm allowed to decline, aren't I? Or did I miss that in the contract? Maybe I'm too stupid to know how this all works."

Munro stared at me as if I'd just grown another head. But I didn't want to talk about it anymore. I wanted to go home and forget about it. "You'd better go, Munro. You've got work to do." I stalked away to where I'd parked my car, leaving him behind.

As I drove away, I slapped my hand on the steering wheel. God, I'd been an arsehole, but why didn't he understand? He was used to being seen, approached, talked to and about. I was itching to call him, but my car wasn't fancy enough to have Bluetooth to connect my phone. I was going to have to wait until I was home to call. And then grovel.

But even when I was back in my flat, the annoyance festered inside me. I had a whole imaginary argument running through my head, and I hated it.

"Fuck it." I grabbed my keys and coat and went to the bar. A few beers would do me some good and, hopefully, blot out the argument.

"Hi, Beck. I didn't think you were working today." Haydn bounced happily up to me.

"I'm not. I'm here for plenty of mind-numbing alcohol." My desire for beer had faded as I looked along the vast liquor shelves. We had just about every spirit known to man. My eyes locked on the tequila. Damn it. It was too early for that. Beer first, then. I'd get to the shots later.

Haydn gave me a strange look but pulled me a beer. "I thought you had your photo shoot today. Didn't it happen?"

I took a long swig of beer, drinking over a third of it. "It happened."

I could see Haydn wanting to ask more, but he left me to serve another customer. I went to sit in a corner, not in the mood to speak to anyone. Oblivion, here I come.

Chapter 29

Munro

I stared after Beck as he stalked down the road, his back straight and shoulders rigid. What the hell had just happened? There was nothing wrong with spending an entire afternoon in bed with the man you loved. Beck had seemed to be completely relaxed, with Lizbeth taking shots of both of us. So what had just gone wrong? Before I could run after him, my phone rang.

"Hello."

"Munro, it's Ollie. We've found more discrepancies. I really could do with your help here." Ollie was the manager of the Well Fit branch in Leeds and had discovered that one of the trainers had been taking money, large amounts of it.

"Okay." I checked my watch. It was already half past four. "It's too late to drive up today, but I can come tomorrow morning."

"That's great. I won't touch anything else until I see you. I'm so sorry this has happened. That I didn't catch it earlier."

"It's not your fault. I'll see you in the morning." After ending the call, I walked back to my car. The urge to drive straight to Beck's was huge, but I needed to speak to Erin to clear my diary. Other trainers had to cover my classes. I called Beck, but he didn't pick up. Damn, he was so bloody stubborn. But that was also something I loved about him.

I walked back into my office.

"Erin, I've got to go to Leeds tomorrow. Can you rearrange all my appointments and calls for two days? I hope I won't be away for any longer than that. And can you ask Tom and Vicki to come and see me as soon as they're free?"

"Of course. Is there anything else you need from me?" She was already making notes of who to contact.

"Yes, I'd like employment records for Andi Partridge, please." I needed to check out all her previous employers. Ollie had interviewed her, and I didn't have any issues with the way he'd made his decision, but now I was keen to know the reasons for leaving her previous jobs.

When I got behind my desk, I called Beck again. Still no answer. What was he up to? Where was he?

The next chance to call Beck was at nine thirty, and there was still no answer. Fear ran through me. Had he been in an accident? Who could I call? Bruno! He'd be able to reach Leo.

"Hi, Bruno, can you do me a favour?" I asked when he picked up on the second ring.

"Sure." I loved how he agreed before he even knew what I wanted.

"I can't get hold of Beck. We had an, um, strange afternoon. I've called him several times, but he isn't answering. Could you ask Leo if he's heard from him?"

"Leo's at work. Give me a few minutes, and I'll find out. I'll call you back."

I waited, nerves and guilt skittering inside me. Why hadn't I tried to track him down earlier? I hated that my work had come first. And whatever was going on with Beck had to go on hold while I was in Leeds.

My phone rang, and I snatched it up. "Hi."

"Your man is in the bar, and Leo said it's getting messy. He's just started on the tequila. He was about to call you to come and collect your man, but Beck said he didn't want you to."

"Shit." What was going on in his head? Why had he gone from happy, fun Beck to get drunk Beck? "I'd better go. Thanks, Bruno."

"You want me to come with you? I was picking up Leo anyway. I can wait for him."

"Yes, thanks. See you there." I grabbed the files I needed to take with me tomorrow and left.

Bruno was waiting for me outside and gave me a smile and a fist bump. I was grateful for his support. I could be dumped and boyfriend-less in the next few minutes. My stomach was in knots, scared of what could happen.

When we walked in, the bar was busy. Happy hour had finished, but people were still drinking. Leo gave us a smile and gestured with a tilt of his head to the corner.

Bruno went to the bar to greet his man as I weaved through the people to where Beck was downing a shot. Beck wasn't alone. A pretty young man was sitting much too close for my liking. I glared at the guy, and he quickly scuttled away.

"Hey, I've been trying to get hold of you. I was worried." I sat down on the opposite side of the table.

"Well, now you've found me. What do you want?" He was drunk, like really drunk, but his voice still carried a punch that hurt.

"I thought we could go home and get something to eat. I have to go away tomorrow morning, and I wanted to spend this evening with you."

He glowered at me, ready for a fight. Then he shook his head, tipped the shot of tequila into his mouth, and stood. "Okay. I need to go and settle my tab."

I wanted to offer to do it for him but held my tongue. I had a feeling this whole cock-up was to do with me.

He was much steadier than I'd expected him to be, and as much as I wanted to touch him, I left him alone. Leo gave me an apologetic smile as if he was to blame for the amount of alcohol

Beck had consumed. Once Beck had paid, I guided him out of the bar with a hand on the small of his back. He didn't acknowledge it, but he didn't push me away either.

"I'm parked over there." I pointed across the street.

The journey back to my place was a silent one. Beck leant his head on the headrest and closed his eyes. I hated every metre we drove, hated the wall between us, and I didn't know how to knock it down. Should I apologise? But what for? It was Beck who had done all the talking before he stormed away, who'd ignored my calls.

Finally, I pulled up to my garage, waited for the door to open, and drove in. As soon as I stopped, Beck was out of the car and through the door into the house. I followed him quietly.

"I need a shower," Beck announced and went upstairs.

I looked through the takeaway menus. What would he fancy? Better to leave it to Beck. I dropped them on the countertop and climbed the stairs, following the sound of the shower. Beck stood with his shoulders against the wall, his head up, and his legs spread as the water hit his chest. I knew I wasn't invited to join him, so I leant back against the sink unit, watching him as he seemed to struggle to pull himself together.

After what felt like an age, he turned his head. He looked so sad, lost even. "I'm sorry," he whispered and closed his eyes for a couple of seconds. Then he stood upright and slathered shower gel over himself. I simply waited for him to finish, and when he shut off the water, I grabbed a towel. When he reached for it, I shook my head and swept the towel over his chest.

Beck stood still as I slowly dried him, wiping the soft cloth over his torso, down his arms, taking my time. His back rippled as I touched him, and he clenched his bum as I slid over his cheeks. I knelt down and stroked the fabric up and down his legs. He sighed as I stood again, leant into him, and pressed a kiss on his shoulder.

Then I moved my mouth over his shoulder blades to his nape and planted a firm kiss on his warm skin.

"Why are you doing this?" Beck's voice was hoarse, thick with emotion.

"Because I love you. You don't have to talk now. Just come to bed." I kissed him behind his ear.

"Okay, I am sorry, though. I was a dick. You did nothing wrong."

"It doesn't matter." I pressed my mouth on his.

With our lips locked, we stumbled back into the bedroom until his legs bumped against the bed. He tumbled down, and I followed. "Let me love you."

As we lay back, our breaths laboured and our hearts beating frantically, Beck looked at me, his eyes still dark, his lids heavy. "I keep waiting for you to realise that I'm not worth it and leave me. And don't give me that don't-be-dumb look. I was overwhelmed all of a sudden. The idea that people out there would want to talk to me fucking terrified me. You make it look and sound so easy, but for me, it's a really big deal."

How could he still think I would leave him, that what we had wasn't forever? "You don't have to do anything you don't want to, Beck. No one's going to put a gun to your head and make you do something you're not comfortable with. That includes me."

"I'm such a dickhead," he muttered and moved in closer. "I've ruined our day, and you're going away tomorrow. How long will you be gone?"

"I'm hoping to be back tomorrow night, but it depends on how quickly I can deal with it. I need to get the police involved. With any luck, it'll go smoothly, and I can come back home."

"The police? What's happened?"

"Theft. One of the trainers has been copying card details of our members and taking money out of their accounts. It started as only a couple of quid here and there, but she got greedy and took larger amounts. When the customers found out, the banks traced it back to our machines."

"Fuck. Does the trainer know she's been discovered?"

"No, she's got a full morning of classes, so I have to be there before she does. And then I'll call the police."

"Do you want me to come? I can ask for time off work."

"I'd love you to, but I don't know how long it'll all take." I kissed him. "Why don't we go away for a weekend? You can pick where."

"I'd like that." Beck's stomach let out a loud grumble, and we both laughed.

"Food. Come on. I'll even let you choose."

BECK

When Munro came home from Leeds on Friday evening, he was a mixture of exhausted and a ball of fizzing anger. I did the best thing I could think of and bundled him upstairs, stripped him down, and took him to the shower. He could tell me about what had happened tomorrow if he felt like it.

As the water pelted down on us, I grabbed the shampoo and squeezed some into my hand. "Lean back, babe."

The groan he released as I massaged the gel into his hair hit my dick, making it pulse and lengthen. Now wasn't the time for that. I willed it down and carried on washing Munro's hair. "Tip your head back." I rinsed the bubbles until the water ran clean through his dark brown locks.

"That felt so good," he said as I ran a sponge over his body. The scent of his shower gel permeated the steam-filled room.

"That was the goal." I kissed him and knelt to wash his legs.

"While you're down there…" He waggled his eyebrows.

"This is supposed to be soothing," I chided him and tortured him by soaping his inner thighs and over his arse. I'd get there, but I wanted his mind on us when I did, not on the stress of the week. It wasn't easy to ignore the large dick sticking straight towards my mouth.

"There's nothing more soothing than a blow job, Beck." His eyes were dark now, full of lust and need.

With a grin, I dropped the sponge. "It would be a shame to waste this." I took his stiff dick in my hand and gripped it tightly.

Munro jerked his hips forward, punching through the tunnel my fingers made. "Stop that and behave. Just feel, Ro."

Then I took him into my mouth. As I swirled my tongue around his glans, I stroked him with slow, short strokes. The taste of precum burst onto my tongue as I sucked only the head, flicking my tongue over the slit. Munro's back hit the tiled wall, and he parted his legs.

"That's so good, but I need more. Stop torturing me, baby." Munro ran his fingers through my hair. A tingle shot down my spine to my neglected dick.

With my tongue flat on the pulsing vein running up the underside of his cock, I took him deep into my throat. I clutched the firm globes of his arse as I let him have what he needed from me. It didn't take long for him to move in a steady rhythm and come down my throat. Letting out a deep-rooted guttural groan, he emptied his load. He shuddered and released the grip on my hair, then slumped down with me on the shower floor.

I wrapped my arms around him, holding him to me until it felt like we might drown. "Come on, we need to get out of here." I shifted and stood, turned off all the jets and stretched out my hand for him to grab. It was my turn to dry him off, wiping the towel over the droplets on his shoulders and chest.

"I can do it. Dry yourself too." Munro took the towel from me and dried himself. I rubbed the towel over my hair and body, then slung it around my waist.

"You hungry?" I asked as we pulled on sweats and a T-shirt. It had become our usual home attire. Sometimes we matched in Well Fit gear, but I tried to not let us be *that* couple, the one that constantly coordinated their clothes in case we were photographed and thrown on social media.

He patted his stomach. "Actually, I am. I don't think I've eaten all day. What shall we have?"

Half an hour later, we were stretched out with our feet on the coffee table and tucked into pizza laden with melted cheese and meat.

"Did you sort it all?" I asked.

"Yes. She admitted it, and the police took over. She'd taken thousands of pounds over a six-month period. Apparently, she'd run up masses of credit card debt and was using the money she took to pay them off. It will go to court, but my part has been done."

"Christ, the lengths some people will go to."

"Let's not talk about that anymore. How was work?"

"Interesting. We think that Jonas and Haydn may be more than boss and employee. Haydn spends a lot of time in Jonas's office and comes out with flushed cheeks and a happy smile that lasts all night." I wanted this to be real. Jonas needed someone to dote on, to look after and protect. I couldn't be that person, but Haydn has vulnerability written all over him.

"I thought so too. I've seen the way Jonas watches him. He only has eyes for him."

"I hope so. They both deserve to be happy," I mused.

"How long were you with Jonas?" Munro asked casually, but I still choked on a piece of pepperoni. I'd never told him about my relationship with Jonas. "Oh, come on, Beck. Do you think I haven't noticed how comfortable you are around each other?"

After a sip of beer, I cleared my throat. "About eight months. It was a while ago. We kept it quiet from the others. Max probably knew but never said anything. Does it bother you?"

"No, of course not. I know you weren't exactly a monk, babe." He paused. "Why didn't it work? You don't have to tell me. It's none of my business."

"It's fine. We had a great time together, and neither of us regrets it. But it wasn't ever going to be more. We wanted different things. I wanted what we've got—an equal partnership. He wanted someone to look after. We're better as friends."

Munro let out a huge yawn and sagged back into the comfy sofa. "I'm beat."

"Why don't you go up? I'll clear all this away and lock up. You still need to be at work tomorrow."

"Yeah, I will. Thanks, Beck." He got up and stretched his arms above his head, straightening his spine, then let his arms flop back down. "Will you be up soon?"

I nodded. When I joined him half an hour later, he was already deeply asleep, his breathing slow and even.

I was halfway through my shift when my phone buzzed from the counter next to the till. I peeked at the screen. An unknown number and I ignored it. I didn't need to speak to cold callers trying to sell me a new phone or a PPI claim. My phone rang again a couple more times, and every time I ignored it. Everyone I wanted or needed to talk to was in my contacts list.

Sawyer had noticed it too. "Who's trying so hard to speak to you?"

"I have no idea. It can't be anything important." I shrugged and served another customer.

Ten minutes before the end of my shift, a person walked in I never wanted to see again: Lucie. A very pregnant Lucie.

The look on her face was one of pure satisfaction. "Hello, Beck. I thought I might find you here. I was hoping your boyfriend would be here too. What a shame. It would've been easier, more satisfying to share the news with both of you."

What did she want me to say? Was she expecting me to believe that this was Munro's baby? No way it could be his. I trusted him completely, whereas I knew this woman was bat-crap crazy and would go to any extreme to get him.

"Go away. You're not welcome in here." It was Max's voice. Behind him stood every one of my brothers. She really was a conniving bitch. She chose to come here at the change of shifts to get the most attention.

"It's a bar, isn't it? A public place?" She narrowed her eyes, and her tone became sharp and loud.

"Not for you. Get out before I ask security to escort you." Max was next to me now.

"You can't throw me out. I'm pregnant, in case you hadn't noticed." She caressed the bump lovingly.

"I didn't say *throw*. I said *escort*. And here's Steve now." He nodded at our bouncer. "Please make sure that the lady leaves the premises safely." I chuckled inside at the derision he infused in the word 'lady'.

"You'll find out all about me and your 'gay' lover tomorrow." The bitch actually put air quotes around *gay*. "Maybe you should tell him to call me before he's ruined."

Steve stepped in front of her. "This way, please, madam."

As soon as she was out the door, I turned to my friends, my brothers. They looked either shocked or furious. Which probably the same expression I was wearing. I grabbed my phone from the counter and called Munro.

"Hey, babe, I was just on my way to you." He sounded happy.

"Don't. Don't come here. Go straight home and don't answer your phone unless it's me. Do not open the door to anyone. I'm on my way."

"Beck? What are you talking about? Why?" Now he was confused.

"Please, Ro. Just do as I ask. I'll be there as quickly as I can."

"Okay, but you're acting really weird, you know that, right?"

I wanted to laugh, but there was absolutely nothing funny about this. "I love you. See you soon."

"I'll drive you." Max had his car keys in his hand. "We can go out the back."

We were soon on our way to Munro's place, and Max let out a sigh. "You don't believe her, do you, Beck? That woman is causing trouble. She wants her ten minutes of fame. That's all it is."

"I know that. Munro never slept with her. He's totally one hundred per cent gay. He's told me all about her, and so have Will and Ed. She's jealous, and it's sad, really, because whoever did get her pregnant has a right to be that child's father."

"Just checking."

Max pulled into Munro's driveway and switched off the engine. "We have your back, yours and Munro's. Don't forget that."

"I won't. And thank you." I got out of the car, jogged up the steps, and used my key to let myself inside.

Munro was pacing the floor, looking more worried than I'd ever seen him.

I hated that bloody woman.

Chapter 31

Munro

I was pacing the living room floor when the front door opened, then closed. "Beck?" I called out stupidly. Who else would it be? I rushed out. He was leaning back against the door with his eyes closed. Shit! What had happened? His family? One of the guys at work?

"What's wrong? What's going on?" I cupped his face, and he opened his eyes.

"Lucie came into the bar, and she's pregnant. Very pregnant. I think she's going to announce that it's yours." He spoke in a whisper. His green eyes had turned almost grey, like a storm, dark and turbulent.

Out of all the scenarios I'd imagined, that wasn't one I could ever have guessed. "What?" He nodded but didn't speak. "It's not true, Beck."

"I know." He leant in and pressed his mouth to mine. As I parted my lips, he slipped the tip of his tongue inside. The kiss became possessive as he dominated my mouth, licking, stroking, and sucking until we pulled apart breathlessly. He rested his forehead on mine. "Something's happening tomorrow. I don't know what, but you need to call your lawyer."

"You talk to him, tell him everything she said. We need Will and Ed here too. They will be able to corroborate my statement. That fucking bitch!"

I called Martin, hating to bother him at home, but this was important. While Beck spoke to him, I called my best friends. Both said they'd come straight away. Then Bruno called—Leo had filled him in—and he was on his way too.

After Beck had told him everything, I spoke to Martin. "How bad is it?"

"Honestly, Munro. Not as bad as you think. We need to have a statement ready as soon as she goes public. We can demand a DNA test, which can be done while she's pregnant, but we can also wait until the baby is born. Her allegation isn't true, so she'll need to prove it. I can get a private investigator to check her out, find out who she's been with. In the meantime, go back to, say, five or six months ago that she could try and say she was with you, and prove her wrong. Think of all the times you saw her with other men within that time frame."

"What about my sponsors?" My stomach roiled, and my lungs didn't seem to get enough air. She could get her own way and ruin me.

"I'll be contacting them. I'll be in touch."

I ended the call. Beck was on his phone, but his eyes were on me. "I just thought I'd let you know....Yes, we think that too.... No, he's okay, or he will be.... Okay, yes, I'll talk to you again tomorrow."

"Who were you talking to?"

"Your mum. I thought she should hear it from us. Otherwise, she'd be on your doorstep first thing tomorrow."

"This is why I love you. You're so put-together, thinking of that. I don't know what the hell to do." The doorbell rang.

Will was the first to arrive, spitting fire. He stormed into the house. "What's the battle plan? Because I've got an idea." He gave me, then Beck a hug.

Over the next ten minutes, more people arrived. Ed and Bruno. Then Max and Gus showed up and brought pizza, and lastly

Sawyer and Devon came. All these amazing people had dropped everything to help or to just be supportive. I could have cried. Less than a year ago, I'd thought I was happy with my life. I had a fantastic career, great friends, parents who loved me, and money in the bank. Then I'd taken one look at a gorgeous, blond-haired, tattooed dream, and I'd known I couldn't keep lying to myself anymore.

Beck made his way to me and copied my stance, leaning back against the countertop. "What are you thinking?"

"My life, you. All these people." How could I explain to him how much my life had changed because of him? "You did this."

Beck stiffened, his eyes sharp. "You think this is my fault?" He sounded brittle, ready to snap.

"What? God, Beck, no. I meant that all these amazing people are here because of you. Well, not Ed and Will. But even they've changed because I fell in love with you. I mean, look at them. Gus is a bloody genius. Bruno is a fucking supermodel. Max owns one, if not *the*, most successful bar in the city. Devon is a giant of a man who seems to be able to calmly dissect any situation. And I wouldn't have known them without you. You've made my life so much richer, and I don't know how to thank you."

"Don't be daft." He nudged me with his elbow. "For a start, you knew Bruno, and the others are just good people. They're your friends, Ro. Maybe it is my fault Lucie is doing this because I took you away from her."

"We were never in a relationship, Beck. You know that. You didn't take me away from her. She could have been a friend and been a part of this group if she'd accepted us. I would never have expected her to do something like this. She's lost the plot, for sure."

"Hey, Munro. Look at this." Ed motioned me over, his phone in his hand.

"What?" I looked at the screen.

"That's Lucie, in the club all over that guy." The picture showed her grinding up to a tall, dark-haired guy.

"That was taken about the time you met Beck. Check the date." Ed grinned. "He could be the father. She left the club with him."

He was right. It was the night I'd waited for Beck and gone home with him. "That was my first night with Beck. I won't ever forget that date." I tapped my finger on my mouth. "She called me in the morning. Beck, you remember that, don't you?"

"Yeah, she cock-blocked us." Everyone groaned and grumbled about too much information.

"Anyway, whatever we were about to get up to didn't happen, and I left. She was here, in the dress she had on the night before and was sobbing that he'd used her for the night. She went off on one because of the hickeys I had on my neck. Thanks to you."

"You're very welcome." Beck sniggered as he waggled his eyebrows.

Ed rolled his eyes. "Can I get back to the point? That could've been the night she got pregnant. The date fits."

Beck reached out his hand. "Can I have a look? I might recognise the guy."

He took Ed's phone and stared at the picture. "I think I've seen him before." He held up the phone to Sawyer and Gus. "Do you know him?"

Sawyer didn't, but Gus nodded. "Yeah, I know him. He's called Adam Fletcher. He works at the uni, something to do with sports. I don't know exactly what he teaches. Sports has never really been my thing. But he seems to be a nice guy."

"It doesn't really matter who the father is. She's going to pin this on me." God, I could strangle her. "Fuck!"

"Hey, Martin said he'd deal with her. Let him do his job." Beck rubbed his hand over my back. The small circles usually soothed me, but I was so wound up now they didn't help.

"I should call her. Ask her to come talk it through."

A chorus of noes erupted, but there was one yes. I could have guessed from whom. Beck.

"What difference will it make? She's not going to back away from the attention this will cause," Will said. "She wants money, Munro. She's expecting you to get in touch. This is blackmail. Not a vendetta."

Chapter 32

BECK

Damn right, I said yes. I wanted him to call her, wanted her to face him in front of us and tell the truth. I wanted her gone from our lives.

All eyes were on me, but I only cared about Munro. "Why?" he asked quietly, almost as if he was disappointed in me.

I took his hands in mine. "Because if one conversation stops her from spreading lies, a potential court case, and a slur on you, then we should take it. She wants the attention, her five minutes with you. Give it to her. We're not going anywhere, so ask her to come over. You've got nothing to lose." I pulled him to me and kissed his knuckles. "I want us, babe. I want to live our lives without her in it."

He shook his head. "Will's right. She wants money. Talking to her is giving in to her."

"I'm not saying to give her what she wants, but you could let her know she could do damage herself more than you if she announces something that's untrue. She has plenty of followers on Insta and TikTok, right? Well, she could lose all of them if they find out she's lying. Especially if you end up having to take legal action against her."

He was giving it some serious thought.

"Okay, I'll do it. But I want to call Martin again first." He pulled his phone out of his pocket, opened the screen, and wandered away. I joined the others.

"I'm not sure about this, Beck," Bruno said, a furrow deep on his forehead. "This could be a huge problem for him."

"Then isn't it better to try and nip it in the bud? Why should he wait until tomorrow, when she blabbers all over social media? He has a right to find out why she's doing this, and yeah, it could go wrong. She could still talk drivel, but at least he'd have tried. But ultimately this is Ro's decision. I'll stand by him whatever he chooses."

"That's what Martin said too." Munro was walking back to us.

"He did?"

"He told me it wasn't the best idea, but it was up to me." He hooked his index fingers into my belt loops and pulled me closer. A collective groan from the others rose as he pressed his mouth to mine.

Exclamations of 'Do you have to?' and 'Not again' came from the kitchen. Munro's lips quirked into a smile against mine. I flipped my middle finger at them while I kissed him.

"What are you going to do?" I asked.

"I'm going to call her."

We all waited with bated breath as Munro called her number. It was on speakerphone, but we'd promised to stay quiet.

"Well, well, well. Your *boyfriend* passed on my message. What took you so long?" Her words dripped with sarcasm.

"What do you want, Lucie? Because we both know that the baby you're carrying isn't mine," Munro snapped.

"That's not the issue here. I want to see you."

Munro looked at me. I shrugged. "It's up to you," I mouthed.

He scanned around the kitchen. Our friends gave him a nod or a thumbs up. Even Will, who had his arms crossed over his chest, his posture rigid as he scowled at the device on the counter, bobbed his head.

"Then you'd better come over," Munro said.

The line went dead.

"I guess we'll wait now." Munro grabbed my hand.

A knock on the door sounded at the same time as Bruno's phone chimed. "It's Leo."

A sigh of relief went around the room. Bruno went to the door to let him in and filled Leo in as they walked back to us.

"Is there a reason everyone is standing in the kitchen?"

"Beer and pizza." Sawyer held up a bottle.

"Cool. Where's mine?" He took Bruno's and had a long swig, then handed it back. As he looked around the kitchen, he chuckled. "Well, this is fun."

We all burst into laughter.

Bang bang bang.

"Showtime," Ed said as Munro walked over to check the screen.

"Ro, keep this on your terms," I said. "We can get her out of here at any time."

His lips were now a thin line. I hated how stressed he was over something he had nothing to do with. He nodded rather than spoke, then opened the door.

Lucie stood on the doorstep, her fist raised, ready to bang on the door again. "You took your time." She strode in like she owned the place.

Her step faltered, and she whipped her head around to Munro. "What are they doing here?"

"They're my friends. Do you remember what that means, Lucie? It means people who stick by you when life gets hard." His voice was cold and hard as he glared at her.

"Whatever." She swished her hair over her shoulder. "Tell them to leave. This is private."

"No, anything you have to say, you can say in front of them." Munro held out his hand, and I moved to be by his side. He smiled, gave my hand a squeeze, then let go.

"God, would you just look at yourself?" She rolled her eyes dramatically. "You're not gay, Munro. I would've known."

The laughter from our friends had her glowering at them. "Why don't you just fuck off. You don't know him as well as you think you do."

"Enough, Lucie. Now please say what you want to say and then leave. We're not friends anymore."

"I want you to admit that this is your baby. To own up and be financially responsible for it. This 'I'm gay' game with him has gone on too long." She gave me a look of such hatred I wanted to push her back out the front door and slam it in her face. I smirked, which she obviously didn't like, as she glared again. "You can fuck off too. You're nothing but a money-grabbing freak."

"Says the person demanding money," Beck said drily.

"You're crazy, you know that, right? We have never had sex, Lucie." Munro glanced from me to her. "I love Beck, and if you hadn't reacted so badly, so jealously, and supported me, you could've been here with all of us. I'll never admit to being the father to your child, so if that's all you wanted, you'd better leave."

"You're a fucking liar, Munro. We were both drunk that night, but you wanted it as much as I did. You were begging me for it. And tomorrow, every one of your fucking followers will know you're a liar and a cheater."

"When? When was this supposed to have happened, Lucie? Because you look about six months pregnant, and I've been with Beck for months." Munro's eyes were blazing now. His voice got louder as he paced.

"Who do you think everyone is going to believe? The guy who lied about himself or his pregnant girlfriend? You'll be ruined."

Will strode up to her. "You're off your head, lady. And I use that word loosely. Everything you thought you and Munro had going on was in your imagination. You were always all over him, but he never gave you any more attention than he did us. He was only ever your friend. And now you're alone, desperate, and needing money."

Her sneer turned her pretty face into an ugly, spiteful contortion. "You're just fucking jealous because he was with me, not you."

"I've never been with you!" Munro boomed at her.

I laid my hand on his back, trying to calm him. It seemed to work as his shoulders, taut with anger, relaxed. He drew in a long breath.

"Lucie, I'm sorry, but I was never more than your friend. Whatever you think happened didn't. We were never together. I don't know why you're doing this, but there's a man out there who *is* the father. Maybe you should be reaching out to him. If you go ahead and spread these lies, I'll have to fight you in court. And I doubt that will be good for you or the baby."

Something flickered in her eyes for a second. Regret? Fear? I wasn't sure, but it was gone as quickly as it had appeared. "You're a fool, Munro. You won't come out of this unscathed. Everything you've worked for will be gone."

Chapter 33

Munro

Why was she really doing this? "Lucie, come with me." I needed to get to the bottom of this.

"Where?"

"My office." I motioned for her to go first, smiling at Beck, who was looking at me like I was mad. "I won't be long."

"Munro." Bruno shook his head. "Not a good idea, mate."

He was right. I needed a witness. "Beck, come with me?" I asked. He wouldn't say no.

I walked in behind her but left the door open. "Why don't you sit down, Lucie? It's late. You must be tired."

She dropped down on the sofa.

"What's really going on, Luce?" I perched on my desk and crossed my feet. Sympathy would go over better than the angry approach.

"I don't know what you mean. All I want is for you to say it's your child." She scowled, but some of the vitriol had dissipated.

"But it's not, and we both know that. Have you spoken to the guy who is? I'm guessing it was the one from the club who wanted nothing more after you'd gone home with him. You came here, remember? It was Sunday morning, and you called me. That was the night I was with Beck, our first night together." I glanced at Beck, who was leaning against the door frame. The soft look on his face told me he was thinking about it too.

Lucie sagged back into the sofa. Tears shimmered in her eyes, and her chin wobbled. I'd been right, and we both knew it. "Oh, Lucie." I crouched down in front of her and took one of her hands in mine.

Her whole demeanour changed as a tear slipped free and slid down her cheek. "I don't know what to do, Munro. He's denying it, refusing to have anything to do with me. And I haven't got a job or any money coming in. I'm scared, Munro."

"And you thought this was the best way to get money? What the fuck," Beck said from the doorway.

Lucie glared at him but stayed silent.

"Why this way? Why didn't you just call me?" I asked her.

Lucie snorted. "We were hardly on speaking terms."

"And whose fault is that? Lucie, your reaction to Beck and to me coming out was unbelievable. I'd never have taken you for a homophobe. So why did you act like that?" I stood. Anger surged through me again.

"You know why, Munro." She peered up at me. "I was in love with you, and you never looked at me the way you looked at him. I hated it, hated that I'd got you wrong, and you'd never want me. I was jealous."

"I never led you on, Lucie. I was so unsure of myself, afraid of what would happen if the news I was gay came out before I was ready. And you forced my hand with that too. Your threat to Beck was so bloody wrong. No one should be forced to expose themselves. You nearly broke us up, and I knew even then that I was falling in love with Beck." I'd walked away from him that night. We'd been apart for a week, and all because of her. I'd hurt so much without anyone to help me. None of this should have happened. "You want to know what really stung?" I didn't wait for an answer. "Your reaction."

"I know," she whispered. "I wish I could turn back the clock because I would do everything so differently. I would never have said the things I did. And seeing you in the bar the night you came out upset me so much. I knew I could've been there with you, just as I know I could've been part of your new life if I hadn't been so blinkered. Beck was always an opponent to me, a threat to what I wanted. I'd seen the way you watched him, and I resented him."

"We're going around in circles, Lucie. But before we try to work out what you can do, I need you to know one thing. My life is with Beck, and I won't stand for you insulting him or us."

"I know it is." She still wouldn't look at Beck.

"Does this mean you're stopping all this crap about me?" She wouldn't continue telling this enormous lie, would she?

"Yes," she said quietly.

"Okay, thank you." I expected her to get up and leave us, but she stayed on the sofa. "What do you want now, Lucie?" I sighed.

"Maybe I could do classes at the gym. You know, for other pregnant women? Yoga, perhaps, or aquafit?"

That was actually a good idea, something I hadn't thought about. Plenty of pregnant women would come to the gym. I'd have to do some research, maybe reach out to the local prenatal groups. "I'll look into it. But this doesn't excuse what you've done. You've explained why, but it really isn't that simple. You hurt me, and you hurt the man I love. Saying sorry is easy. I'm not sure I'm ready for you to be my friend again. I'll need time and space."

Lucie gave me a small smile, but her eyes were still cold.

Bruno appeared in the doorway. "We're all going to head out."

"Sorry. I'm coming." I pressed a kiss on Beck's lips. "I love you," I whispered.

"Love you too."

I left Lucie to get herself together. The kitchen was empty, but voices drifted in from the living room. When I walked in, all heads turned in my direction.

"What's going on?" Ed asked.

"She's not going to say anything. It seems that the father doesn't want anything to do with her. She has said sorry, but it's not that easy, is it?"

"Do you believe her?"

"I believe she won't do it. But it's going to be difficult to trust her. I want to thank you all for being here tonight. I never thought I'd have such amazing friends. I don't know how I'll ever be able to pay you back."

Bruno's mouth curved into a huge grin. "Don't be a dick. It's what we do."

With that, they all stood, gathered the empty beer bottles, and brought them to the kitchen.

Beck joined me at the front door. He wrapped his arm around my waist and shoved his hand into my back pocket. After a flourish of hugs and goodbyes, they all left. I shut the door and leant back on it, closing my eyes. A wave of exhaustion rolled over me.

Beck rested his hands on my hips. "You need to sleep, babe."

"We need to get Lucie home. I don't think she drove here, so we need to call her a cab. Then we can go to bed, and I can lose myself in you."

"I don't want her here, Munro. You need to call a cab."

"It's okay. I've called an Uber." Lucie's voice came from the office.

We went to her. "Will you be okay?" Beck asked.

"You don't have to be nice to me, Beck. I don't deserve it. And yeah, I'll be fine." Sadness had replaced the bitterness from earlier. And while I appreciated the change, it didn't make up for the pain she'd caused us.

Outside, a horn beeped. Lucie gave me a tired smile. "I'll see you around, Munro."

"Yeah, okay."
She left without so much as a glance.
"Please look after yourself, Lucie, and the baby."

BECK

The next couple of weeks went by quietly. Everything had returned to normal. Munro hadn't heard anything from Lucie, but he was looking into the prenatal exercise classes. Whether Lucie would be able to run them posed an issue, something to do with how pregnant she was and insurance, as well as Munro still not trusting her. I didn't get involved.

The door of the bar opened, and in walked Lizbeth. As usual, she was dressed like a Nirvana groupie biker chick. The edgy look she carried off so well softened when she smiled at me.

"Who. Is. That?" Haydn asked as she made her way to us.

"That's Lizbeth. She's awesome."

"I might have to turn straight," he whispered.

"Watch it, boy," Jonas growled at Haydn. It was no longer a secret that they were into each other. Not that they'd announced anything, but it was obvious.

"Hey, Beck, I wanted to hand this to you personally." She passed me an envelope made of thick, expensive paper. "Your official invitation."

I'd got over my strop about not being good enough to be at the opening. Munro had persuaded me that I was worth meeting. "Thank you. I don't have to show up in a monkey suit, do I?"

She laughed her rich, almost dirty-sounding laugh. "No, wear whatever you feel most comfortable in. Can you give me the names of who you're inviting so that they can be added to the list?"

I wanted all the guys to come, but I didn't know how they'd manage it. It wasn't like they could close the bar. And I wanted Munro's parents to be there. That was it. "Sure, there aren't many. These clowns and Munro's parents, and maybe Craig, the guy who'd made my skin so beautiful."

She frowned. "Not your family?"

"They are my family." I crossed my arms around my stomach.

"That sounds great, Beck. I'll see you a week on Thursday." With a wink and a wave, she was gone.

I turned the envelope over in my hand. Should I open it now or leave it until I was with Munro?

"Open it, Beck." Haydn nudged me. He was so eager about everything.

"I know what it is."

"But you don't know what it looks like. I bet it has your name on it."

"You're such a dork." I grinned at him, slipped my thumb under the seal, and pulled out a gorgeous, embossed card: *Art in Motion* by Lizbeth Houghton. Holy smokes. In the top right corner was a small glossy square photograph of the lotus on my neck. *Introducing Beck.*

The card also mentioned the date and the venue, but I could only focus on my name. No surname, just Beck, as if I were someone famous. The colours were so vivid, so stunning and striking, it looked like the flower was real. I couldn't wait to show the others.

"Wow! That's so cool. I told you it would have your name on it."

It did, but why only my name? Lizbeth had said she was going to be using other people's tattoos as well.

"Are you going to be able to come?" I asked Jonas.

"I wouldn't miss it for the world." His smile was so warm, and the look of pride in his eyes surprised me. He hugged me. "You deserve to be happy and successful. I'm so glad you found your person," he whispered.

"And maybe you've found yours," I said softly. He deserved to be happy as much as I did. Jonas was always the quiet one in the background. Max was much more outgoing and, well, loud. People tended to forget Jonas was the older brother and the one behind the scenes keeping everything running.

"Maybe. I hope so." He let go of me and turned to Haydn. "You'll get your turn." With a wink, he walked into the staff corridor.

Haydn followed him with his eyes, and when the door closed behind Jonas, he sighed. "He's so gorgeous."

"Yes, he is. Be good to him, Haydn." I patted his shoulder, then glanced back at the invitation. I grabbed my phone and sent a photo of it to Munro and his parents.

Emma messaged me back instantly, with a line of fanfare trumpets and congratulations.

My phone beeped with another message.

Munro: I'm so fucking proud of you. And tonight, I'll show you.
Me: I can't wait. Love you x
Munro: Love you too.

I got back to work, trying not to watch the clock or the door.

Finally, Munro strode in, his smile lighting up his face when he saw me. I bent over the bar, and his lips met mine. It was way too brief for my liking, but I still had thirty minutes to go before my shift finished.

"Let me see it." He held out his hand. I picked up the envelope and gave it to him. "Ooh, very fancy."

"I told your mum. She was very excited. Some of the guys will be coming too. I don't know why it only says my name, though."

He shrugged. "I don't know. Maybe because you're new and the others are already known. We'll have to wait and see."

I checked myself out in the full-length mirror in Munro's bedroom. Lizbeth had said to dress in whatever I wanted, but this was a swanky art gallery. I would look like shit in my faded black skinny jeans compared to everyone else. So I bought a pair of charcoal-grey trousers. They were skinny too, but I didn't feel like myself in them. Even with my old Stone Roses T-shirt, I still feel weird, overdressed. Or maybe my nerves were getting to me.

"Damn, your ass looks good, hot as fuck." Munro stepped up behind me, put his chin on my shoulder, and kissed my neck.

I scowled at our reflection. "I look like a dork." I fiddled with the waistband. Should I take them off and put my jeans on?

"Oh no, you don't. You look like a cool hipster. I can imagine peeling them slowly off your hips and sucking your cock." He bit my ear lobe, tugging it between his teeth.

I shivered. "There's nothing stopping you." My dick was already getting hard.

"Only time. We have to go, babe. The cab will be here in a minute."

"Does my hair look all right? Oh hell, this isn't going to work. No one will like me. They'll laugh at me for having covered myself in ink. I can't go. This isn't a good idea." I shook my hands as if I could get rid of the nerves through my fingertips.

Munro clamped his mouth shut, but his eyes sparkled. The bloody man was trying not to laugh. "It's not funny. Ro, I'm freaking out here."

"You look perfect, and they will love you. Everyone will find you as interesting and cool as I do. And if you're still worried, my mum will be there to hug the shit out of you."

Okay, that was funny, and strangely, I did feel better. I grabbed the jacket that went with the trousers and stalked out of the room. "We have to go now before I change my mind."

Munro let out a bark of laughter, and when he caught up with me, he slapped my arse. "Ow!" I glowered at him. "That hurt."

He stopped me and cupped my face, his expression serious. "Tonight is going to be awesome because *you're* awesome. I love you so much, Beck, and this will be the start of something huge. If you want it."

What did he mean by that? Did he know something I didn't? Before I could ask, a car horn honked.

Munro held my hand tightly the whole ride while the driver chatted away. When he needed a cab now, Munro always called the man with the gay son, and they talked about him and how much he loved the gym.

He pulled up outside the gallery. "Have a fabulous night, guys."

Munro opened the door and pulled me out.

The huge glass windows were lit up, displaying two enormous photos of me, of my tattoos. Stunned, I stared at them.

Munro grabbed my other hand. "Take a deep breath, babe."

I closed my eyes, pulled in a long breath, held it for a couple of seconds, then let it out. When I opened my eyes again, Munro was studying me. The intensity of his gaze took my breath away.

"You've got this, Beck. Let's go celebrate the beauty of you and your ink."

Chapter 35

Munro

To say I was surprised when Lizbeth called me was a huge understatement.

"Christ, Lizzie, I'm not sure it's a good idea. He's not keen on secrets."

"Think of it as more of a surprise. Munro. These images are breathtaking. The interest I've had in them, in him, is incredible. Please, Munro, let me do it this way."

"Fine. But if he hates you, don't blame me."

Her answer was a throaty chuckle. "He's going to love me."

The images of Beck and both of us were going to be the entire show. Her idea for the show had changed direction when she saw just how much potential Beck had. But she had wanted it to be a surprise. She knew he'd freak out and want to cancel it.

"Time to be the star of the show." I squeezed his hand, then let go and walked him to the door. "I want to kiss you so hard right now."

Beck swallowed hard, and a small smile lifted the corners of his lips. "Later, babe."

He grabbed the handle, pushed the door open, and walked in.

And stopped in his tracks. Every one of his friends from the bar—his family—were here.

"Beck!" Leo was the first to spot him.

A rosy glow of embarrassment spread over Beck's cheeks, but he smiled. "I can't believe you're all here. How? What about the bar?" He hugged Leo.

"We decided this was more important, Beck," Max said and clapped him on the back.

Jonas was grinning from ear to ear. Their relationship might have ended, but he held genuine affection for Beck, as Beck did for him. It would never be more than that. "I wouldn't have missed this for the world."

He embraced all his friends, then took a glass of champagne from a passing waiter. This gave us the chance to walk around the room. The pictures were spectacular. The ink seemed to have come alive, the colours were so bright. I found some of my favourites, the ones I'd run over with my fingertips and my tongue as I took my time worshipping him. I dragged him over to the photos of the two of us. "Wow! Babe, we're hot." I grinned at him, but he wasn't looking at the pictures or me. He darted his eyes over all of them. Shit.

"What's going on?" he asked and cast his gaze around the room. "Where's Lizbeth?"

She must have either heard him or been looking for him because she walked over to us at that moment. "What do you think, Beck?" Lizbeth greeted him with her arms wide as she gestured around the room.

"I think you're crazy. Why are there only pictures of me? That's not what you told me. You said some pictures of me and some of other people, a mix of diverse images, to open up inclusivity." He ran his hands through his hair. Some of the pictures were bordering on explicit, showing hints of his groin, his arse. "You should have told me, Lizbeth. It's a lot to take in. I feel exposed."

She hesitated. "Why do you think? You're incredible, Beck. I'm sorry I didn't tell you, but I'm not sorry for only using you.

Representatives of model agencies are here and eager to talk to you. They can change your life. People are buying these images."

Beck looked at me. "Did you know about all this?"

I slid my hand around his hip and gave him a squeeze. "I didn't know about the model scouts or people buying the pictures. But I knew the show would be only of you. I did warn Lizbeth it wasn't a good idea."

Beck walked back to the images of himself, clenching his fists as if he were stopping himself from touching them.

A hand landed on my shoulder. "Is Beck okay?" my dad asked. "He doesn't look too happy. The photographs are beautiful. Lizbeth has done a wonderful job."

I filled my parents in on what had happened.

"Oh, the poor boy. It must have been a shock, but he should be proud of the gorgeous pictures," my mum said.

Beck spun around as if her voice had somehow pulled him from his thoughts.

"Beck, sweetheart." My mum took hold of his hand. "Those tattoos are beautiful. They are you, and you wear them with such pride. So be proud of them now that they are on the walls. Look around. So many people want to see your art. Don't be cross with Lizbeth or Munro. They love you."

He looked at my mum for a long time. I knew he'd come to love her and respect her. Then he nodded and returned my mum's hug.

"I really want to be pissed off with you, Lizbeth. These photographs are great, but the ones of Munro and me aren't for sale."

"They've already sold." I cupped his face in my hands. "I bought them. No one is seeing us wrapped in each other's arms."

Resigned, Beck turned back to the photographer. "So, Lizbeth, what percentage do I get from the sales?"

"Forty. Now come and meet some people who are desperate to get to know you better."

I went over to the guys from the bar, who were joking and laughing. They were always such a happy bunch, and I loved that they'd accepted me so easily. "He's being chatted up by model agencies."

Bruno nodded. "I know a couple. In fact, one of them used to represent me. If Beck's interested, he'd do well to sign with him."

"Go talk to them. Let them know he's got you in his corner. They may think twice about selling him cheap."

I smiled as Bruno walked up to them and seamlessly joined in the conversation. "Do you think he'll go for it?" Sawyer asked.

"Probably not, but he may like being asked."

"Beck didn't look too happy earlier," Max said.

"No, he wasn't. I'll have a lot of grovelling to do later." I already had the perfect way in mind.

"Have you heard anything more from Lucie?" Gus asked. "I saw the guy from the picture on campus the other day. I couldn't help wondering if it's his baby or that he doesn't care."

"I haven't. I don't want to appear callous, but I don't need her in my life. She wasn't there for me when I could have used her support. The fact that she was willing to cause me so much trouble and damage what I'd spent years building really hurt me. If she'd approached me at any time and apologised, I would've forgiven her. What's that expression? 'You've made your bed. Now lie in it.'"

I rubbed my neck. "I've researched her suggestion of exercises for pregnant women, and it's a great idea. But I can't set up classes in time to have her as an instructor. She'd be too close to having the baby. I'm not dismissing it, and if it happens, I may contact her."

Beck put a hand on my arm. "Ro, your parents are getting ready to leave."

"Hey, what did you think?"

"It's been a wonderful evening, such a success for you, Beck, and for Lizbeth," my mum said.

"Thank you so much for coming," Beck said to them both. "And for your kind words, Emma. I needed to hear that."

"Anytime, Beck. You're family, and we love you." She pulled him in a hug, flushed cheeks and all.

I said goodbye too and agreed to Sunday lunch this weekend.

"Have you finished schmoozing?" I asked Beck as we walked back into the room.

"Yep, they were interested and had lots of propositions for me. Bruno was cool, asking them questions I would never have thought of."

"Are you considering it?"

Beck shrugged. "I'm not sure yet. I'd like to earn a bit more money, but I don't want to leave the bar. I love my job there. But maybe a couple of jobs wouldn't hurt."

"Good for you, baby." I dropped a quick kiss on his mouth. "Let's have a wander around. Then we can go home and celebrate."

It took another half an hour to get around the room as everyone wanted to congratulate Beck. Finally, we said goodbye to our friends and got out.

We drove home in silence, Beck resting his head on my shoulder as he played with my fingers. He had plenty to think about, but not tonight. He could revisit it all again in the morning.

When we got indoors, he headed straight for the stairs. I locked up and followed him. He was splayed out on the bed. All he'd managed to do was kick off his shoes.

"Whatcha doing?" I tickled under his sole. "Not taking your clothes off?"

He raised his head, a wicked glint in his eyes. "Too tired. You'll have to do it."

"What a hardship, stripping my gorgeous boyfriend out of his clothes. Can I play as I do it?"

"You can do whatever you want." He dropped his head back down. A sweet, lazy smile spread over his lips.

So I did. I slowly removed his shirt, kissing over every inch of exposed skin as I hitched up his shirt. As I grazed my teeth over his nipple, Beck pushed his chest up into my mouth. I tugged his T-shirt over his head and threw it over my shoulder. Then it was time to rid him of the sexy-as-hell trousers.

"Your arse looked so fucking hot in these, babe." I looked up at him from between his legs.

"It'll look even better out of them. Get a move on. I want your cock in it. Pronto."

I grinned. Hell, yeah. I yanked the trousers and his briefs down his legs, then sent them in the same direction as his T-shirt. "Stroke yourself," I ordered as I stripped off my clothes.

He spread his bent legs wide, his feet flat on the bed, his tight hole on display. God, I loved being inside him, the clench of his muscles as I thrust in and out of his body. "Stop staring and get back here."

I snapped out of my daze and grabbed the lube. "You need to stop looking so fucking sexy." I crawled back up between his legs and leant in to get a taste of his cock. The head was already shiny with precum, which I licked away. My blow jobs skills had improved since my first fumbled attempt. I could even play with the beads that ran up the underside of his dick as I sucked him. Beck had always been more than willing to let me practice on him.

It didn't take long before he thrust up into my mouth as I sucked him. "Stop," he groaned. "I'm going to come, and I want you inside me."

I slowly slid my mouth up his thick length, teasing him. I also took my time stretching him.

"I don't need much prep, Ro. I just want you," he snapped.

"Shush." I added a third finger and worked him open slowly. "Fucker."

I chuckled and pulled my fingers free. "So demanding."

I squirted more lube into my hand and slicked up my aching and impatient dick. Beck grabbed his knees and pulled his legs up to his chest, giving me full access. As I lined my dick up, I bent over him and whispered, "I'm so proud of you. You were amazing tonight, and I'm sorry I let Lizzie talk me into keeping it a secret."

"Less talking, more fucking. I want it hard." He wrapped his legs around my thighs and dug his heels in.

In one smooth movement, I pushed inside him, pulled out, and slammed back in. I smiled as he growled and grumbled. Over and over, I drove into him, sweat dripping down my face onto Beck's chest. But it wasn't enough. I wanted to be deeper.

I pulled out of him and flipped him onto his stomach. "Get on your hands and knees." He instantly obeyed and was up with his knees spread wide and his gorgeous arse in the air. I slapped my hand down on it, which left a red imprint blossoming on his skin, and pushed back inside him.

This was the way I wanted him. I grabbed his hips and rutted hard. "Grab your cock, babe." Beck dropped his chest to the mattress and curled his hand around his dick. "Fuck your fist. I'm getting close."

Beck was making the most guttural sounds as I pounded him, hitting his prostate every time. "Gonna come, Ro. Fuck, yeah."

As his cum burst free, splattering the bed, the muscles in his arse clamped down. They squeezed me so hard I seemed to explode inside him, filling him, flooding his channel. My cry ricocheted around the room as I collapsed onto his back.

Beck's knees gave way, and he flopped down onto the sticky mess. My dick was still throbbing inside him. I waited until it softened, then withdrew. I rolled off his back and lay looking up at the ceiling, panting.

I turned my head. Beck did the same. He was beautiful, with his eyes glassy and his cheeks flushed. I grinned. "Was that hard enough for you?"

His smile was dopey. "Best fuck ever."

Chapter 36

BECK

I woke up with Munro plastered against me. Puffs of his breath warmed my neck, and his morning wood nudged against the crack of my arse. My sore arse. No way was he going there for a couple of days.

Last night had been surreal. I'd been so pissed off that Lizbeth hadn't told me, but I couldn't deny that the photographs were fantastic. But the people from the model agencies had been too enthusiastic for my liking, gushing adjectives like a bloody waterfall. I hadn't believed half the words that had come out of their mouths. Thankfully, Bruno had known what to say, what to ask them, but it didn't sound like my kind of thing. Putting on those bloody trousers last night had been bad enough.

But I'd told them I'd consider it because flatly refusing would have been stupid. How much different could it be from the the photo shoot with Munro?

Munro stirred behind me, shifting away from my body but staying asleep. He was going to be late for work if he didn't wake up soon. I rolled over and trailed my hand down his smooth, firm chest to the thin dark line of hair beneath his belly button. He swatted my hand away.

"Time to wake up, babe," I murmured in his ear as I travelled lower and circled the head of his semi-hard cock with one finger.

"Hmm, that's nice." He squirmed. "Keep doing that."

"Only if you wake up." I wrapped my fingers around his length and stroked him firmly. "Open your eyes, Ro."

As his eyelids fluttered, I pressed a kiss on the corner of his mouth. "Good morning, my love."

Munro thrust his hips up, his cock slowly fucking my fist. Precum wetted my thumb, and I spread it over the head.

"Nice?" I rubbed his slit again. I loved these early-morning sleepy moments. Then why wouldn't I agree to move in? I was here so much. Why should I still be paying for my flat?

Munro canted his hips again. "So good." I let go. I had something better in mind, so I moved over him and kissed my way down his body until I reached his dick.

"Watch me." I waited for Munro to prop himself up and meet my eyes. One slow lick up from the base had his eyes rolling back. I took him into my mouth and sucked, hollowing my cheeks until he bumped the back of my throat. As I pulled back, a burst of precum soaked my tongue. This would be over way too soon unless I tortured him. Unfortunately, we didn't have time for any edging this morning, so I deep throated him again.

"Christ, Beck, that's it. Fuck yes."

I wrapped my hand around his length and jacked him as I sucked, working him faster and faster until he arched his back and cried out my name. His load flooded my mouth, and I swallowed and swallowed. I licked gently, cleaning him up. He twitched and laughed, complaining about sensitivity.

Munro hauled me up by my armpits and smashed his mouth to mine, then delved his tongue inside and licked any remnants he could find. "Now that's a way to wake up." He smiled and kissed me again. "Y'know, we could do this every day if you lived here."

"Okay." How long would it take his orgasm-fogged brain to realise what I've said?

"Think how much money you'd have if you sold your flat. The property market is booming. It's a perfect time for you—"

I placed two fingers over his lips. "Munro, I said okay. I'll move in."

His eyes went wide, as did his smile spreading over his face. "Really?"

"You're right. It's stupid to keep my flat, and I love being here with you. So as long as we split all the bills, then yes, I'll move in with you."

"Okay, we can do that. This is brilliant. When do you want to start moving your stuff over here?" His whole body buzzed with excitement.

"The weekend, although I don't have much left in my flat. Most of my clothes are here already. I'll have to decide what to do with all the furniture, though."

"Maybe you could rent the flat out rather than sell it?" He jumped out of bed. "Let's shower."

I followed him into the bathroom, pressed my chest to his back as he turned on the water, and slipped my fingers around his waist. "My arse is going to be out of action after you pounded it last night," I growled in his ear, loving the shudder that ran through him. "Maybe it's your turn."

"Anytime, baby."

I walked into the bar, ready for a late Saturday night shift. Munro had a meeting tonight, something to do with sponsors, so he wouldn't be coming in later.

"Hey, look at you all smiley and shit." Sawyer laughed. "What's brought that smile out?"

"I'm going to move in with Munro."

"That's great, congratulations. I thought you were going to tell me you were going to take the modelling world by storm."

"Oh, that. Bruno has a friend, Gideon, who apparently was more successful than him. Hard to believe, right? Anyway, we're going down to London to meet him. He spent a year travelling the world with his husband but is now running his own agency."

"The show last night was incredible. I guess all the hours and hours you getting inked have paid off."

"We'll see."

We hadn't any more time to talk. The bar was packed wall to wall. And even though we were rushed off our feet, it made the time go quickly, and it was two o'clock before I could blink.

When I got home, Munro was fast asleep. I tiptoed through his room—or our room now, I supposed, or did I have to have all my belongings here before it was official?—to the bathroom and softly shut the door behind me. I considered skipping the shower, but I hated having alcohol fumes surrounding me, so I made it a quick one.

I slipped under the duvet and lay down, knowing it wouldn't be long until Munro turned in his sleep and snuggled into me. And like a magnet, he moved to my side, threw his leg over my own, and rested his head on my chest. He let out the cutest *hmm* but didn't wake. His journey had been so different from mine. What would've happened if my parents had accepted me? Maybe I would've made it to university. Would I now be a teacher like them? Maybe. Or perhaps I'd have stayed with one of the guys I went out with at eighteen. God, that idea horrified me. To not have Sawyer and Leo in my life was a sad and scary thought. I didn't regret anything I'd done. Even the crappy exes and bad decisions had taught me something. And everything had brought me here, to now. To Munro.

And through him, I gained new parents who loved me more than my own. Whatever was going to happen with Bruno's friend, I'd be happy. I *was* happy.

I took a sip of coffee as Munro explained why he thought it was important for him to come with me.

With a sigh, I put down the cup. "It's not practical. Both you and Bruno have ridiculous two-seater cars. How will you fit in? I don't fancy having you sit on my lap for the journey."

His scowl made me chuckle. "You're so adorable when you're cross."

"I'm not cross." The crinkle between his eyes as his eyebrows knitted together proved the contrary. "I just want to be with you. This is exciting, important to you."

"I'm not even sure it's for me. I like being in the background. I don't want to be noticed, especially not after what happened to Leo and Bruno."

"Okay, I'll stay here when you go with Bruno, but I want to hear everything when you get back."

"Of course." I hesitated for a moment. "Would you be disappointed if I decided not to do it?"

Munro was already shaking his head. "No, babe, of course not. This is your life, your decision."

Could I tell him the main reason I was even considering this? He'd never mentioned money and how we would decide on who paid what. I had to be honest with him. If I turned this opportunity down, I would only have my salary from the bar. And that was nothing compared to what he earned.

"Come on, Beck, talk to me. We don't have secrets, do we?"

"I'm worried I won't have enough money to pay my way when I move in with you. This is a big house, and the utility bills must be crazy high."

Munro looked at me as if he'd never even thought of it. "Why would you need to do that? I pay those bills monthly by direct debit. I thought we'd just split the groceries and things like that. You moving in won't make a noticeable difference to the gas and electric bills."

"That's not happening, Ro. We'll be splitting all the bills fifty-fifty. That's not negotiable." I stood and walked to the sink to wash out my coffee cup.

Munro pressed his front to my back and placed a kiss on my nape. "I'm not going to argue with you, Beck. I just want you with me. I don't care if you work at the bar for the rest of your life. If it makes you happy, keep doing it. Maybe taking Bruno up on his offer will give you more money, but I don't want that to be the only reason you're thinking about it."

I swivelled around to him. He gazed at me with nothing but genuine concern. "Thank you."

"You don't need to thank me for telling the truth."

Chapter 37

Munro

I'd been staring at my computer screen all morning and not really getting anywhere. My mind was on Beck and how he was getting on. If only I'd gone with him. I would've liked to have met Gideon; I'd followed him and his husband through their year of travelling. They'd had some amazing experiences as they moved around the world.

My phone vibrated across my desk, and 'Bad at Love' filled the silence. Lucie. Groaning, I picked up the phone. "Lucie, this is a surprise."

"Oh, Munro, I need your help."

Oh, crap. I didn't need this. "What do you need?"

"Can you help me get some shopping done? I'm so big now. Everything is a struggle. I don't have anyone else to ask." The whine she always used when she wanted something was back.

"When?" I looked at the time in the corner of the computer screen. Beck should be finished by now, and I wanted to speak to him.

"Could you come now? It won't take too long. I need to pick up a few things from the baby shop. You'd be doing me a huge favour."

"Okay, but I'm waiting to hear from Beck, so I can't be long." Why was I even agreeing to this?

When she let out a heavy sigh, I almost changed my mind. "Okay, fine. Can you pick me up? It's hard to get in and out of my Mini."

I doubted she'd find my car any easier, but if it would get this over with, then fine. "I'll be with you in twenty minutes."

I closed my laptop and grabbed my keys, all the while grumbling about annoying ex-friends and why I was a sucker for not being able to say no. Beck wouldn't mind me helping her. Hell, he'd probably come with me.

The drive over to her place was a short one, and she was waiting outside her door. She had got huge. It had been a few weeks since we'd had our confrontation, but I hadn't expected her she had grown so large.

I pulled onto her drive and stopped. She met me at the front of the car, and for a split second, I thought she was going to kiss me. The moment passed. Thank god. "It's not going to be easy to get you in, Lucie. And we're going to need a shoehorn to lever you out."

"Gee, thanks for making me feel good." But she smiled. Honestly, she did look good in a pair of black jeans and a grey cashmere jumper that clung to her bump.

We laughed as I helped her into her seat. Then I got back in as well. "Where to first?"

"There's a baby shop in the little mall I like to go to. I've got to order the heavy stuff to be delivered, and they have the cutest clothes."

Please kill me now. Too bad no one was listening. As we walked through the intimate, upmarket mall, she looped her arm through mine, telling me her balance wasn't as good as it used to be. She talked as if we hadn't had months of silence and an acrimonious last meeting. She told me she was having a little girl but hadn't decided on a name yet. That she had started a vlog about her life and pregnancy and already had a huge following. But nothing about contacting the father again.

"This is it," Lucie said when we stopped in front of a double-fronted but small boutique. It looked expensive. How could she afford to buy here?

She pushed open the door. "I have an appointment with one of the nursery advisers."

"So you don't need me here? I can grab a coffee while you sort it out." I wanted out of here fast. This place was giving me hives.

"Don't be silly. I want your opinion." She gripped my arm again.

I stood back when she strutted up to the counter and gave her name. The assistant glanced at me and smiled. What had Lucie just said to her? I had a bad feeling about this. Lucie was acting weird, like she once again decided I was the father. She motioned for me to join her.

The assistant introduced herself as Sophie and shook my hand. "We're going to have fun. Come this way."

I took hold of Lucie's elbow, stopping her from following. "What the hell is going on, Lucie? This isn't what you asked me to do. Help with your shopping, you said. I expected us to go to Sainsbury's."

"This is shopping, Munro. And I do need your help." Her smile was as false as her eyelashes, and I wanted to turn around and leave. "It won't take long, I promise."

"I'm not helping you choose bloody prams and cots, Lucie. This has nothing to do with me." We were both whispering but apparently loud enough that Sophie looked back at us.

"Please, Munro." Her eyes brimmed with tears.

Again, I gave in and nodded, and the tears disappeared. Shit. Crocodile tears designed to make me feel guilty, and what was worse was that it worked. "Fine, come on."

For the next thirty minutes, the two of them talked about cribs, cots that turned into beds, and nursing chairs—whatever they were.

I pulled out my phone. A little flutter zapped through me. Beck had sent me a message. I swiped my thumb over the screen, then froze. What the hell? Did I just get called baby daddy?

Sophie smiled at me. "What do you think, Papa?"

Papa? God, that was worse than baby daddy. "Oh, I'm not the—"

"I think the cream and pink," Lucie blurted out, her cheeks red. Was she embarrassed or angry?

"I'm only here to carry the bags. This is all Lucie's decision."

Eventually, the shopping nightmare ended, and Lucie seemed happy. I just wanted to get the hell out of here, determined never to step inside again. Would Beck want children? We'd never talked about it. I'd like to have them, or maybe just one, if this is what was needed.

I waited by the door while Lucie picked up a whole wardrobe worth of clothes and put them on the counter. It looked like my torture was about to be over. Sophie wrapped the clothes in tissue and placed them in expensive glossy bags. Jesus, could this day get any worse?

Of course, it could because this was Lucie. Again, she summoned me back to the counter.

Both Lucie and the assistant looked embarrassed. "What's wrong? Please don't tell me you've changed your mind."

"There's a problem with my card. It won't go through," Lucie fake whispered. My blood ran cold. That was why she asked me to go shopping. That bloody woman.

"Maybe you should choose which items you need the most. Then you can pick up the other stuff another time." How could I have fallen for this? Why had she done this to me?

"I need them all, Munro." Her voice was clipped, defiant. Was she really going to push me on this? I was as angry with myself as I was with her.

I looked at the pile of bags and did the most stupid thing ever. "How much is it?"

Lucie had gone silent now. Sophie gave me the figure. My mouth fell open. "Three and a half thousand pounds? How the hell can a baby need that much? Where was the pram made, Aston Martin?"

Both of the women didn't say anything, but the pressure radiating from them was suffocating.

I tugged Lucie away from the counter. "Is this why I'm here, Lucie? You knew this all along? I thought you'd stopped playing this stupid game. Why the hell are we in the most expensive shop in town? You don't need everything to be so exclusive."

Lucie narrowed her eyes to slits. The spiteful expression was back on her face. "If I still had my job, I could've afforded all of it."

"You quit, Lucie. You couldn't accept who I was, and you walked out, leaving me with a mountain of classes I had to cover." I clutched her shoulders, forcing her to look at me. "If I do this for you, Lucie, this is it. I don't want anything more to do with you. Don't call me or come to me again. And for the love of god, tell the bloody father that he needs to pay maintenance to you."

I stalked over to the counter and pulled out my wallet.

BECK

Today had gone so much better than I'd expected, which wasn't difficult when I'd had no idea what would happen. Bruno's friend, Gideon, was a great guy and had said he could absolutely find me some work. Another man called Jasper had been there. He was a photographer and Gideon's best friend. He'd taken loads of shots to put a portfolio together for me. After that, we'd gone out for a late lunch. Now we were on our way back.

"Have you heard back from Munro?" Bruno asked as he easily negotiated his way through the London traffic.

"Not yet. I'll shoot off another message that we're on our way home."

When I opened up my screen, a ton of messages popped up. And Twitter and Instagram notifications. "Something's going on. I've got a load of messages from the others. Has Leo messaged you?"

I opened the first one. It was Leo freaking out about Munro and some photos on Twitter. I clicked on the picture he'd attached, and my heart stopped. Lucie had her arm through my man's arm as they looked at a baby boutique.

"Munro's been with Lucie," I told Bruno, hardly recognising my hollow voice.

"No way." Bruno shook his head.

"There are photos of them on Twitter." I scrolled through the pictures Leo had sent me. The last one was of Munro carrying several bags and Lucie walking next to him. He didn't look happy. In fact, he looked furious. Something wasn't right.

Well, look here. Gay fitness influencer Munro Sylvester with his very pregnant friend, Lucie Enderby, shopping for baby clothes. Is he the baby's daddy?

I brought up his number and pressed Call. "It's not what it seems," Munro said before I could speak.

"Then what is it? Because it's all over social media, Munro. What the fuck were you doing?" I could strangle that woman.

"I know it's everywhere, and I'm just as pissed off as you. Lucie played me, and like the bloody idiot I am, I fell for it." He sounded so heartbroken, but I believed him. I needed to be there with him. "I'm sorry, Beck."

"We're on our way home. We're just out of London now. Have you spoken to Martin?"

"Yeah, he's putting together a statement and has some shit for Lucie to sign. I wish you were here, babe. It's everywhere."

"We won't be long. Bruno's put his foot down. We've got a lot to talk through, Munro."

"You believe me, though, don't you? You know there's nothing between us. Please, Beck."

Yes, I believed—I knew—he wasn't the father, but I didn't understand why he would put himself in that situation. That was why I was annoyed with him. Okay, Lucie forced him back into the spotlight, but why didn't he walk away? And now we had to sort it all out before I could share my news. Lucie had managed to push me into the background.

"Beck?" Munro said my name again.

"I know you're not the father, Munro, but this hurt. Have you spoken to your parents?"

"Not yet. I'm hoping it'll be over with before they find out." How could he be so flippant? Of course they would find out. Emma had never liked or trusted Lucie. She would be livid.

"Call them, Munro. Before your mum turns up on your doorstep." I looked out the window to check where we were. Bruno was indeed driving fast, and we should be home in less than an hour. "I'll be home soon. We can talk then."

I dropped my phone onto my lap. "What the fuck was he thinking?"

Bruno's fingers tensed around the steering wheel. "Munro is a nice guy, Beck. He's one of those people who helps others. I doubt he thought it would cause this problem. And Lucie is very manipulative towards him. She knows how to work him."

Yeah, all that was true. Munro had proved his kindness over and over. He'd given the cab driver's kid a lifetime membership. But that didn't explain why after everything Lucie had done, he'd go shopping with her.

"He's also one of the most honest people I know. He would've told you about this, even if it hadn't hit social media. He loves you so completely, Beck, and he would never do anything to hurt your feelings."

"He sure managed it. I'm so bloody angry with him. Anything I do now will be overshadowed by this. I'll be the guy Munro cheated on. He'll be the one who got his 'ex' pregnant. And Lucie will get all the pity."

"It may not be as bad as that. You know Leo and I went through a ton of shit, and it went away. Without being flippant, I'm sure this won't be news tomorrow."

As much as I wanted to believe Bruno, it wasn't that simple. It hurt that Munro had so easily gone with her, that he hadn't even messaged me, telling me his plans. Would he have told me if his pictures hadn't been splashed across social media? Was this the first time, or had he done this with her while I'd been working? I didn't know the answers.

My stomach churned and clenched, and I couldn't stop myself from searching the internet for any mentions of him and Lucie. The same photographs Leo had sent me were all over social media. Whoever had taken them was happy to spread them everywhere.

At last, Bruno pulled into Munro's driveway. The door seemed to fly inward, and Munro stepped out. He must've been waiting for me. Our eyes locked, his full of pain and confusion. Dammit, I had caused that. I'd left him unsure of my feelings. Because I was. I didn't know what to think.

Whatever we talked about and decided would totally kick my meeting this morning into touch. It could even affect whether I was ready to move in with him. For fuck's sake, I wanted to be here with him. I also wanted to trust him not to rush off to Lucie whenever she clicked her fingers.

Bruno left the car idling, the high-performance engine purring gently.

"Go talk to him, Beck. Don't let that damn woman ruin what you have together. I'll call you tomorrow, but don't hesitate to get in touch if you need to. I'll try to keep Leo away this evening." He gave me a dry smile. "You did amazingly today. Don't forget to tell him that."

"Yeah, that's going to be the top of the things we need to talk about." I rolled my eyes as the sarcasm dripped off my tongue.

"Maybe not. But don't let it be the bottom of it either."

I nodded, then reached for the door handle. "Thanks for everything, Bruno."

"Anytime, Beck."

I climbed out of the low car and closed the door, not moving until he'd driven away. I wasn't sure I wanted to move even then. Munro stepped down and waited again.

No time like the present to fuck up my life again. I walked towards him, but neither of us spoke, not even once we were inside and the door was closed and locked.

I headed straight for the kitchen and grabbed a beer from the fridge. Munro's lips on my nape startled me.

"I'm sorry, Beck. Please let me tell you everything," he whispered. Even quietly his voice was hoarse, pained.

I straightened and turned around, and he took a step back. "You're going to have to because I don't understand what the fuck you were thinking."

"Can we go and sit down?" God, he looked wrecked.

I followed him into the living room and took a seat at the opposite end of the sofa to him.

He talked for twenty minutes, telling me everything that had happened. He spoke with nothing but truth and transparency in his words. What she'd done had hurt him. Bruno had been right. Munro was generous to a fault. His kindness and honesty were some of his best traits. And she'd abused those. I could sit here, feel sorry for myself, and drag this out, or I could get over it, be the supportive boyfriend, and help him sort out the mess of his social media.

"So what do we do to stop the gossip?" I asked him. He blinked a couple of times. "What? You thought I was going to turn this into something horrible? To have an argument that could break us? Yeah, she'd love that. Don't look so surprised, Ro. I love you, and with that comes trust. You should've messaged me, but you know that. But please, please don't have anything to do with her again. She planned this, arranged to take so much money from you, from the moment she picked up her phone."

Chapter 39

Munro

I let out the breath I felt I'd been holding since I'd seen the post. The weight lifted off my shoulders when Beck gave me a small smile. It wasn't a full-blown happy smile, but I'd take that over an argument or a break-up.

"God, Beck, you're amazing. I love you so much. I should've said no to her in the store. It would've embarrassed her, and she would've hated me for it. But I was more concerned about what crap she could spread and bring up the whole baby daddy again."

Beck grinned. "Baby daddy? Really? I don't think that suits you."

"Fuck off." I threw a cushion at him. "I don't think our group needs another Daddy in it. Martin emailed her a notice to leave me alone. That if she approaches me or says shit about me, we will sue her. She has signed it already. I won't be seeing her again."

"Come here." Beck crooked his finger, and I clambered over the sofa to him.

I hovered over him, waiting for him to take the lead. I didn't have to wait long. He snaked his hands over my hips and pulled me down onto him. As soon as our lips touched, he slipped his tongue between them and stroked alongside my own. I groaned as I matched him stroke for stroke, sigh for sigh. I grappled at his clothes, eager for more, desperate to feel his skin.

Beck got the message and broke off the kiss. "Naked now."

Our clothes flew everywhere before we crashed back together. I lay under him, and he rolled his hips over mine so our cocks rubbed deliciously together. Beck's mouth found my throat. He licked and nipped over the taught skin, sucked on my Adam's apple. His lips were hot over my heated skin. I shuddered as he scraped his teeth over my jaw until he was by my ear.

"I love you so much, baby," he murmured, then bit down on the lobe.

"Then get that big, fat cock in my arse."

He chuckled. "Not yet. You need to be punished. To learn your lesson. I'm going to take my time."

Beck sat up, straddling my thighs, cock pointing straight up. It was a beautiful sight, the crown dark with engorged blood and slick with our combined precum. He was looking at me with the same adoration I stared at him. His thumbs were back in the crease of my thighs. A sensitive spot he'd found early in our relationship that always made me wild. He teased my high ball sac with his fingernails, and precum spurted from the slit and dripped down my length.

"You're so beautiful, so responsive. I could play with you all night." As he leant over me, he slid his hands up to my chest, to my nipples. He tweaked and tugged on them as he pressed a kiss to my lips. I writhed beneath him, bucking my hips up, begging for more. More of his touch, his taste, his...his everything. I wanted all of him.

He sat up again and shifted sideways so he could reach the wooden box we kept on the coffee table. We'd learnt early on we needed lube in every room in the house. With his fingers slick, he moved between my legs, stroked my cock with one hand, and stretched my hole with the other.

"Enough," I barked as he twisted three fingers inside me. "I'm ready."

With more lube applied to his dick and my legs up by my chest, he pressed inside me. Our mutual groans filled the room as he slid in and out of me.

The pace was slow, steady, his steel-like shaft slick inside me as he grazed over my prostate. Our gazes were fastened on each other. He was so fucking gorgeous with his lips slightly parted and his cheeks flushed. I locked my legs around his waist, and he changed the tempo. Faster, he plunged into me until sparks ignited in my spine and legs, racing towards my groin and firing into my balls.

"You close?" I said. "I can't hold on."

Beck nodded and grabbed my dick. His tight fist shuttling up and down my dick was enough. My orgasm fired my release over my stomach and chest. He swelled, his rhythm faltered, and he cried out. Heat filled my arse as he came hard. The tendons in his neck tight, he dropped his head back and pumped the last of his seed into me.

My legs flopped ungraciously from his waist, and Beck collapsed onto me, sandwiching the sticky mess I'd made between our bodies. Beck buried his head in my neck as he caught his breath. I wrapped my arms around him and held him against me.

It was far too soon for my liking when Beck pushed off me. "We should shower."

After untangling our limbs, Beck led me upstairs to the bathroom. As the hot water poured over us, we soaped each other and washed the remnants of our lovemaking away. Beck's soft hands slowly caressed my skin. I had never felt so cherished. He has proved over and over that he loved me and trusted me.

"Thank you," I whispered.

"What for?"

"For being here with me, for loving me. For trusting me when you could've walked away."

"No, I couldn't. Walk away, I mean. I love you too much. You're it for me, Ro. Whatever life throws at us, we'll face it together."

"God, you're amazing."

Beck gave me a wink and a slap that stung on my wet arse. "And don't you forget it."

I turned off the shower, grabbed two towels, and gave one to Beck. We dried off and got dressed again, then went back downstairs.

I opened the fridge. "What do you want to eat tonight?"

"I don't think there's much in there. Do you want to go out?"

I gestured at the old grey sweats and faded Well Fit T-shirt I'd put on after our shower. "Not really dressed for eating out."

"Pizza it is, then." Beck pulled his phone from his pocket and ordered our favourite pizzas. "Twenty minutes."

Beck gave me the rundown of his day, telling me all about Gideon and Jasper, how it sounded like their group of friends were just like ours.

"It was fun, but I'm not sure it's for me, especially after hearing the dramas and bitchiness that seems to go on. I'm happier here with you. We're just about to move in together, and I don't want to travel. I don't want to lose my job at the bar to try something I don't think is really me."

"I'd love that too. But don't dismiss Gideon's ideas just yet. They could be something new and positive in your life."

"How?" He took a bite of his pizza.

"Because you deserve to be known as your own person. I want you with me, but I want you to be so much more than 'Munro Sylvester's boyfriend'." If only he could see himself the way I and so many others saw him. Lizbeth had seen it as soon as she met him. As had the sponsors. They had wanted him then and had approached him since, but he'd brushed off their offers.

The furrow in his forehead deepened as his eyes became stormy. "Is that how you think people see me? How *you* see me? Because my friends don't think of you as 'Beck's boyfriend'." He air quoted the last words.

What? How could he think that? "No, of course I don't. But that could be how every photograph of us is captioned. And you're not just my boyfriend. You're my partner. We're equal in this."

"So why does it matter? I know I'm more than someone holding your hand, and so do you."

"Okay." I raised my hands in defeat. "Don't do anything, Beck. I'm not going to argue with you. It's your choice."

Beck dropped the rest of the pizza slice, picked up a paper napkin, and wiped his fingers. "I know it is, and I didn't flatly refuse to take it further. If I felt like that, then I wouldn't have wasted everyone's time. But if I do, it's not because I feel any need to validate who I am in some stranger's eyes. Munro, I'm thrilled that I'm your boyfriend. It's not a moniker I will ever hate." The anger from before has dissipated, and he gave me a shy smile. "I'm never going to be excited about being looked at. I'm not as confident as you, and I wouldn't be able to brush off the hurtful comments that are bound to come. Thanks to Lizbeth's show, my tattoos are everywhere, and I can't hide them anymore, but they are mine, my life, my journey. If someone hates me, even without knowing me, because of them, it'll hurt. I told Gideon the same thing, and he promised me that he would contact the right people. I'll decide what to do when—if—they reach out to me."

"Anyone who judges you because of your tattoos doesn't deserve to know you, babe. I do understand you, and I'm sorry if I made you feel pressured."

BECK

As I stepped into the breakroom at work, my phone rang, and I pulled it out of my back pocket, then paused. Gideon's name flashed on the screen. It had been three weeks since I went to meet him, and apart from a call the following day, I hadn't heard from him. That must mean he wasn't interested in me, and that was fine. I really wasn't bothered about taking it any further.

I swiped the screen to accept the call. "Hi,"

"Beck, hello. I'm sorry I've not been in touch. I've had a hectic time here. And that's because of you." He chuckled. What was so funny?

"Um, do I need to apologise?"

"Hell, no. You're in hot demand. I've had so many people calling about you. I wanted to determine which one was best for you. Are you still interested?"

The swirl of excitement in my gut surprised me. Maybe it would be good to try it. At least once. "What's it for?"

"A show for Kate Richards. They're desperate to have you at the show for the latest designs. First a runway show and then a shoot for Vogue. This is huge, Beck. She doesn't always pick the most well-known and professional models."

I dropped down on the sofa. Kate Richards was the designer of the moment. Everyone who was anyone from rappers to sports stars wanted to wear her clothes. "I don't know what to say," I croaked. Even I knew this was huge. "When is it?"

"Friday. And yes, they're aware it's short notice for you, but they really want you." Gideon sounded cool and calm, but a buzz seeped through in his voice.

"I'll see if I can get the day off work. Fridays are busy here." I was sure Max and Jonas would be fine with me swapping my shifts. "Could Munro come with me? Will you be there?"

Gideon chuckled again. "Beck, I don't think they'd care if you brought your whole family as long as you agree."

"When do you need to know my decision?" I wanted to talk to Munro. "I mean, can you give me time to call Munro."

"Of course. Give him a ring, and I'll be waiting for your answer."

We said goodbye, and I stared at the picture Lizbeth had taken of me and Munro in bed. It was one of my favourites and hung above our bed. After taking a deep breath, I called Munro.

"Hi, can you talk?"

"Hi, babe, of course. What's up? Is everything okay?" However much we'd pushed all thoughts of Lucie aside, he still expected her to try something else to upset him.

"Yeah, it's all good. Gideon just called. He's got a job for me and asked if I'm interested. It's on Friday. Could you come with me?"

"That's great. What's the job? And of course, I'll come."

I could tell he was smiling, and I had a feeling I was about to make his smile bigger. "It's, um, it's Kate Richards."

The phone went silent. I checked if we were still connected. "Munro, are you still here?"

"Fucking hell, Beck, you sure know how to go big. I hope you said yes." He let out a nervous laugh. "I shouldn't be surprised. You're exactly her type."

"I told him I needed to speak to you first. Was that stupid?"

"Tell him yes. And I'll come with you. Bloody hell, babe. Kate Richards. I can't believe it. I'll see you later."

"Okay. Ro, thank you."

I called back Gideon, who whooped with excitement. "You're going to be a star. I'll email you all the details. Don't hesitate to call me with any questions."

"What do you think?" Gideon asked in the busy room, people rushing around, shouting orders.

"It's incredible." Young men and women with lithe bodies stripped down to nothing but the smallest scraps of flesh-toned underwear. The clothes were bright, garish, risqué, and exquisite. I couldn't wait for my turn. Munro was talking to Jasper, but he kept stealing glances at me from time to time. Gideon had spent all morning teaching me how to walk and turn. I'd also had to learn how to have an expressionless face. Which was harder than I'd thought. I was used to smiling as I greeted people in the bar. Of course, Munro took it on himself to make me laugh, and I'd got it sorted now.

"Good, because it's your turn." Gideon handed me over to a team of dressers, makeup artists, and hairstylists.

The next ninety minutes went by in a daze. I was in and out of outfits too many to count. Camera flashes blinded me, but I made it. When it was over, everybody hugged me. Then Jasper whisked me away for the Vogue photo shoot. Which was equally as exhausting. Was it always like this?

I was bone-tired. All I wanted was a long, hot shower and a comfy bed.

Munro squeezed my hand. "I think they're done. Jasper is happy with the pictures, and so is the editorial team from the magazine."

"How do you know?"

"I heard him tell them."

I rested my head on his shoulder and closed my eyes. I'd never thought falling asleep standing was possible until now.

"Beck, we're done." Jasper's voice forced me to open my eyes. "You can go home," he said with a wry smile on his face.

"We're staying here tonight. Bruno gave us the keys to his place," Munro said.

"Great, maybe we can get together for brunch tomorrow. You can meet our husbands," Jasper said. "I'll call you in the morning."

He turned to me with a serious look on his face. I stood a bit straighter, bracing myself for the news the photographs weren't what they wanted. That *I* wasn't what they wanted.

"You've been amazing, Beck. A natural. All the shots are incredible, with hardly a bad one. Many people try so hard to do this, and you did it effortlessly. Well done. I hope I get to work with you again."

"It's been an eye-opening experience. I can't quite believe it yet. Thank you."

"There's a car waiting outside for you."

After he hugged us both, we left and headed outside to the sleek black car waiting at the kerb. I happily slid into the back seat and rested my head back.

Munro got in beside me and placed his hand on my leg. We were silent, both deep in thought. I felt his gaze on me, and I turned to him.

He smiled. No, he beamed. A smile full of what looked an awful lot like pride, and that wasn't something aimed at me often. "You're an incredible man, Beck. I can't believe what you did today. You entered an exclusive lifestyle like you were made to be there. I knew you were nervous, but it never showed. I overheard what the people who do that craziness every day were saying about you. And they had nothing but praise and admiration for you. One or two were a bit smitten, and the guy who did your makeup was in full-blown lust for you." He squeezed my thigh. "You're going to be a huge hit, and designers will be clamouring to have you. I'm so fucking proud of you."

I leant into him and pressed my lips to his, my heart full of love for him, while my head tried to cope with his compliments. Our tongues tangled for a brief kiss, and when I pulled back, his eyes were dark. "You have no idea how much you saying that means to me. Not what the others were saying, but that you're proud of me. You're the only person who's ever said that to me."

"I'm more than happy to tell you that every day. How do you feel about today? Are you going to do it again?"

I laughed a little and shook my head. "Today was so many things. It felt like a dream, like I wasn't really there, if you know what I mean. Stepping out onto the runway was unreal. The loud music, the lights, and the flashes from the cameras were intoxicating. All I could do to get me moving was remember what Gideon had told me. I'm so glad I got the opportunity to do it, but I'm not sure I'll be doing it again."

"Really?" Munro's eyebrows shot up.

"Yeah, it was fun, but it's not how I want to live my life. I want to wake up with you every morning. If I travel, I only want to do it with you. We should be making plans for us to do together. And that was a crazy circus. I'd go mad. I'll have to think about it if Gideon calls again."

"Trust me. He'll be calling you."

Chapter 41

Munro

We never made it to brunch. When Jasper called, I'd told him Beck was too tired. What I hadn't told him was that Beck didn't want everything rehashed and dissected before he made a decision. Instead, we'd slept in late. Now we were in the car on our way home. I squirmed in my seat.

"I'm so sorry, babe. How sore are you?" Beck squeezed my thigh as he apologised for the fourth or fifth time.

"Stop it. I'm fine. And I'm pretty sure I was the one shouting 'harder' at you." I laughed. And that was exactly what he'd done to me in bed this morning. I clenched my ass, which still tingled from the drag of his piercings as he'd pumped in and out of me.

"I do remember that, but I should've remembered that we had to drive home."

Beck's phone rang.

"Hi, Leo," he answered.

His high-pitched shriek came through the device loud and clear, followed by him demanding to be on speaker.

"Oh my god, Beck, you're everywhere. Every newspaper's fashion section has a photo of you strutting your stuff. You even made the front page on some of them. They describe you as 'perfection on two legs'."

Beck groaned loudly. "You're kidding me? That's all I need."

"But you're famous now, so what's with the grumpy attitude?" He spoke still four octaves too high.

"It's great today, but I can forget it happened when I wake up in the morning. We're on our way home. I'll call you when I get in."

"Okay, but we're going to celebrate, Beck. Consider yourself warned." Leo sounded more normal now.

They said goodbye, and he dropped his phone in the cupholder. "He's not going to let this go, is he?" He looked at me.

"Nope, probably not." I placed my hand on his leg, and he covered it with his own.

Beck was quiet, still tired from everything that had happened yesterday, and as we drove up the motorway that carved through the countryside, I left him to his thoughts.

I wanted him with me just as much as he did. He'd fully moved into my place—our place now. He hadn't decided yet what to do with his flat, and that had bothered me at first. As if he were keeping a bolthole in case we didn't work, but after a heated but short argument, I'd stopped acting like a dick and believed him when he told me he was in it for the long haul. The sex after that had been pretty fucking hot. It had been almost worth pissing Beck off for that alone.

"What are you doing?"

Beck was scrolling through his phone.

"Looking at what Leo said. He wasn't bullshitting me. The papers actually show pictures of me. How crazy is that."

"Does it say you're perfection on legs?" I couldn't hold back my smile.

"It does. Would you like me to read it to you?" He was smiling too, the first genuine smile he had given me since last night.

"If you want to, but not if you're going to go all diva on me."

He clutched his phone to his chest and gasped. "How dare you? Don't you know who I am?"

"Yeah, yeah, whatever." I laughed.

His mood lifted, and we chatted for the remainder of the way home. Although the huge sigh of relief he let out when we walked through the front door gave away his true feelings.

"How about we go upstairs and get to bed? You're still tired." I wrapped my arms around his waist and pulled him to me. He slowly blinked, his eyes dark and heavy-lidded.

"I'd rather go to bed and let you fuck me." He slid his hands down over my arse and squeezed. "It's time for you to make me scream."

I pressed a kiss on his soft lips, then grinned. "Let's go, then."

Beck bolted up the stairs and into the bedroom, me hot on his heels. His clothes hit the floor at record speed. He fell down onto our bed and let out a contented groan. He looked as if he'd be asleep any minute. Maybe I'd better let him sleep. But Beck didn't share the same idea as he fisted his swelling cock. The sight of his leisurely strokes made my dick plump up, and all thoughts of being the sensible one flew out the window.

"What are you waiting for?" Beck taunted me by placing his feet flat on the mattress and spreading his legs. With my eyes on his tight hole, I threw my clothes off.

"You're going to regret teasing me when I don't let you come." I crawled up the bed and settled between his parted thighs.

I pushed his legs up to his chest. "Keep them there." Beck held on to them, and I flicked my tongue over and around his tight pucker, earning a deep groan.

I licked, kissed, and sucked over every centimetre of his arse, taint, and balls. Precum oozed down his cock and spread over his tight sac. I hadn't touched his dick yet, ignoring all his pleas. I wanted him out of his mind when I eventually fucked him.

Beck snarled at me as I stopped and got the lube. "Quit teasing me and fuck me."

"Nope. I'm enjoying myself way too much." I squeezed the cool gel onto my fingers and rubbed them together to warm it up. Then I relented and grasped his cock. I was used to the ladder of piercings that ran up the underside of his length, and I slotted my fingers between the small, metal balls and tugged the skin up. His foreskin covered the slick crown, but I slid it back down and exposed the head. A pearly bead of precum slipped free. Beck groaned and grunted as I worked his cock with one hand and pushed a finger into his hole with the other. The speed of my finger matched the slow pumping motion of my hand, and soon Beck was begging me for more.

After stretching him with three fingers, he'd had enough, and I laughed when he ordered me to get my cock in his arse. "I'm getting there, babe."

As soon as I pushed inside him, Beck released his legs and slung them around my arse. His heels dug into the top of my thighs as I sped up, slamming into him. He begged for more, for harder, for it to never stop. I wasn't going to last long. Playing with him for so long had been torture for me too.

"Stroke your cock, Beck. You feel so good." I leant over him and kissed him, sliding my tongue over his as we worked to bring ourselves to climax. I wanted Beck to come first, and with a flick of my hips, I hit his prostate. Game over.

Beck went rigid. The tendons in his neck were taut as he arched up. He looked so fucking beautiful, with a sheen of sweat covering his skin. Cum flew from his dick over his stomach and chest. That was all I needed, and with a shout, I came, firing deep inside him until I was a shuddering mess and collapsed down onto him.

"Fuck, you're good at that." Beck puffed and wrapped his arms around me.

I chuckled, pressing a kiss into the crook of his neck. "I had a great teacher."

Carefully, I pulled out, grabbed a cloth, and cleaned us both up. We snuggled down under the duvet. Beck laid his head on my chest, stroking his fingers up and down my stomach. He was so relaxed. If he were a cat, he'd be purring.

"Do you think I'd be stupid if I didn't do any more modelling?" he asked, his voice hushed. "The money would be useful for us, don't you think?"

"We don't need the money, Beck. You don't have to do something you don't like."

"I didn't hate it. I just want to be with you and pay my way." He stopped stroking me and rested his hand over my heart.

"We've already been through this, and you're already paying enough." I kissed the top of his head. "And if you really want to earn more, then accept the offer from the drink sponsor you did the shoot with me. In fact, I'd bet that after your face has been all over the internet, more companies will be clamouring to sponsor you."

"Do you think Martin would help me too?"

"I'm sure he would."

"I need to have a proper think." He pressed a kiss to my chest, and his fingers resumed their stroking. "Are we having lunch with your parents tomorrow?"

"We are. I'd forgotten about that. It's a good job one of us has a brain that works."

"I've got work tomorrow night too. That's going to be really weird."

"You'll be fine."

BECK

After another delicious, calorie-laden lunch with Munro's mum and dad, I was on my way to work. I had no idea what Leo had planned, but to say I wasn't looking forward to it was an understatement.

At the front door, Steve grinned at me. "Good luck, Beck."

"Oh, god," I groaned. "How bad is it?"

"Leo and Gus have done it all." As if that were encouraging. Steve patted my shoulder.

I stepped up the few steps into the bar and pushed open the door. Photographs of me from the papers decorated every inch of wall. Balloons and streamers hung everywhere. It was utter chaos.

Leo and Gus were grinning like idiots behind the bar while Sawyer shook his head at me. I scowled as I walked up to them. "You two are bloody nuts. How the hell did you get permission to do this?" I waved my hand at the streamers above my head.

Gus waggled his eyebrows. "You've got to bribe the boss with blow jobs."

"Gross. Go away." I shooed him away. "You're not even supposed to work here anymore." I strolled through the door at the back and down to the breakroom.

As I passed the office, Jonas called out. "Congratulations, Beck."

He was sitting in his chair, his hands behind his head. He was much more laid back lately, and I was sure it was because of Haydn. "Yeah, thanks."

He dropped his hands and became serious. "That doesn't sound too positive. Beck, are you regretting doing it? Because you looked like you were made to be there."

With a sigh, I propped myself up against his door frame. "I don't know, Jonas. It was frantic, a little crazy. The noise was incredibly loud, as everyone spoke at the same time. The speed you had to work at behind the scenes was lunacy. I'm not going to say I hated it. Parts were great. But it didn't feel real. I'm just me. I've never travelled or got a great education. I felt like a fake, a fraud."

Guilt washed over me. I hadn't told any of this to Munro. But Jonas was a safe place for me. He knew all about my past and the struggles I had had to go through. Munro knew the newer version of me. The me who'd grown into his own skin.

"What does Munro think? He knows a bit about being in the public eye."

"I haven't talked to him much. He knows I'm not sure about continuing, but not everything. It's only been a couple of days, and he watched it all happen, and I could see how proud he was of me. He wants me to find my success if I want to. We're thinking of doing more stuff together. He said he never wants me to be seen as just his boyfriend."

"That's understandable, Beck. He loves you and knows you're an amazing man with so much to give. He wants the very best for you."

"But what if the best for me is working here and loving him? Will it still be enough in six months, a year? When is he going to realise I'm not ever going to be as good as him?"

"I don't think that's fair on him, Beck. He fell in love with you. He knows about your family. He knows *you*. And he knows you're his equal. Don't ever doubt him. He was prepared to lose everything he worked for to be with you. You may have forgotten that."

"Yeah, you're right. I had forgotten that. Anyway, sorry for dumping my shit on you." I pushed off the frame. "You look well, Jo. Haydn is good for you."

He smiled. "Yeah, he's great. I like him a lot."

"Good, you should be happy."

"Oh, and before I forget. There was a man in here earlier asking for you."

"Who? Did you know him?"

"Nope, never seen him before. He was in his thirties, looked a bit like a rugby player. He seemed okay. Said he'd come in again."

"Okay, thanks." I continued down to the breakroom. Who could it have been? Did I know anyone who looked like a rugby player? Not that I could think of. I brushed it off. If it was important, he'd be back.

The shift was even livelier than usual. My friends all took the piss on me, but it was all in good fun. The congratulations I received from the regulars made me feel a little better. Maybe I could manage to split my life. I didn't have to lose my job or Munro. Gideon was happy to have me pick any work I wanted. More talks were definitely needed.

About fifteen minutes before we closed, my life came crashing around me.

My brother, Peter, stood in front of me.

Neither of us spoke. I had nothing to say, but he obviously did, as he fidgeted, his hands deep in the pockets of an expensive-looking pea coat. But I wouldn't back down. He was the first to lower his gaze, but not before I noticed something flashing across his face. He looked uncomfortable, unhappy even.

What was he doing here? I could wait all night. If he had anything to say, he would have to speak up. Leo stepped up next to me. Sawyer came to my other side. Both laid a hand on my shoulder in silent support.

Finally, Peter lifted his head. "Um, hi, Beck."

"Who are you?" Leo snapped.

"He's nobody. And he's about to leave," I replied but kept my eyes fixed on my brother. He looked good, a little bit heavier than when I'd last seen him, but over a decade had passed since then.

"Beck, please. I'd like to talk to you." He took his hands out of his pockets but shoved them back in as if he didn't know what to do with them.

"Why? What on earth could we possibly have to say to each other? No, go away." I turned, stalked to the end of the bar, and collected up a couple of empty glasses to put in the washer.

"Beck, come on. Please don't be like this. It's important." Peter put his hands on the bar.

I couldn't do this, not here, not now, and maybe not ever. I'd got enough going on in my head without my brother adding more to it. I was positive that after all these years, he wouldn't have anything good to say. And why now? Why the hell had he come here, at eleven o'clock on Sunday night, for Christ's sake? I looked over to the doorway, where Sawyer was talking to Steve. He gave me a nod. He'd have me covered if I needed it.

Leo was on his phone. Hopefully, he wasn't calling Munro, but knowing Leo, he was. Peter drummed his fingers on the bar, a nervous gesture I couldn't remember seeing him do. What could I say to him? How had he found me? I'd moved away, far away from them all, as soon as I could. Saved every spare penny for a ticket out of there. The last thing I'd wanted was to bump into any of them in Sainsbury's.

"Beck?" Leo's voice broke another staring competition.

He bit his lip. He hated confrontations, and we might look like we would be at each other's throats in a minute. "He's my brother, but it's okay, Leo. He was just leaving."

"No, I'm not. I need to talk to you." Peter was getting stroppy now and folded his arms across his chest. He really did look different. The stubbornness was new. As a child, he was a crawly bumlick at home, the biggest tattletale everywhere else. Katherine hadn't been as bad; she would just do as she was told.

"No!" I slapped my fist on the bar. "You don't get to decide if I talk to you. It's been years, Peter. You were part of the problem. The way you treated me doesn't give you any right to walk into my place of work and demand we talk. We have nothing to say to each other."

Movement over by the door caught my attention. Munro was talking to Steve and Sawyer. Then he looked to me, his concern apparent by the deep furrows on his forehead. I gave him a small smile as he made his way to me. When he reached me, he leant over the bar and kissed me, something we had always done. The fact that he did it now, after everything he knew about me, meant the world to me.

"What's going on?" Munro said, looking at Peter.

"This has nothing to do with you," Peter replied.

"It has everything to do with me. Beck is my boyfriend, and he's told you he doesn't want to talk to you. Before we get Steve over here to remove you, you should leave."

"Not until I tell him why I'm here," he snapped back, not even looking at Munro.

I'd had enough of whatever game he was playing. "Just spit it out."

"There was an accident—a car crash. Mum and Dad are dead," he said, his voice cracking at the end.

I stared at him for a full minute. Was that it? I felt...nothing. Absolutely nothing. He could've been talking about two strangers.

What did he want from me? Him coming here served one thing at least. Now I had the chance to say what I had bottled up for a decade. "They were dead to me from the day they turned their backs to me. You've wasted your time, Peter. I don't care."

"I know, and I can understand that. But I'd like to say a few things too. Can we please meet up? Tomorrow, perhaps?"

Munro squeezed my hand. What was he thinking? I didn't have a clue what to do next. Apart from telling my brother to fuck off and never come near me again.

Chapter 43

Munro

When Leo said Beck's brother had shown up, I was out the door before he stopped talking. I was grateful for the quiet Sunday night roads. I parked right outside the bar and jumped out.

"Is he still in there?" I asked Steve at the door.

"Yeah, I'm watching him. He was here yesterday too. Not sure if he spoke to anyone, though. He came back out soon after he entered."

"Thanks, Steve." I patted his huge, muscled arm. He was a regular at the gym now. I walked over to the bar. His bigoted, arsehole brother wasn't going to stop me from greeting Beck with a kiss. "Hey, you okay?" I whispered. Beck was shooting daggers at his brother.

Peter's reaction to my question did nothing to put him in my good books, and I set him straight that Beck was my boyfriend. He ignored me after that, which was fine with me. I waited expressionless until he answered Beck's order: talk or fuck off.

I hadn't expected the words that came out of his mouth. Beck's parents were dead.

Now Beck was looking at me for guidance.

"This is your decision, babe. You don't owe your brother another second of your time," I said, then turned to Peter. "You have no right to demand his time."

"And I wouldn't if it wasn't important. Half an hour, Beck, that's all I'm asking for. After that, you don't ever need to see me again if you don't want to."

"Where's Katherine? Does she know you're here?" Beck asked.

"No, we're not in touch so much now. We had a difference of opinion a few years back, and it broke us apart. Please, Beck, I can explain it all tomorrow."

"Fine." He nodded. "Where are you staying?"

"The Crown," Peter said. Holy smokes, The Crown was an incredibly expensive hotel.

"We'll be there at twelve," I told him.

Peter left, and Beck let out the longest sigh. He looked drained, exhausted by the whole encounter.

"Take Beck home," Sawyer said. "We've got this under control."

"Thank you."

I wasn't surprised when Beck was quiet on the drive home. I would be too.

Not until we were lying in bed, my arms wrapped around him, his head resting on my chest, did he speak.

"That was one hell of a surprise."

"Do you want to talk about it? It's late. We can do it in the morning." He might want to get his thoughts out tonight, but sleep could give him a better perspective in the morning.

Beck's huff of laughter was dry, his discord apparent. "I don't think I could sleep if I didn't. I never thought I'd see him again. I never wanted to. He's five years older than me and was at uni when it all kicked off. Old enough to make his own decisions and was bound to have met gay people there. But he still complied with my parents' instructions to ignore me. By the time I got out of their house, he was about to leave uni. I don't know what he did then, but he never went against their wishes. Katherine is only two years older than me and did what she was told to do."

He lifted his head. I leant into him and kissed him softly.

"Should I care they're dead? I haven't given them a single thought for years. Only talking to you about them brought everything back."

"No, babe. They don't deserve your grief. Don't worry about it." What was he thinking? I would be devastated to lose my mum and dad. Our relationship was the opposite of Beck's.

"What do you think he has to say?"

"I have no idea. Maybe it's to apologise. He did look pretty contrite. I don't like the idea he's messing with you and could hurt you all over again. That's why I want to come with you. If he starts with any homophobic shit, I'll stop him. I won't let him hurt you."

"I know. I wouldn't be meeting him if you didn't come with me." Beck shifted so he hovered over me. "Love me, Ro. I need to feel you inside me."

I pulled his head down to mine and kissed him deeply, then rolled him over and did exactly what he'd asked.

"Do you think he saw me in the papers? Is that why he got in touch? I mean, it's bad that my parents have died. It must be tough for Peter and Katherine, but is that really why he came here?" Beck had been firing questions to me the whole drive to the hotel. I didn't think he'd slept much with so much going on in his head. The only way I could stop him from talking this morning was to suck his dick.

"You'll be able to ask him everything in a few minutes." I patted his thigh as I pulled into the hotel car park.

As soon as I stopped the car, he turned to me. "I don't think I can do this. I don't need him in my life. So the rest doesn't matter, does it?"

I cupped his face and ran my thumb over his cheek. "You'll always be wondering what he had to say. We're here now and can do this as quickly as you want."

"Okay." He took a deep breath and opened the car door.

We walked into the grand foyer and over to the desk, where we gave our names and my car's registration to the receptionist. She told us with a friendly smile we were expected in the lounge.

We found Peter in a secluded corner of the room, looking as nervous as Beck. I was glad the lounge was empty except for another man and an older couple.

Peter stood, smoothing his crease-free trousers. "Thanks for coming." He gestured for us to take a seat. We chose the small sofa that faced his chair.

"I really don't know why I'm here. Why I care what you have to say, but I have some questions too," Beck said and grabbed my hand.

"Do you want to go first?" Peter asked.

"No, you can. You're the one who asked to meet up. What's so important that you finally bothered to seek me out?"

"I've known where you've been for a while now, but I've never had the courage to contact you. My partner has been pestering me, though. Then when Mum and Dad died, I had the perfect reason. But I knew what you would think of that, and this isn't about that."

Hmm, *partner*. Interesting. He was wearing a wedding ring, so why didn't he just say his wife? Also, he'd looked over our heads immediately after he mentioned it. My stomach clenched. Peter was gay or bi or any of the colours in the pride community. This wasn't going to go well. I could already imagine Beck's reaction.

"Okay, I'll bite. What's so important that it's happened now."

"Can I go back to the start? Do you have time?" Peter looked at me.

"Nothing is more important than Beck. You can carry on."

"I was terrible to you when you came out. I was away at uni and could come and go as I pleased. I think it was because it didn't really make any difference to me. I wasn't ignoring you because I was told to. Honestly, Beck, I wouldn't have paid you any attention anyway. You were fifteen. I thought you were annoying before you came out. I didn't care what was going on. I was a dick, a self-centred arsehole, who was enjoying being away from home. It wasn't until I'd finished uni and had to move home until I found a place that I'd found out you'd gone. No one seemed to know where, and they cared even less. I didn't know what I could do." He picked up his coffee cup and sipped at it. It must've been cold by the grimace on his face.

"Let me order some more drinks." I stood and went over to the reception. When I came back, it seemed they hadn't said anything more. "Coffee is coming."

"Anyway, I soon found a place to live and started work. I met a wonderful woman called Sara. We dated for a few years, then got married. Then Sara and I had a baby, a little boy called Archie. He's wonderful. He's seven now. Then one day two years ago, we were at a birthday party for one of Archie's school friends. And my life changed."

"What happened?" Beck asked, his voice cold. I held my breath. I had a feeling about what Peter was going to say.

"I met someone else. I couldn't understand what was happening or why. But I couldn't stop myself. I knew I had to take the chance. Mum and Dad were horrendous, and I suddenly realised what it had been like for you. Only you were so young. At least I had some years on my side and somewhere to live. Even Sara behaved better than them."

"Why? Because you cheated on your wife? I wouldn't have thought that would have any parallels to what those bastards put me through. Oh, poor you, Peter. You obviously have a great job and financial stability. Otherwise, you wouldn't be staying here. Don't you dare compare what they did to me, a child, to how they reacted to your dirty affair." Beck made a move to stand, but I put my hand on his leg.

"I think you should let Peter finish, babe."

"The reason they reacted so dreadfully was that the person I fell in love with was a man." Peter looked over our heads again. "That man."

Beck went still.

BECK

I looked at Munro. "You knew?"

"I guessed. He said partner, not girlfriend or wife. And he looked over our heads to someone else when he did."

Peter appeared to be having a silent conversation with his husband, then turned to us again. "His name is Jake, and he'd like to meet you."

"No." How could he think that would be a good idea? "Your life is your own, Peter. And like you said about me at fifteen, I don't care what's going on. What did you want to happen? Did you suddenly see us arm in arm in the PRIDE parade?"

"I wanted to see you and say sorry. Sorry for not standing up for you. I'm sorry that our parents were so shitty. I'm sorry for staying away from you for so long." Anguish flashed in Peter's eyes. He seemed genuine. Did I really need to be a total dick about it all? It must have taken a lot of effort, and yes, courage, for him to approach me after all these years. Besides, I wasn't a kid anymore. I was in a serious, forever relationship and not totally skint.

"Okay." I sent him a tiny smile. "I get why you're here. Maybe you should've started with the apologies. I'd like to meet your man."

"Really? Oh god, Beck, thank you. Wait here." Peter jumped up and hurried over to the man on the other side of the lounge.

"Hey, you okay? You did good, babe. I'm so proud." Munro wrapped his arm around my shoulders and kissed my cheek.

"Proud that I didn't punch him?"

"That's one of the reasons. But this is okay, right? You're not just doing what he wants?"

"No, I just decided that it was okay, that he made a tough choice coming to look for me. It would've been easy to stay away from me for the rest of his life. Maybe it would be okay to have him in my life, to have one member of my family who doesn't hate me."

"You have my family, and I think my mum loves you more than she does me."

"It's true. She does. She told me." I laughed, and the last bit of tension eased.

"Beck, this is my husband, Jake," Peter said.

Both of us stood. I held out my hand. "It's good to meet you, Jake."

"Thank you. Pete's been so worried about this." He glanced at my brother with so much love in his eyes.

"This is my boyfriend, Munro," I introduced Ro, who smiled and shook his hand.

"I know who he is. I'm a huge fan." Jake blushed, and Peter put his arm around his shoulders.

"Oh, please. Don't tell him that. He's famous enough." I nudged Munro with my shoulder.

"Says Mr I-model-for-Kate-Richards," Peter said.

My cheeks heated.

"That was just a one-off. I haven't decided if I want that kind of life. I like beer and pizza too much. And I don't like the idea of being away from Ro."

They both nodded as if understanding our desire to be together. We moved on to more obvious questions about what they did for work. They told us they'd left their jobs to start their own marketing business. They had custody of Archie, since Sara wanted to go travelling for a while, but they shared when she was back in the UK. It was easy to talk to them both, maybe because Peter really was a stranger to me.

Eventually, I brought up the topic of our parents and their deaths. "I said I didn't want to know, but maybe you could fill me in on what happened to our parents."

"Of course. It was only a couple of months ago. Katherine told me. They'd been on holiday in Scotland and were driving home when an articulated lorry jack-knifed in front of them. They didn't stand a chance. The funeral took place a couple of weeks later. Katherine didn't want us there. She and her husband don't approve of what she calls our lifestyle choices, and she made it very clear that Mum and Dad wouldn't want me to go." Peter leant a little closer to Jake, who kissed his temple.

"Obviously, we didn't pay any attention to her because I wanted to say goodbye. They were awful to me and Jake, but that was their problem. It was a simple boring service, everyone in black, no funny stories or moments to make people smile to honour their memory, but maybe that was how they were. A few days after the funeral, their solicitor called and informed me that they had left everything to Katherine, apart from money for Archie they had put in a trust, which he can access when he turns eighteen. That was fine by me. I didn't need anything from them. Katherine is welcome to the lot. I hope she doesn't end up as sad and bitter as they were."

"There's nothing you can do about that, and I doubt you'll ever see her again," I said. "You have a new life now. You don't need her, so let her go."

Munro squeezed my hand and whispered, "You've got to be at work in a couple of hours, babe."

I checked the time on my phone. Wow, we'd been talking for hours. "I'm sorry, Peter, but I have to go. I've got to work tonight." I stood and smiled at him. "It's been really good seeing you. I'm glad you looked me up. Good to know at least one of my past family doesn't hate me."

Peter and Jake shared another silent conversation. "Could we swap numbers? I'd like us to stay in touch. If you'd like that?"

"Sure, and you know where I work, so you can always reach me there." I opened my phone and passed it to him. He punched in his number and handed it back, I quickly sent him a text so he had mine, and then that was that.

"How long are you here for?" Munro asked as we walked back out of the room together.

"Just two more nights. Archie is with my parents, and we don't like to leave him for too long," Jake replied.

"Would you like to come and have a look around the gym tomorrow?" he asked them, and Jake's face lit up.

"I'd love to. I've followed you on Instagram since you started."

We arranged to meet them there tomorrow, and after a hug, we walked back to the car. When I sat in the passenger seat, I let out a laugh that sounded just a little bit crazed.

"That wasn't what I'd expected." I glanced over at Munro and caught just a glimpse of him looking at me the way Jake had looked at my brother. Warm flutters tingled through me. He loved me. I knew he did, but to see it so clearly always took me by surprise. "I love you so much, Ro. Thank you for coming with me today. I wouldn't have gone if I had to do it alone."

"I love you too, and I wouldn't have let you go alone." He started to engine and pulled onto the road. "It's been one hell of a day, Beck. You've got a lot to process. Are you going to be okay at work?"

"Yeah, I'll be fine. It'll give me some time to let it soak in. Besides, if I don't go in, the guys will be at my door or blowing up my phone all night long."

He chuckled. "That's very true. Haydn's enthusiasm may be a bit too much for me today."

When I walked into the breakroom, all the guys were waiting for me, concerned looks on their faces. "What's this? I didn't know we were having an intervention," I joked.

"We were worried about you," Jonas said. Haydn stood next to him, a happy smile on his face. The others nodded in agreement.

"Thank you. Surprisingly, it went way better than I'd expected. It was difficult to hear about him and why he did what he did, but I can understand why. Still, it hurt that he didn't think about me until he knew I'd left. Then"—I paused—"he introduced us to his husband."

Heavy silence descended in the room.

"WHAT?"

"Yep. And believe me, I was as shocked as you. Especially when he told me he's married and has a child. Jake, his husband, has been pressuring him to come clean to me. To be honest, Peter was more of a stranger than a brother, and I realised I had to treat him as such, as someone I'd just met who had the potential to become a friend. I liked them, and I think we have a chance to make it work."

"Good for you, Beck. I do hope you didn't make it too easy for him," Sawyer said. "He was a shit last night."

"I promise I didn't make it easy. There were a couple of moments I nearly walked out."

"Good." His serious face morphed into a smile. "As long as you don't like him more than you like us."

"Never going to happen. Although Jake is a little bit in love with Munro. Apparently, he's been a fan for years. Ro is going to show them around the gym tomorrow."

"You don't have anything to worry about, Beck. Munro only has eyes for you," Jonas said.

"Can I go and work now, or is there more?" What would I do without such an awesome family around me?

"You're good to go." Max laughed and grabbed Gus's hand. "We're out of here. We've got plans for tonight."

The guys who weren't working left as well, each giving me a hug.

I almost expected to see Peter and Jake in the bar tonight, but they didn't come. Not that I minded. Munro had been right. I had a lot to think about.

When I got home, Munro was still up and had the TV on some kind of drama. "Hey, I didn't think you would still be up. Is everything okay?" I walked over to the sofa and kissed him.

"Yeah, I'm fine. I wanted to make sure you were all right. Did you fill them in on what happened?"

"It was like a fucking intervention. They were all there. Like a bunch of old ladies clucking and fussing over me."

"Because they care, babe." He stood and held out his hand. "It's been a tough day for you, but you've been amazing." He kissed me softly, then bit my lip, giving me a hint of more to come. "Are you ready for bed?"

I picked up the remote and switched off the telly. "With you, I'm always ready. It's my turn tonight."

Munro grinned. "I was hoping you were going to say that."

As I slid inside his body and he clenched around me, I had everything I needed. We made love slowly, murmuring how much we loved each other, and it was perfect. After, we lay back panting, covered in a sheen of sweat.

"I'd like to marry you," I said simply.

Munro smiled slowly. "Are you asking?"

I stroked a finger over his cheeks and across his kiss-swollen lips. "Yeah, if you'll have me, I am."

"Good, because it's a yes. I'd like to marry you too."

Epilogue

Munro

One year later

I watched Beck as he woke up. The sun was shining on his chest, making the heart and my name tattooed over his heart glow. I touched the ink on my skin. Having his name be my first and probably only tattoo was beyond special. I let my gaze drop lower to the thin line of hair that travelled down from his belly button and disappeared under the duvet. I loved every piece of this amazing man, and in the last year, my love had only grown stronger.

When we got engaged, the reactions were incredible. My mum had cried and hugged Beck so hard he'd squeaked, but he'd laughed too. He loved her as much as she loved him. I'd never realised how much she'd worried about me being alone. Our friends had all scrabbled and argued over who would be the best man.

I'd thought we would be the first to get married, but Sawyer and Devon had beaten us to it. They did what Beck had always said they would. They had done it quietly, with only a few of us present, plus some of their family. The party at the bar had been epic, as had been the hangovers we all had afterwards.

Beck's eyes slowly opened. He blinked a couple of times in the bright sun. Then a lazy and sexy smile spread wide over his face. "Morning," he croaked. He cleared his throat. "How long have you been awake and perving on me?"

"I don't perv. I appreciate." I gave him a quick kiss. "And your body is perfect." And it was. In the past year, he'd worked hard at the gym. The biggest surprise was his addiction to kickboxing. He now taught his own class, and his defined muscles brought out the artwork on his body even more. No wonder Gideon offered him more work.

"Is it now? I'm not sure you've looked all over it." He pushed the duvet down, exposing his hard cock. The rows of piercings on the underside of his length glinted in the sunshine. I loved them. At first, they had scared the fuck out of me, but now I could play with them for hours.

"Hmm, as much as I'd love to examine every inch, we have something to do today, and we can't spend the morning in bed."

"It's our day, Ro. We can do whatever we want. And I want to do you." Beck grasped his dick. After only a couple of strokes, a bead of pearly precum appeared in the slit. My mouth watered, wanting to taste it. "You don't have to rush today. We're the stars of the show. Everyone will wait." He shuttled his cock through his fist again.

"You make a very good point, Mr Thompson, and that shouldn't go to waste, not really." I slid down the bed until I was level with his hip. "Spread your legs, babe. I want to taste all of you."

Once he'd complied, I lay between his thighs and batted his hand away from what was mine. "God, I love your dick." I ran my tongue from the root to the tip, taking my time to circle each bead, flicking them as I went higher. Beck was moaning and begging for more, and after more than a year of sucking this man's cock, I had got very good at it. Which meant I knew every trigger point that would have him crying out my name.

I took my time licking, sucking, and teasing the head, lapping up the precum before it had time to leak out. When he was cursing for me to just fucking suck him, I moved farther between his legs and pushed his arse up. Rimming had become another talent of mine. I had always loved watching rimming scenes, and doing it to Beck didn't disappoint.

"Fuck, Ro, cut it out. I'm going to come if you carry on, and I want to do that inside you," Beck snarled as I teased his hole with my tongue and finger.

I looked up from between his legs. "You have such a pleasant way of asking, babe." I kissed his thigh, then sucked hard enough to leave a bruise. I clambered up his body and straddled his waist. He was already squirting lube onto his fingers, ready to stretch me. I didn't need as much prep as I used to. I relished the pleasure-pain threshold.

I reached behind him and grabbed his dick, then positioned it at my entrance. "God, that's so good." I sank slowly down on his length, taking my time to take him all inside. When I was bottomed out, I bent forward and kissed his tattoo, then bit his nipple.

Beck grasped my thighs and pumped up his hips. He was on the brink after all my edging. The heat in his eyes was scorching as he fucked up hard into me. "Don't make me wait any longer, Ro. Stroke yourself."

I closed my eyes and let the sensations take me over the edge. By some chance, or maybe Beck worked it that way, we came together, crying out our names as our orgasms consumed us. I lifted off him and rolled onto my back next to him. My heart was beating its way out of my chest as I tried to slow my breathing down.

I burst out laughing.

"What? That's not how you usually react to my epic dick." Beck raised his eyebrows.

"I need to clean up thoroughly, or I'll have cum in my ass as we walk down the aisle."

He grinned. "Why do you think I wanted to top?"

"You fucker!" I lunged for him and soon had him pinned face down on the bed. "I'm sure I could take you before we have to leave," I whispered in his ear.

My phone ringing stopped us from getting any messier.

"Saved by the bell. I bet that's your mum." Beck wriggled out from under me. "I'll start the shower."

"Hi, Mum. Everything okay?"

"Of course, dear, I just wanted to let you know we're at the front door. It sounded like you'd finished." She ended with a snort of laughter, my dad chastising her.

"Oh, for god's sake, Mum. You could've stayed at home, or at least in the car with the radio turned up loud. If you mention this to Beck, I'll never talk to you again."

"Tell me what?" Beck was leaning on the doorframe.

My mum's voice carried up through the open window. "Morning, Beck, great finish, although I hope you haven't lost your voice with all the shouting."

Beck looked from the window to me, and all colour drained from his face. "Noooo!" he mouthed to me as I nodded solemnly. "Kill me now."

"Dad, take her home. She's not invited anymore," I shouted, then bustled Beck into the bathroom and the shower.

"How am I ever going to look her in the eye again?" Beck lamented as I took control and washed him and his hair. "I'm so embarrassed."

"You're embarrassed. That's *my* mother. She's just heard me come and god knows what else." I scrubbed my body hard enough to take the top layer of skin away.

Beck was biting on his lip, holding back his grin. I glared at him, but it was no use. In seconds, we were hanging off each other, howling with laughter.

What better way to start the day than loving and laughing with the man I would soon be promising to love and spend the rest of my life with.

BECK

The garden of The Crown hotel was decorated so beautifully. The rows of navy padded chairs each had a flower attached to the back. They were some kind of lily, but I didn't know what type. The matching carpet led down to a simple dais on which we would declare our love and intent to all our friends and family.

I'd got over my embarrassment from this morning, but only just. I wasn't completely able to look either of my soon-to-be in-laws in the eye just yet. Gideon was fussing about the incredibly expensive and stylish suits that my favourite designer, Kate Richards, had gifted to both me and Munro. They were made of midnight-blue fabric with amethyst silk lining, and we had matching ties and waistcoats. Hopefully, the day wouldn't be too hot for us to wear it all. Guests were arriving. Munro was refusing to look, afraid it would make him too nervous.

"You can't stand too close to me, Bruno. You're too bloody good-looking, and I'll look like something the cat dragged in," he told his best man.

"You're way better looking than him, babe." I blew him a kiss. Munro smiled at me. All my insides went gooey. God, I loved this man.

"How do you think I feel? I have to stand next to you, and in case you hadn't noticed, you're now hot as hell," Leo grumbled. I grabbed him and pulled him into a hug.

Jasper poked his head around the door, asking for entry. Gideon waved him in, and Jasper took photographs of us all getting ready. We finished up amid glasses of champagne and lots of laughter. Before we went downstairs, I took Munro's hand and pressed a gift box into his palm.

"I thought you might like to wear these.".

"Oh, Beck, thank you." He pulled out one of the white gold Cartier cufflinks and, with a shaking hand, held it out for me to fit through the holes on his cuffs. My hands were trembling just as much. Bruno took pity on me and deftly attached one, then the other while muttering about sappy grooms.

After Jasper had declared he had enough photographs for now, we were ready to go down to the garden. The chairs were all full, and my nerves ratcheted up another notch. Together, we walked down the aisle, and as I squeezed Munro's hand, I whispered, "Whose idea was this again?"

"Yours. Now let's do this so we can get to the kissing part." Munro winked at me, and I kissed him.

The rest of the ceremony went by in a daze. I said the correct words at the right time, and I didn't drop the ring as I slid it down Munro's finger. Munro seemed to be calmer than me, but then again, he was always more put-together.

At last, the registrar announced us Mr and Mr Sylvester. I was already reaching for Munro before she'd finished speaking.

"You may kiss your husband," she said with a small laugh as I kissed him hard, dipping him down to the cheers and applause from our friends.

After we'd finished signing everything, we walked back down the aisle to more applause. "I love you, Munro."

The rest of the afternoon and evening was perfect, the food was incredible, and the cocktails were almost as good as ours at the bar. When the day came to a close and night drew in, the lights hidden in all the trees and flowers twinkled, and the dancing started. The bar's resident DJ was here and kept us on our feet all night. At some point, I lost my jacket and my tie, but I didn't lose hold of Munro.

"Let's go, babe," Munro whispered when we were dancing slowly together. The music played a more upbeat number, but we didn't care. This felt right to us.

"Yeah, I'm ready." I cupped his face in my palms. "I'm yours until I take my last breath."

It took us another thirty minutes to say goodbye to everyone. My brother was the last to come up to me. Jake was behind him, looking fondly at us both.

"Thank you, Beck. Thank you for letting me back into your life and allowing me to share this day with you. I wish the two of you nothing but love, laughter, and happiness." He pressed a kiss to each of my cheeks, then hugged me so hard my breath hitched. Although I wasn't so sure that was because of the hug.

"I'm so pleased we have each other again, Peter."

BECK

Five years later

I pushed Munro towards the automatic doors. He was tripping over all the bags he was carrying. "I don't think you needed to bring all that right now, babe."

"You asked me to get the stuff together, so I did." He finally stood upright. "Where do we need to go?"

I directed him down the hallway. Our shoes squeaked on the polished floor as we walked to the lifts. I pressed the Call button, and the doors swished open. As we stepped inside and the doors closed, I took his hand and gave it a squeeze.

I found the door we'd been directed to and knocked lightly. It was opened by a lady with a smiley face. "You must be Beck and

Munro. Come in, come in. Kayleigh and Tegan have been talking about you so much."

We entered and left all the bags on the table, then went through to the next room. Tegan lay in the bed, strapped to all sorts of machines, but she waved happily. Her wife, Kayleigh, came to greet us.

"Are you ready?" she asked.

I said yes at the same time Munro blurted out no. We all laughed. "You'll do just fine."

"Are you sure you're okay with us being here through this part?" Munro asked. He was already looking a bit green.

"Of course. You need to be here," Tegan said, then winced a little.

"Another contraction, sweetie?" the smiley nurse asked. Tegan nodded. "Let me see how you're doing. We can get that topped up if you're about ready."

Kayleigh stood next to us. "She had the epidural early. We wanted this to be pain-free through it all."

"God, yes. Why would you suffer when the pain can be taken away," Munro said.

The nurse pressed a button by the top of the bed, and soon more people were in the room than I thought a baby being born would need.

I leant back on the wall while it all went on around me. It had taken us a year to find the perfect surrogate for us. The fact that she lived in the States didn't bother us. We'd spent the first four years of our married life doing what we wanted. We'd travelled as much as work would let us. Which luckily had been quite a lot. Then I'd got the need for something more—a child. I knew Munro had always wanted them but had never thought it would happen for him. We didn't know which of us was the biological father, and it didn't matter.

We'd been over here for two weeks now, waiting for this moment, and we had another three weeks before we'd travel back to the UK. Munro clutched my arm, dragging me out of musings.

"Beck, Munro, come over. It's time to meet your baby." Kayleigh grasped Munro's sleeve and drew him closer to the bed. Thank god for the sheet covering Tegan's legs, allowing her some dignity from all the prying eyes.

"Who's the catcher?" the nurse asked with a towel in her arms.

"Um, me, I think." I glanced at Munro, who nodded.

"You'd better have this then and get ready."

Less than two minutes later, the tiniest human I'd ever seen was placed in the towel, and instinctively, I wrapped my daughter into my arms. And then I cried. Munro pulled down the towel, peered at the little scrunched-up face, and laughed through his tears. "That's our baby. Like for real. We get to keep her." He lifted her tiny hand and kissed it.

"We do, babe. She's ours." I held her for a couple more moments before they took her away to do all the usual stuff I guessed they did to newborns. My arms already ached to hold her again. I looked over to Tegan and Kayleigh as they shared some private time. "Thank you." It wasn't enough, but what other words sufficed when someone had done something so selfless.

We had used donor eggs, so it wasn't as if Tegan had given us a biological part of herself, but she had changed her whole life around for us. The fee we'd paid they would use for their own child to go to college, and I would gladly have paid more if they'd asked.

"You're so very welcome. Have a lovely life with her," Tegan said. She would be moved to a private room, while we could stay here for a while until the doctor was happy for the baby to leave.

Kayleigh was holding Tegan's hand and held out her other for Munro. "Do you have a name for her?"

Munro nodded. "Aster," he said. "They are my mother's favourite flowers."

"It's a beautiful name," Tegan said.

The next three weeks flew by in the blink of a very tired eye. I never knew exhaustion like this existed. I couldn't remember what day it was, but thankfully Munro was better at functioning on less sleep than me. We had the car loaded up and all the passports and Aster's birth certificate ready. It was time to go home.

I didn't know who to thank for the offer of a private flight home. Possibly one of the friends of Jasper's husband. But it meant we didn't have to worry about upsetting any other passengers if Aster cried.

In the early-morning hours, we walked into our house, which was warm and clean, thanks to Emma. She'd also arranged all the things we'd need for breakfast in the morning. Munro gave Aster her bottle while I got her crib ready. When we had her settled by our bed, we collapsed into it and wrapped our arms around each other.

"We made it." I kissed Munro.

"We really did. Thank you for every day of the last six years, Beck. You took a chance on a scared and lonely, closeted man and gave him the whole world."

"You taught me to be brave and to trust again. I love you so much, Munro."

The End

Are you interested in Gideon's story? Then check out A New Chapter

Or maybe more from Jasper? Then look up A Safe Heart

Just two of the four books in the Redemption series

JJ Harper

About the Author

You will normally find her in the living room—typing away—with her wayward puppy, Siddiqi. As a hopeless romantic, JJ dives into her stories, always falling in love with her men, making sure they get the happy-ever-after they deserve, even if they do have to work hard for it.

JJ lives in a small, very quiet, village in Lincolnshire, UK, with her husband and dogs, and spends all daydreaming up stories full of really hot men.

If you like the book, please leave a short review. It really makes a difference to indie authors, and it makes JJ smile.

You can get more information about upcoming releases from JJ on her website: https://www.jjharper-author.com

or sign up for her newsletter

and in her reader group

Follow

Twitter

Instagram

BookBub

More by JJ Harper

The Reunion Trilogy
Reunion
Reunited
Elysium
Reunion the Complete Series

The Troy Duology
Troy Into the Light
Troy Out of the Dark

Narrow Margins

Cooper's Ridge Series
Denver's Calling
Here Without You

Standalones
Reckless Behavior
Square One
Trulli, Madly, Deeply (Destination Daddies)
Not Just For Christmas

The Redemption Series
Home to You
Family Ties
A Safe Heart

Beck

A New Chapter

HeavyLoad! Series
My Kind of Man
Your Kind of Man
His Kind of Man
Our Kind of Man

Escape Series
Not Your Boy
Ronan's Boy

BAR 28
Gus
Sawyer
Leo
Beck
Haydn (Coming soon)

Wild Oak Series
Awakening
Reckoning (Coming soon)

Always Series
Anything, Anytime
Everything, Always

The Finding Me Series (M/F)
Rising Up
My Turn
Missing Pieces
Set to Fall

Printed in Great Britain
by Amazon

23654454R00145